The Portland Contract

To Sharon,

I hope this brings back memories of your old stomping ground. Hope you enjoy the book,

Warwick

Warwick Payne spent a decade in newspapers and is former chief reporter of the *Hampshire Chronicle*. Winning regional and national awards, he cut his teeth writing university, pub and hotel guides and *The Portland Contract* is his debut book.

He left journalism in 2012 after being invited to join Southampton City Council's cabinet as executive member for housing and leisure.

His interests include emerging live music, cycling, golf, real ale and classic cars. He lives in Southampton with his wife, Louise, who is also a former news and music journalist, and their daughter, Tabitha.

The Portland Contract

Warwick Payne

The Portland Contract

Olympia Publishers
London

www.olympiapublishers.com
OLYMPIA PAPERBACK EDITION

A CIP catalogue record for this title is
available from the British Library.

ISBN: 978-1-84897-290-2

(Olympia Publishers is part of Ashwell Publishing Ltd)

This is a work of fiction.
Names, characters, places and incidents originate from the writer's
imagination. Any resemblance to actual persons, living or dead, is purely
coincidental.

First Published in 2013

Olympia Publishers
60 Cannon Street
London
EC4N 6NP

Printed in Great Britain

Dedication

For my grandparents

Jim and Dot Payne along with Bill and Mary Harding
...who always enjoyed a good story.

Acknowledgement

Special thanks to my wife, Louise, for her support and encouragement, and also my late mother, Marnie, who passed away soon after the first draft of *The Portland Contract* was finished.

Thanks also to the rest of my family and friends, colleagues at the *Hampshire Chronicle* for printing so many of my stories, Claire Lewis and Juliet Howland for their valuable advice, and also to Olympia Publishers.

She never heard the shot that killed her. Nobody ever does.

Carmel knew she was being watched. In troubled times, surfing was her escape. She packed her bags and fled to Cornwall, but did not visit Newquay as usual. Instead she chose a smaller resort a few miles away called Perranporth, in the hope of throwing her pursuers off the scent.

Carmel was a newspaper reporter… a good one. During a decade on the nationals in London she had landed several scoops. However, none came close to the Portland Contract. The story was so incredible that she hadn't even told her editor, in case it slipped through her fingers or was handed to a more experienced journalist. The police also didn't know, as Carmel realised that they would not believe her without more evidence. She had to prove her story. It was the exclusive that would set her up for life.

However, Carmel knew she was being followed, and it would be hard to find the proof she needed while being watched. As a result, she took several days off, and drove overnight to Cornwall to lie low. She checked into a bed and breakfast under a false name, switched off her mobile phone, and started to read the first of several books in her luggage.

Only the lure of surfing the Atlantic waves at Perranporth tempted Carmel outside. It was on the fourth day that she hired a wet-suit and a board and headed for the beach. It was late July and the golden sand stretched out like a warm carpet in the sunshine. The waves were rolling onto the beach, which stretched on for miles. Carmel took to the water and went to find the best wave of her life. It would also be her last.

Carmel headed around fifty yards out to sea. Despite the warm sunshine, the water was still cold and ripped through her in constantly aggressive surges. Each wave was like a gauntlet being thrown down, challenging her to ride it until she plunged back into the sea. A few surges passed by, but then Carmel saw a crest of water on the horizon. It was the biggest wave that day, and the moment had come. She changed direction and began to swim towards the shore, building up speed. Then she launched herself and was standing on the board. Just for that brief moment she didn't care about anything. It didn't matter if her pursuers saw her; they would only report her movements back to their employers. The story could slip through her fingers or make her name, but when the wave came, she didn't care a single bit. She felt the board rising beneath her feet and lifting her towards heaven.

Around two hundred yards away, hidden by the grass of the windswept and barren sand dunes, a silenced sniper rifle was pointing out to sea. A small puff of smoke rose from the barrel. The firearm was then taken apart and packed away.

The crest of the wave was stained with blood. A body was floating on the currents. It came ashore a few moments later, with a surfboard close by. The lifeguards rushed to the scene, but hordes of curious holidaymakers arrived first. What they saw would haunt most of them for the rest of their lives.

***

The parcel was too large for the letterbox. It had also been sent by recorded delivery, which meant that a signature was required.

Oliver Dart was usually in during the day. Being a children's writer, he could work at home. Indeed, few things dragged him away from his apartment, but his passion for cycling was one of them. Needless to say, he was riding his hand-built machine when the postman knocked on his door.

Oliver found the Royal Mail card on his doormat. He muttered a bad word and took a few weary steps towards the sink. He poured a glass of water then drank it dry. He wiped his mouth with his right hand, the cycling glove feeling coarse against the stubble on his face. He needed a bath and a shave. His apartment was perfectly decorated and tidy but for one thing – himself. His knees were dotted with specks of mud and his Lycra top was laced with beads of sweat.

Oliver glared at the Royal Mail card. It summoned him to the post office in the centre of town to fetch his parcel. Parking was tricky nearby, and it was slightly too far to walk. It was a journey tailor-made for a bicycle. However, he had already ridden forty miles and didn't want to move another yard until he was clean from head to toe.

A coin was tossed in the air. If it came up heads, Oliver would enjoy a long bath. He would also place the radio beside the sink and count out several pieces of chocolate, which he could savour as he listened to the music.

The coin landed and glared its result at Oliver. He frowned back, ruing his misfortune that the Queen's head was not visible. Fate had forced him back on the bike.

Oliver lived in Torquay. He chose it because it was pleasantly far from London where he'd toiled for years. His escape came in the form of Spib. Around three-foot tall, lime green and wearing blue sunglasses, Spib was a children's favourite. Brave and stylish, he was a super-sleuth who unravelled crimes such as jailing the culprits who stole the world's entire supply of lemonade. The villains who tried to suck up most of Europe's custard reserves with a turbocharged vacuum cleaner were also doing porridge thanks to Spib.

His first adventure was written when Oliver came back to his microscopic London flat one night after several post-work drinks. For years he'd struggled to find a publisher for his crime novels so, as a joke, Oliver opted to write a children's book instead. The next day he woke on his couch to find several drawings spread across the floor. He gathered them into some sort of order and, to prolong the wheeze, mailed the sketches to a publisher.

One month later, Oliver had a book deal, and Spib's first adventure was about to go into print. Other tales followed and enough cheques appeared on Oliver's doorstep to allow him to leave London and go elsewhere. He hadn't settled upon Torquay immediately, indeed he was a very different man when he fled the capital from when he sought sanctuary in Devon. Oliver left London in his late 20s with a girlfriend called Michaela. A few years later, his bank account looked respectable, but nothing else in his life was right. How Oliver came to be alone was a long story, but Torquay had struck him as a quiet enough place to hide and lick his wounds. It was scenic, there were countless steep hills to cycle up and down, and nothing exciting or unexpected was likely to happen.

Oliver chained his racing bike outside the post office and plodded inside. The queue stretched into the distance, so he left, bought a copy of the *Herald Express*, and returned to stand in line with the local paper. He scanned its pages to check that it was all quiet on the Torquay front. Reports of turgid parish councils meetings and Women's Institute cake sales reassured him to some extent, although the story about bicycle thefts in Paignton caused a little anxiety. However, his main concern was the national news page. One story caught his eye, stating that a female journalist from London had been shot while surfing in Cornwall.

Oliver had worked as a news reporter in London for several years, and knew many journalists in the city. He also remembered one who enjoyed surfing. Her name was Carmel Rawlings. They'd worked on the same paper for a couple of years. Oliver liked her, indeed, they made a half-hearted attempt to become an item. They dated for a while, but finally the pressures of work drove them apart. They parted on good terms, but Oliver needed time to write his crime novels, and Carmel wanted to surf in Cornwall.

Frustratingly, police had not identified the murdered woman, which left Oliver fearing the worst. If the last five years were any indicator, when things could go wrong, they usually did. The Royal Mail card in Oliver's hand was further evidence, having been unlucky enough to miss the postman. Along with the surfer's identity, another mystery fizzing around Oliver's mind was who had sent him the parcel and what it contained. He was none the wiser when it was presented to him at the counter. After checking it wasn't ticking, or sporting an obvious warning along the lines of "fatally toxic", he signed his name grudgingly.

Oliver cycled back to his apartment. It was on the sixth floor of Edenhurst Court, a seven-storey building perched awkwardly on a slope above the harbour. With pastel colours and light blue concrete pillars, it resembled a 1960s council tower block, but with lipstick and white stilettos. Naturally the letting agent hadn't described it as such on the phone, but once Oliver saw the view from the balcony, he fell madly in love with the place.

After locking up his racing bike, Oliver returned home and placed the package on the coffee table. He was moments away from his bath and neatly arranged line of chocolates. However, the parcel was staring at him, almost taunting him to unwrap it and expose the contents. The sofa was also calling, sending a telepathic message that its soft cushions would be much comfier than sitting in the bath. Within seconds Oliver had cracked, and he was wrestling with the package. He couldn't remember the last time anyone had sent him a parcel, and he was dying to find out what was inside.

Once the packaging was conquered, Oliver stared at a collection of scruffy pieces of paper. The parcel had also contained a journalist's notebook. There was no name inside it, but Oliver knew that a reporter was nothing without their pad; it was like a gunslinger without a pistol. The dates inside the notebook covered the previous two months, and there were a few pages spare, which meant that it was still in use. No journalist would send anyone, much less a former reporter, an active pad. It was like hacking off a cherished limb and mailing it to a distant cousin. Something was wrong.

Oliver sifted the paperwork, which was a dreadful mess. He began sorting it into four piles, which he christened 'unreadable', 'unprintable', 'uninteresting', and 'unclassifiable'. His task was nearly complete when part of a document caught his eye. It was an application made under the Freedom of Information Act, which from Oliver's experience, was designed to cover up Government gaffes. There were more than twenty ways to block a request, and this particular one, which sought details about Royal Navy bases in Dorset, had satisfied just about all of them. However, it was not the predictable refusal that caught Oliver's attention but the name on the application. The request was from Carmel Rawlings.

The paperwork would take ages to digest, so Oliver called a halt in order to enjoy his long-anticipated bath. He turned on the taps and was poised to remove his Lycra top when the doorbell rang. Oliver sighed; one drawback of living alone was that nobody else could answer his calls. He trudged to the door, hoping that the faint smell of perspiration and cycle oil would excuse him from any long conversations about politics, God or double glazing.

"Daddy?"

Oliver stared at the boy on his doorstep. Panic filled his veins. He had no children, at least to his knowledge, and the boy was a stranger. However, the youngster, who was about eleven-years-old, seemed to believe that Oliver was his father. The only crumb of comfort was the question mark at the end of the dreaded word 'daddy', which suggested a degree of uncertainty on the boy's part. It was possible that he had the wrong apartment, which was certainly true if he wanted to avoid a conversation with a sweaty man in skin-tight shorts.

"I'm Kieran," added the youngster.

Oliver wouldn't have chosen the name himself, although deciding what to call a son was a problem he had never anticipated. He was still excused the responsibility, seeing as somebody had already given Kieran his name, and that somebody was probably the absent father that the youngster was seeking, and not him.

"Who are you looking for?"

The youngster fell silent, then reached for a piece of paper in his back pocket.

"Oliver Dart," he read from the sheet, before reciting the address for good measure. The revelation struck Oliver like a thunderbolt. He couldn't be a father, much less to a boy knocking on the door of secondary school. He swiftly went back a dozen years in his mind to when he arrived in London. He tried to recall if he had a girlfriend at the time, and one name immediately shot into his mind.

However, just because Oliver was dating, it didn't mean that he was a father. He had been cautious with his sexual health to the point of embarrassment. One night still haunted him when he treated a significant other to dinner. The meal was extortionate, but Oliver was reviewing the restaurant for his paper, so his meagre wages remained intact. However, he had neglected to come out with enough change for the condom machine in the men's room, or more accurately, had brought the exact amount, but had not reckoned with the dispenser rejecting one of his coins. In desperation, he fed the offending coin into the machine several times until he had a small audience. Eventually one of his more drunken admirers took pity on him, but rather than offering Oliver a substitute coin, he ventured into the restaurant and loudly asked the occupants of each table if they could help. The Samaritan returned with the necessary amount, generously donated by the "blonde on table six". She was Oliver's date that evening, and her name was Carmel Rawlings.

"Who's your mummy?" Oliver asked the youngster. He realised that the question was blunt, but he needed to know the answer. However, there was none forthcoming, as Kieran simply looked at the floor and quietly snivelled. It then struck Oliver that a young boy should not be alone, and he amended his questioning.

"Is anyone with you?"

Kieran stayed silent, but this time there was an answer. Oliver heard a heavy pair of footsteps approaching his door.

"Mr Dart?" Boomed a huge woman in a tent-like summer frock. "I'm Mrs Lightbody."

The name struck Oliver as ironic, but he resisted poking fun and politely extended his arm to shake hands, which left him with numerous squashed fingers.

"I'm Kieran's case officer at Surrey social services."

"What's he done?" asked Oliver.

"Nothing, he's a lovely lad," stated Mrs Lightbody, patting Kieran on the head with the deftness of an all-in wrestler.

"He called me 'daddy' when he arrived," stated Oliver, hoping for some clarification.

"Yes, we need to discuss that," said the social worker, squeezing herself through the door with Kieran in tow. She then deposited the youngster onto the sofa before taking a seat at the kitchen table, hauling her oversized bag onto its polished surface.

"There must be some mistake, I don't have any children," stated Oliver.

"They all say that," muttered the social worker, delving into her bag.

"But I'd be a hopeless father. I've no experience dealing with kids, and doing one set of chores is more than enough," Oliver protested. As he did so, he noticed warm liquid at his feet. He turned around to see water seeping out from underneath the bathroom door.

"I see what you mean," chuckled Mrs Lightbody.

Oliver was about to indulge in a luscious binge of bad language, but stopped when he remembered that a child was present. He stared at Kieran for a moment. Could the boy who was fiddling idly with his remote controls really be his son? It seemed impossible. What was certain, however, was that Oliver's longed-for bath was now gleefully overflowing and oozing over his marble floor. He stomped into the bathroom and turned off the taps before grabbing every towel from the rack to mop up the floor. As he was crouched over the floodwater, Oliver felt Mrs Lightbody's shadow looming over him.

"Kieran's watching television, but we still need to talk."

"What about?" Oliver protested, adding that Kieran was not his son.

"His mother believed that you were," replied the social worker, smugly.

"Who is this mystery woman?"

"Carmel Rawlings."

Oliver nodded in grim resignation, pausing briefly before he returned to mopping the floor on his hands and knees. Mrs Lightbody then asked if he'd heard about the 'accident' in Cornwall.

"I read something in the paper," Oliver muttered.

"The police would have told you, but it wasn't until we studied Ms Rawlings' will that your involvement came to light."

Oliver replied that he only dated Carmel for a few weeks, and while omitting the story about the condom machine, maintained that he couldn't be Kieran's father.

"He's coping well for an eleven-year-old," said Mrs Lightbody. "Given that his mother raised him single-handed, he's virtually an orphan now."

"But he's not my son," insisted Oliver, "I'll happily take a paternity test if you like."

"It's not a question of paternity, it's a matter of law."

Oliver tried to recall if he'd ever signed anything to make him an adoptive parent. The only realistic culprit seemed to be competition entries when you had to mark a box to avoid receiving tons of junk mail. Perhaps one of them said "if you don't want social services to dump a little brat on you without notice, tick here", and he'd forgotten to do so.

"In Ms Rawlings' will, you were made legal guardian of Kieran Dart."

"She named him after me?" Oliver asked, flabbergasted.

"You see, it makes no difference if he isn't your biological son."

"It matters to me."

"But not to the law," stated Mrs Lightbody.

Oliver was about to ask if Carmel had any relatives that could look after Kieran, but the question stuck in his throat. Not only did it sound callous, but he also knew the answer. Carmel's parents were dead, and she was an only child. Indeed, apart from doing the same job, a lack of close family was Oliver's only similarity with his deceased old flame.

"I've checked your background," revealed the social worker, brandishing a battered folder, "and you have no criminal record or drug problems."

"Hardly a proper journalist, was I?"

"Six years at a gutter tabloid, and then you started writing children's books."

"It seemed a natural progression," Oliver observed.

"Engaged once,"

"Okay, you've done your homework," interrupted Oliver. "So what's your diagnosis; am I Mary Poppins or Hannibal Lecter?"

"My conclusion would be 'a spoonful of sugar helps the fried lower intestine go down'. Your legal record is spotless, and your parenting experience is hopeless."

"Sounds accurate," stated Oliver, mopping up the last of the floodwater.

"That's why I'm watching you closely," warned the social worker.

"You mean I'm supposed to look after him?"

"Catch on quick for a tabloid reporter, don't you?"

Oliver was ruing his luck. He'd missed the postman, then had the misfortune to be in when the social worker from Hades arrived with her pint-sized cargo. All he wanted was a bath, some music, and few pieces of chocolate. A reunion with a previously unknown son was not on his wish list. He hadn't a clue how to look after a youngster. They needed food, clothing, somewhere to sleep, and an education.

"You needn't worry about schools yet," said the social worker.

"Of course, the summer holidays began last week."

"Which gives you time to get acquainted," declared Mrs Lightbody, adding that Oliver needn't worry about Kieran's education as a secondary school in Dorking had accepted him.

"I'm not driving two-hundred miles, he'll get an education down here."

"Becoming possessive of Kieran, are we?" Mrs Lightbody noted smugly.

"He can't live here, there's no space."

"You must have a guest room, surely?"

Oliver replied that his second bedroom was converted into a study.

"What happens when people stay with you?"

"They don't," he muttered, wringing out the sodden towels over the sink. The social worker sighed, and opened the bathroom door so that Oliver could see Kieran in the lounge.

"He doesn't have anybody else," said Mrs Lightbody.

"What happens if I turn him away?"

"Kieran would go into care," muttered the social worker. "Some kids manage, but not all of them. He's being brave now, but he's clinging to the hope that you'll accept him."

"That boy can't have any affection for me, we've never met."

Mrs Lightbody closed the door again, in case their conversation was overheard.

"Carmel told her son all about you, but never informed you about him, in case you felt guilty. Kieran wants to meet you, it's what keeps him going."

"He really has nobody else?"

"No, he's just like you in that respect," observed Mrs Lightbody. "Maybe you could be a bit of company for each other."

***

Five minutes after the social worker left, Kieran and Oliver were sitting at the kitchen table. The conversation was stunted at times, and non-existent at others.

"Would you like a coffee?" Oliver volunteered.

"Do you have any Coke?"

"No."

Silence returned once more. Oliver scrutinised the youngster who had invaded his life. He looked for any physical similarities. There was nothing conclusive, but he didn't look much like his father either, so it was difficult to tell.

"Mum says you're a journalist."

"I used to be," nodded Oliver.

"What do you do now?"

"Children's books," he replied, before realising that his job might be of some interest to Kieran, given his age. "I write the Spib adventures."

"No you don't, they're done by Trevor Dial."

"I know, that's me," stated Oliver, picking up a nearby book and pointing at its spine.

"That's not your name."

"It's the one I use for publishing, it's an anagram."

"What does that mean?"

"It's what happens when you rearrange letters to make up new words, so Oliver Dart becomes Trevor Dial."

"Why don't you put your own name on the books?"

Oliver replied that he liked to shun publicity, although the actual reason was that he thought his Spib adventures were crap. However, Kieran had other ideas.

"I used to love these books," he stated, thumbing through the instalment where Spib caught the reprobates who kidnapped the entire England football squad. "Mum bought this one for me during the last World Cup."

"Really?"

"We did so badly, the kidnappers should have just kept them," stated Kieran. Such dry cynicism brought a smile from Oliver. It seemed that Carmel had raised him well.

"Was your mum still working at the same paper?"

"No, she left three years ago."

"What's she been doing since?"

"Working freelance."

"Oh, unemployed then," muttered Oliver, getting up to boil the kettle. As he selected which brand of coffee he wanted, Kieran revealed that his mother had recently taken a part time job with *The Times*, and was working as an investigative reporter.

"What was she looking into?"

"She never told me, said it was best if 'I didn't know'," sighed Kieran.

Oliver was about to make his coffee, but then glanced over his shoulder. The open plan design of his flat meant that he could look all the way across to the lounge area. On the coffee table he noticed the bundle of paperwork which had arrived that morning.

"Did your mum say anything about sending me a package?"

Kieran said she hadn't, which increased Oliver's curiosity. He went to the bundle and started sifting through the papers. Before long he found a lined page ripped from a reporter's notepad. Very little was written on it, and everything was in shorthand. Oliver struggled with the symbols, having not used them for several years. However, he decoded the first outline straight away. It was his name.

Oliver then started to translate the rest of the page. It appeared to be a note from Carmel, warning him about a major story she had uncovered. There was no mention of her life being in danger, but she said she was "being watched". The single page also gave no details about the story she was working on, except for a name. The first symbol contained the letters 'P and R' followed by a 'T or D', then 'L and N', finishing with a 'D or T'. One of the drawbacks with reporter's shorthand was the omission of vowels. Oliver was equally stumped on what the second word, which contained 'C', perhaps followed by 'N' then a 'D' or 'T', a further 'C' and another 'T' or 'D'.

"What are you trying to tell me?" Oliver muttered under his breath.

The rest of the page revealed that Carmel was going to Cornwall, and had sent him a copy of her paperwork 'in case something bad happened'. It struck Oliver that being gunned down in broad daylight certainly came into this category. The note added that the rest of her research was hidden in a metal chest buried on a beach.

"Was your mum into pirate stories?" Oliver asked.

"No," muttered Kieran, surfing channels on the widescreen television.

The chest's location was given precisely, having been buried three feet below a sign saying 'Dangerous tides'. Frustratingly, though, Oliver could not translate the name of the resort. It started with a 'P', followed by 'R', 'N', 'P', 'R', and what could be 'H' or 'TH'.

Oliver was about to consult his atlas to identify the resort, but then remembered what dragged him away from the paperwork in the first place. He needed a bath, urgently in fact. After locking the front door, to ensure that Kieran didn't waltz off with most of his belongings, Oliver headed into the bathroom and left his new flatmate watching television.

Once in the tub, Oliver had a chance to reflect – aided by music and chocolate – on the day's events. He was a father. At least in legal terms, anyway. A potentially lethal story had also dropped into his lap. Several years ago he would have been delighted to take up the chase. Landing a major scoop, along with the associated publicity, could have launched his career as a crime novelist. Instead he wrote children's books, and forty minutes ago, had taken delivery of a child as well.

Reaching out of the bath, Oliver grabbed his mobile phone and rang his old paper to find out what they knew about Carmel's death. They were aware of the shooting, but nothing much else. Owing to a rapid turnover of staff, few people at the tabloid remembered Carmel, and even fewer recalled a crime correspondent once employed there called Oliver Dart.

Kieran's revelation that his mother had been working at *The Times* gave Oliver one more line of inquiry. He rang the editorial section, and spoke to one of the reporters.

"It's terrible what happened in Cornwall, isn't it?"

"Yes," Oliver concurred, "do we know why she was targeted?"

"We're looking into it," the reporter replied, which Oliver recognised as code for 'we don't have a bloody clue'.

"Was she on a dangerous story?" he asked.

"No, Carmel did fashion features, so apart from the designers of Littlewoods' autumn range, nobody could possibly want to kill her."

Oliver shook his head; his inquiries were getting nowhere. However, he did have one final question.

"One more thing," he ventured, "did Carmel mention anything about a son?"

"No, she was the private type. I didn't even know she had kids."

"Makes two of us," muttered Oliver, who thanked the reporter before hanging up. His attention then transferred to a letter that Mrs Lightbody thrust onto him just before leaving his flat. He'd taken it into the bathroom, as the social worker had advised him to read it when Kieran wasn't around. The letter was from Surrey social services. Its headed notepaper had a telephone number and an address in Dorking. However, Oliver was more interested in the letter's contents. In a nutshell, it advised him to contact social services if he wanted them to take Kieran away. It was tempting to make the call. However, Oliver didn't want the guilt of hanging a young lad out to dry, even if they weren't related.

Once dressed, Oliver returned to the lounge and found Kieran watching a report on the previous weekend's league fixtures.

"Do you like football?" Oliver enquired, rubbing a towel through his hair.

"Not much, I'm just waiting for the van."

"Van?"

As Oliver spoke, his doorbell rang again.

"Kieran, you don't have any other siblings, do you?"

"No, it's probably the removal guys."

To say that Oliver raised an eyebrow was an understatement – one entire side of his face suffered a localised earthquake. Once the aftershocks passed, he summoned enough courage to open the door. Two burly men in overalls were skulking in the corridor with a vast assortment of toys and small pieces of furniture caked in science fiction stickers.

"Social services?" grunted the larger man.

"What?" shrugged Oliver, hoping that the last hour was just a bad dream.

"Delivery for Dart," muttered the second removal man, who wafted a clipboard under Oliver's nose in the hope of gaining a signature. Before putting pen to paper, Oliver asked Kieran to step forward and identify his belongings.

"Cool, where's the rest?" the youngster chirped, inspecting his mountain of goods.

"The second truck's downstairs," muttered the larger gentleman in overalls.

Oliver did not have the slightest clue where to store Kieran's possessions. Nowhere obvious sprang to mind, with the possible exception of the seabed. It seemed unbelievable that a youngster could accumulate so many things. If the social services phone number was burning a hole in Oliver's pocket beforehand, it had now set his leg on fire.

"Sign here," urged the second man, still wafting his clipboard expectantly. Oliver asked how much it would cost, and the reply finally brought some good news.

"It's free, social services are paying."

"Okay," Oliver conceded, his decision influenced by the fact that Kieran had already dragged several boxes of toys into his lounge. The removal men headed downstairs to fetch the second truckload while Oliver retreated to his sofa in shock. The paperwork sent to him earlier that day was still lying on the coffee table, begging for attention.

"Can you help me please?" Kieran asked.

"No, daddy's working," muttered Oliver, settling effortlessly into the role of a negligent father. "If you want to make yourself useful, store your things in the study."

"Is that my bedroom?"

"Probably," sighed Oliver, thumbing through the countless sheets of paper. He tried to concentrate, but the disruption caused by the removal men, coupled with the excruciating din as Kieran dragged his things across the polished marble floor was too much to blot out. Trying to make sense of the paperwork was virtually impossible anyway, with half of it buried three feet beneath an unknown sand dune.

"Are you getting tired of dragging things around?" Oliver enquired of Kieran, knowing that his eardrums were already significantly fed up. The youngster nodded, and Oliver rose to his feet. He then picked a road atlas from one of his many bookshelves, and gave it to the eleven-year-old. Oliver then wrote the letters 'P', 'R', 'N', 'P', 'R', 'TH' on the cover.

"Right, find a coastal resort in Britain containing those consonants in that order."

"Why?"

"Because if you find it within one hour, we'll go there."

"Brilliant," enthused the youngster, who promptly began to devour every page of the atlas with a coastline, including the Lake District. Oliver then trudged into the hall and started to carry the remaining boxes of toys into his previously pristine study.

It took Oliver some time to salvage his possessions and billet them elsewhere in the flat. He then shoved Kieran's bed, games consoles and clothes boxes into the room. It was a horrible mess. Tidying seemed pointless, as if Kieran was a normal boy, he would turn his quarters upside down within a heartbeat. Oliver checked his watch; he'd been a father for eighty-four minutes and it was not much fun. It had also been fifty-nine minutes since Kieran had been set the challenge of finding the elusive town.

"Time's up," he announced, returning to the lounge.

"I've found the resort," beamed Kieran, holding up the atlas.

"Impress me."

"Perranporth," said the youngster, passing the book to Oliver. He studied it and found the town on the northern coast of Cornwall.

"Well done," he muttered, conceding that Kieran was not an idiot after all.

"So are we going there?" the youngster asked expectantly. Oliver glanced into the bomb-site that was once his study, and couldn't face bringing order to the chaos.

"Pack an overnight bag," he advised. Kieran immediately leapt up and dashed into his new room, but then stopped in his tracks.

"This place is a tip," he complained.

Oliver allowed himself a smile; maybe his new companion would be easier to tolerate than expected.

***

The Gordon Keeble GK1 glided out of the garage, its deep red paint gleaming in the afternoon sunshine. Thanks to the success of Spib, his creator travelled in style. The vehicle was a 1960s sports tourer, built in Hampshire with continental looks and a throaty American V8 engine. Oliver loved the car, and it was the only thing in his life that he really trusted.

Kieran opened the passenger door and placed his bag in the footwell.

"Seatbelt," Oliver muttered. The youngster strapped himself in and the car rumbled forwards, the automatic garage door closing obediently as it moved away.

"I saw your bike in the garage," said Kieran.

"You don't miss much."

"Do you like cycling?"

"It keeps me fit."

"What else do you do?"

By this time, Oliver had negotiated the twisty drive leading from Edenhurst Court and was in Parkhill Road, a narrow street perched high above the marina. Torquay was teeming with steep climbs, and as Oliver intentionally brought the car to a halt by the kerbside, Kieran could see several flights of intimidating steps towering uphill towards the horizon.

"That's how I stay fit apart from cycling. I run up that."

Oliver's passenger greeted the revelation with stunned silence. The steps ran beside Edenhurst Court, and the top of the climb was virtually level with its seventh floor. Oliver then informed his passenger that it took him forty seconds to reach the summit.

"If you're going on this adventure, you need to be quick," said Oliver.

"I am."

"Okay, you have sixty seconds."

"To do what?"

Oliver didn't reply, and merely gazed up the hill. Kieran began to look pale.

"Clock's running," encouraged the driver, starting his stopwatch. The youngster leapt from the Gordon Keeble and stormed up the first dozen steps.

"Swift little sod," muttered Oliver, who then released the handbrake. His car began to roll forwards majestically and out of view. Fifty yards down the road, he engaged first gear, and placed his foot on the accelerator. However, he didn't apply any pressure.

"Come on, you're not that much of a bastard," he reminded himself.

The reverse lights on the Gordon Keeble blinked into life. Parkhill Road was usually quiet, and Oliver backed the car up to the foot of the steps. He arrived as Kieran reached the summit. He was jumping in celebration. Oliver gestured for his colleague to descend the stairs. He noted that Kieran was hardly out of breath on his return.

"Did I make it?"

Oliver checked his watch, and realised that it hadn't been stopped. However, it was less than two minutes since Kieran had begun his challenge.

"Close enough."

"Now can I go on your trip?"

"If you insist."

***

The car was heading west. Oliver skirted around the gloomy heights of Dartmoor and then skirted around Plymouth on the dual carriageway. The vehicle then neared the River Tamar, which separated Cornwall from the rest of England. A massive road bridge spanned its estuary, and beside it, the Victorian magnificence of Isambard Kingdom Brunel's railway bridge carried locomotives over the river far below.

"Is Perranporth in Cornwall?" asked Kieran, a little apprehensive. Oliver nodded, then remembered that Carmel had been killed while surfing along its coast. Taking her son to the murder scene was perhaps inconsiderate, but the journey was vital. Oliver had to know why Carmel had been shot. He wanted to identify the culprit, not only to bring them to justice, but also to avoid the same fate himself.

There was an awkward silence in the car as it left the Tamar Bridge and slipped into the darkness of the tunnel below Saltash. Enclosed by concrete walls, there was nothing to hear but engine noise until the vehicle emerged from the gloom a mile down the road. It was at this point that Kieran found the courage to speak.

"Do you know who killed my mum?"

"No, but the police will find them."

"If the police are looking, why are we here?"

"The detectives are only hunting a killer. We need to find who hired them and why."

"It's because of mum's story, isn't it?" Kieran asked.

Oliver was impressed; the youngster had a sharp mind. He was also showing a great deal of bravery, given the circumstances. He was beginning to realise that Kieran was not a child that had to be humoured and patronised, but someone who could help.

"What was your mum working on?"

"Something about the navy."

"Did she discuss it much?"

"No," sighed Kieran, adding that the police had asked plenty of similar questions.

"We'll need the rest of your mother's notes then."

"Where are they?"

"Buried under a beach."

Oliver then recounted the story of the package arriving at his flat earlier that day, and how its contents were frustratingly incomplete. To fill the blanks, they would have the find the rest of Carmel's paperwork.

The Gordon Keeble wriggled through the twisty roads between Saltash and Bodmin, squeezing through valleys and thundering over hills.

"Mum used to bring me down here," Kieran observed.

"Did you come with her last week?"

"No, I was on a school trip in France."

Oliver reflected that Kieran would have returned home expecting to see his mother. Instead, he was probably greeted by a social worker. It must have been unbearable for him, and for that reason, Oliver wasn't surprised that his passenger sometimes wiped away a few tears. He couldn't begin to imagine what the boy was going through. He had lost his mother.

***

Waves rolled in from the Atlantic Ocean. The engine fell silent and Oliver stepped from the vehicle. He had never been to Perranporth. It was scenic town with golden beaches shielded by rugged cliffs and endless sand dunes. The seafront car park was nearly full, and the small town was a hive of activity. Surfers and less adventurous holidaymakers were all meandering through the town with its eclectic mix of souvenir shops, eateries and bars.

"Ever been here before?"

"No," Kieran replied, as he stepped from the vehicle.

"Shame about the beach," sighed Oliver, opening the boot of his car, and removing a shovel. "I'd hoped it would be smaller."

Kieran then walked onto the beach. Almost everyone else was heading the other way as the incoming tide herded the holidaymakers towards their dinner tables. As the families with countless buckets, spades, Frisbees, and inflatables headed for dry land, one boy stood out from the crowd. He was followed by a man carrying a shovel and a set of written instructions. They were looking for a container underneath the beach, and with high tide fast approaching, they did not have long.

Oliver felt the sand becoming saturated beneath his shoes as they ventured further away from the seafront. They were heading towards a narrow channel between the craggy cliffs and a small island, which was defiantly perched at the western end of the beach. Oliver could see a sign mounted on the rugged outpost. With each step, he was moving closer to the ocean, which was advancing angrily in their direction.

"I think we've only got a few minutes," he warned. Kieran was still a few steps ahead, and had reached the rocky island.

"Dangerous tides," he announced, reading the sign.

"That might be it," said Oliver, who plunged the shovel into the sand next to the rock. The beach was sodden, and the rumble of the ocean was growing louder by the second. He continued digging, but the task was daunting. Three foot didn't sound much, but it was more than half the height of a grown man. As the waves advanced, more sand flew out of the hole that Oliver was creating, but there was no sign of the container. His arms were now burning, and he was ready to concede. The hole was now filling with water, and the waves were only a few metres away. Oliver plunged the shovel into the depths for one final time. He then felt the handle judder as he struck something hard in the ground.

"That must be it."

"Let's dig the box out," said Kieran, reaching down into the hole.

"We can't now, the tide's coming in."

"What if the container gets flooded?"

"I'm sure it's waterproof," wheezed Oliver, throwing the shovel aside. It then occurred to him that a container impervious to water might be made of plastic. In addition to that, if it only contained paper, it would be lighter than water.

"Hang on, it might float away," warned Oliver, who picked up the shovel once more. "You better get back to the car."

"I want to stay."

"It's safer on dry land. I have to get this box."

Oliver started pushing sodden sand away from the container, but could not release it, and was rapidly losing sight of it as water poured into the hole. Both his hands were around the box, but it was trapped. Two more hands, younger than his own, then appeared and grabbed the container. It then came free, and Oliver tumbled backwards onto the saturated beach. He felt waves lapping at his side, and he struggled to his feet. Collecting the shovel, and holding the container with his remaining arm, he staggered away from the hole. Kieran was beside him, trying to outrun the waves that were chasing them every step of the way. It was a race between the ocean and the two of them. However, on this occasion, the sea was thwarted, and Oliver and Kieran made their escape.

They were both tired as they reached the safety of the sea wall. A bench was nearby and they rested for a moment. Kieran then asked if he could open the box.

"Not here, somewhere quiet," Oliver replied, picking sand out of his hair. He needed a bath again, and it was a long drive back to Torquay. Once home, he would be confronted by the disastrous mess that masqueraded as Kieran's room. He couldn't face it, and the only escape would be to find a hotel.

Oliver also needed to eat. He spotted an ice cream van across the car park, and was about to leave the bench and buy something. However, he then remembered that he was buying for two people. He would also have to purchase dinner, breakfast, lunch and snacks for Kieran every day from this moment forward. The financial implications of fatherhood were now sinking in. He would also need to pay for Kieran at the hotel, and was unsure if a twin room or separate ones would be appropriate. Eventually he chose the former, as he could keep an eye on Kieran, and more importantly, it was cheaper.

They booked into a bed and breakfast near the beach. They entered the room eating ice creams from the van. Oliver set the box, which was still unopened, on the coffee table.

"You have the first bath."

"I don't need one," the youngster protested, his hair caked in sand.

"You do."

"I don't, I had one four days ago."

"I had one four hours ago, but I need another."

"That's because you stink."

Oliver avoided raising his voice, and simply planted his ice cream on Kieran's head like a dunce's hat. Sweet melting liquid started to seep through his light brown hair.

"Leave me some hot water," advised Oliver, who started to unpack his bags. Kieran removed the cone and stomped into the bathroom, slamming the door as he went.

Kieran's departure allowed Oliver to study a vital document that he didn't want the youngster to see. Far from being secret, it was a copy of *The West Briton*, the local paper. Oliver had directed his colleague away from the newsstands, given the headline of "Female surfer shot dead". Police had named Carmel as the victim, but her killer was still at large. It then struck Oliver that relying on papers for updates was unnecessary. The case was being handled by Devon and Cornwall Constabulary, where he had a friend. In his London reporter days, Oliver had a mole in the Metropolitan Police, who was a superb source of stories. He was Detective Sergeant Kwame Ebwelle. Sadly for Oliver, he headed to Devon for a quieter life and a promotion to inspector. His decision had influenced Oliver's decision to go west.

"Detective Inspector Ebwelle please," said Oliver, having dialled Exeter CID. As usual he was off duty, which always happened when he needed him in a crisis. Thankfully the two were on drinking terms, so Oliver had his mobile number.

"Kwame, it's Oliver."

"Hello mate, long time no see."

"Are you on duty tomorrow?"

"The day after."

"We need to meet, I've got a story."

"I thought you'd retired."

"Yes, but I'm coming out of hibernation."

"Must be important. What's it got to do with me?"

"Are you handling the Carmel Rawlings case?"

"Who?"

"I guess not," sighed Oliver, who then told Kwame about his relationship with Carmel, and her assassination on the Cornish coast.

"I'd like you to investigate it," he added. "Carmel was onto something big, maybe concerning the navy. It was damaging enough for someone to kill her."

"Oh, great," sighed the inspector, "and to think I came here for a quiet life."

"I know the feeling, see you later."

Oliver hung up, and then stared at the container. He had brought the paperwork from his flat, and hoped that the contents of the box would fill the gaps. He walked to the coffee table, placed his hands on the lid, took a deep breath, and opened the container.

"Incredible," he muttered to himself. Oliver then heard water draining from the bath next door. He was about to replace the lid, when an idea came to him. Oliver took a sachet of sugar from the tea tray. He then jammed a corner of it inside the container as he replaced the lid. He then slid the box against the wall, so that the sachet was not visible.

Kieran emerged from the bathroom wrapped in a towel. His expression was that of a dejected refugee. Somebody had forced him to wash, and it was a painful experience.

"We'll have dinner after my bath," Oliver announced.

"I'm starving," grumbled the youngster.

"Have the biscuits on the tea tray."

"I'm bored."

"Watch the television."

Kieran replied that nothing good was on, listing the schedules for all the main stations for the next hour. Oliver was simultaneously amazed and appalled that the boy had watched so much television that he'd memorised all the shows between 6 and 7pm on Tuesdays.

"Don't you ever read anything?"

"Comics," muttered Kieran.

"What about your Spib books?"

"They're for kids," snorted the eleven-year-old. "I could read your paper."

"Not yet," said Oliver, scooping the copy of the *West Briton* off his bed before Kieran spotted the headline.

"Why not?"

"I haven't finished with it," muttered Oliver, desperate for a better excuse.

"But I'm bored."

"Okay," he sighed, removing the property section and giving Kieran a pen. "See how many words you can make out of 'Perranporth'."

"Boring."

"It's either that or dull television."

"What about the box?" asked the youngster. Oliver glanced at the container, pressed tightly against the wall on top of the writing desk.

"No, and I want you to promise that you won't look inside it until I'm back."

"Okay."

"I can't hear you."

"All right, I promise," protested the child, snatching a pack of custard creams from the tea tray. Oliver then went into the bathroom. At first he could hear Kieran through the door, listing the words he could make from Perranporth.

"North, near, ear, pear, parp."

Every few moments a new combination of letters would surface but before long there was silence. Oliver could hear the youngster moving about. He'd set the trap with the sugar sachet in the container to see if Kieran could be trusted. If the sachet was missing, it would be a clear sign that the youngster had opened the box.

37

When Oliver left the bathroom, he found Kieran perched on his bed, eager to go out and explore.

"How many words?"

"Seventeen," Kieran replied, handing over the property section, now garnished with countless semi-legible scrawls in every margin.

"'Perp' isn't a word."

"Sixteen then."

"Did you look in the box?"

"No."

Oliver headed towards the container. He lifted it, and noticed that the sachet was still jammed in the lid. He was a little surprised to find it there, but pleased all the same.

"Right, let's open it," said Oliver. As he detached the lid, Kieran looked excited, but his expression soon turned to disappointment. Oliver already knew why. He reached into the box and removed the contents. It was just a single sheet of paper. Oliver knew what it said, but read it aloud for Kieran's benefit.

"'Oliver, sorry to mess you around, but I couldn't risk my notes falling into the wrong hands. You'll find another container fifty miles away. As a clue, it's hidden beside a large river in a building that Isambard Kingdom Brunel would have found convenient'."

"What does that mean?"

"We've got another box to find," sighed Oliver. He then sealed the original container. While its meagre contents had been a disappointment, the box had at least taught him that Kieran could be trusted. The youngster was also feeling pleased. After all, it had taken ages to clamber around on the floor and retrieve the sugar sachet after it fell behind the desk. ***

"Did your mum say much about me?" Oliver asked.

Kieran peered up from his ice cream. The two were finishing a massive meal at The Tywarnhale Inn, one of the pubs in Perranporth's main square. Their table was outside and the relentless waves of the Atlantic Ocean could be heard in the distance, crashing onto the beach. The only other sound was the muffled music inside the bar along with the occasional clatter of air-cooled Volkswagen engines as surf wagons wheezed by. The conversation had been stunted, firstly by the onset of food, and by the tension between the diners.

"She said you were a reporter."

"I write children's books these days."

"I know," muttered the youngster, taking another spoonful of raspberry ripple. Oliver returned to his pint, and planned his next move. He wanted to learn about Kieran, but hardly knew where to begin.

"Carmel never told me about you," he said. "If I'd known I would have visited."

"That's why she didn't tell you."

The response raised an eyebrow with Oliver. The boy was blunter than a seasoned hack after his fourth whisky. He asked Kieran if he had any half-brothers or stepsisters, but the youngster shook his head, and spooned another glob of ice cream.

"Did mum see any other men after me?"

"A few," he muttered, chasing a glacé cherry around his sundae glass.

"But nothing serious?"

Kieran seemed thrown by the question, and shrugged in ignorance.

"I guess if you had a stepfather, you'd be with him now," muttered Oliver, trying to fill in the blanks. His inquiries about Kieran's past were not revealing much. However, as the boy finished his dessert, the tables quickly turned.

"Why did you leave my mum?"

Oliver nearly choked on his pint. As he recalled, it was Carmel that started to ignore his calls, not the reverse. His official line on the relationship was that they mutually agreed to part. The reality was that she had grown tired of him, but Oliver had never liked that version.

"It was complicated," he sighed, immediately regretting his use of such a cowardly, and in this case, wholly inaccurate cliché. The situation was remarkably simple. They dated, Carmel got bored, and they split up. However, during this fling, it appeared that his normally careful approach to bedroom antics had been pointless. The evidence was sitting on the opposite side of the table, and it wanted answers.

"Your mum decided, for whatever reason, that I wasn't 'Mr Right'."

"Why?"

"I don't know," Oliver sighed, genuinely lost for a response. He opted to find solace in his pint of ale while Kieran finished his cola. Had the youngster not been there, Oliver would have returned to his room to sip scotch and drunkenly scribble another Spib adventure. He tended to produce his best stories towards midnight, but there would be no time to write that evening. Kieran had been fed and watered, and now he had to be entertained.

"What do you like to do?"

"Go-karting," replied the youngster, adding that computer games, television, and the odd game of football were also favoured.

"Right," sighed Oliver, instantly regretting his lack of a go-kart, computer, or football. According to his pint-sized colleague, the television shows that night were also nothing much to write home about, unless they wanted to complain.

"What did you do with your mum?"

The question triggered a blank expression from Kieran. It appeared that entertaining her son had not been a priority, and Sky One had been left to pick up the pieces, with Marge and Homer Simpson acting as foster parents. It certainly explained Kieran's conversational shortcomings, which rivalled a monk with a sore throat. At that moment it struck Oliver that if he wanted to uncover what Carmel was searching for then he needed to change his tactics with Kieran. If he was simply along for the ride, he would slow them down. He had to pull his weight and help to unmask his mother's killer.

"Right, we've got work to do," Oliver announced, finishing his pint.

"Work?"

"Yes, we need to understand your mum's notes to track down the bad guy."

"Who's he?"

"That's what we need to find out, and before he finds us."

***

The next day Oliver and Kieran left town. They'd spent the previous evening trying to make sense of Carmel's notes. The initial suspicions that she was investigating the Royal Navy were partly true, but didn't tell the whole story. The paperwork also included confidential documents from Détente, a leading defence contractor. Oliver had no idea how Carmel had got them, but he was pretty sure that they wanted them back.

What the Royal Navy and Détente had done, or intended to do, was unclear. The situation was made hazier by the time difference between the documents. Most of the naval papers referred to incidents thirty years ago. The Détente information was contemporary, but its subject matter was confusing. The documents referred to chemical tests, property deeds and personnel matters. The naval papers were dominated by disciplinary and discharge issues, but the names were all blacked out. How they were connected was a mystery, and Carmel's remaining paperwork was starting to look like the missing ingredient.

Oliver loaded his rucksack into the car, climbed into the driver's seat, and started the ignition. He was about to pull away when the passenger door opened. He'd almost forgotten Kieran, not having adjusted to his sudden switch from bachelor to single parent. Once the youngster was aboard, the car glided away from the hotel. They were soon heading down St Piran's Road, the main street in Perranporth. Most of the shops were crammed with holiday souvenirs. Others offered fish and chips, pasties and even surfboards. It was a comfortingly odd place, but Oliver couldn't escape what had happened in this sweet little resort. A murder had been committed, and the case was unsolved.

Oliver was heading east. While Carmel's notes had been hard to decipher, the clue over where to find the missing papers was easier. The references to Isambard Kingdom Brunel and a large river suggested that one of his gigantic bridges might be involved. With that in mind, Oliver had a good idea where to start looking.

The Gordon Keeble rolled into Saltash just before lunchtime. It was the last town in Cornwall before crossing the border back into Devon. Making the trip by road was impressive, but it was even more dramatic going by train. Two majestic bridges spanned the River Tamar and the one for the locomotives was a Victorian masterpiece. Not only was it designed by Isambard Kingdom Brunel, but his name was engraved on the huge structure.

Oliver parked near the bridge. He decided to begin his search on the Cornish side, determined that he'd leave no stone unturned, and therefore only have to pay the toll on the road bridge once. He stared up at the rail crossing, which was perched on sturdy columns of pale stone. The bridge towered over Saltash and soared across the river as if held there by magic. Underneath it, the town was perched on a steep slope, cascading down to the river. Oliver had chosen to park near the water, driving down a hill that was virtually a sheer drop.

"Are mum's notes up there?" Kieran asked, staring into the sky.

"I hope not," Oliver replied, stepping from the car. His theory was that the notes were underneath the bridge, and not on it, as anyone who walked along the structure would risk a major disagreement with a speeding express train. In terms of where to look, Oliver had a feeling that 'convenient' was the key word in the clue, but was unsure what it meant. It fell to Kieran to provide the answer.

"I need the toilet."

"You went in Perranporth," sighed Oliver.

"Yes."

"And Bodmin."

"I was desperate."

"Then Liskeard."

"I couldn't wait."

"And finally in a pop bottle."

"I didn't wait."

The fact that Kieran had needed the toilet five times in one morning suggested that buying him a three-litre bottle of cola for a treat was unwise. Oliver had much to learn about parenting, like where to dispose of a three-litre bottle of lukewarm piss.

Underneath one of the massive columns supporting the railway bridge was a toilet block. The exterior looked as if a bomb had struck it, which had been laced with manure.

"After you master bladder," prompted Oliver, hovering by the door.

"Aren't you coming?"

"No, you obviously don't know the 'urinal code'."

Kieran's expression was blanker than a whiteboard containing a list of Nobel Prize winning footballers. Oliver explained that the 'urinal code' stated that two men should never visit to the bathroom together. It also instructed males to find a urinal as far away from other users as possible, and to keep conversation to a minimum.

"Has nobody ever explained this?" Oliver added. Kieran shook his head, which was not a huge shock, seeing as his mother was unlikely to know how male toilets worked. From Oliver's experience, male toilets rarely worked, if at all, and their hygiene was usually poorer than a radioactive swamp.

Kieran emerged from the bathroom after a couple of minutes.

"Did you wash your hands?"

"There wasn't a hand dryer."

"Use the toilet paper."

"All gone," shrugged the youngster.

"You could have shaken your hands dry."

"There was no sink."

Oliver sighed and trudged into the toilet block. It had the atmosphere of a poisonous planet in decaying orbit around a toxic sun. The light was broken, the floor was sodden and the air was nauseating. Oliver poured the contents of the pop bottle into a toilet bowl, which he flushed before heading towards the exit. As he was leaving, he spotted an ancient sign clinging awkwardly to the cracked wall tiles. It read 'conveniences', and pointed towards the hellhole that Oliver had just vacated.

"A building that Isambard Kingdom Brunel would have found convenient," he recited to himself. Oliver shook his head in disbelief.

"Kieran, could you come in please?"

"What about the 'urinal code'?" came the faint reply from outside.

"Skip it, there's nobody else here anyway."

Kieran slouched into the festering abyss, his nose twitching in disgust. Oliver broke the news that Carmel's notes were probably hidden somewhere in the toilet block, and they would have to search from the cobwebs on the ceiling down to the saturated floor.

"And you want me to keep watch?"

Oliver was impressed with Kieran's attempt to dodge the nauseating search, but he wasn't escaping that easily. He was soon put to work inspecting the urinals, while the grottier business of searching the cubicles rested with Oliver. He investigated the cleaner ones first, then moved onto the more distasteful stalls. On each occasion he tried to flush the contents of the putrid bowls, but the mechanisms were all broken, and one chain snapped off in his hand. Each time he stood precariously on the slippery porcelain, lifting the lids of the ageing cisterns, and dreading what he might find. The short answer was nothing at all.

Oliver and Kieran left the toilet block, taking deep breaths of fresh air to purge their polluted lungs.

"Find anything?"

"Dead rat," muttered Oliver, "yourself?"

"Chewing gum."

"It's a bad habit throwing gum butts into urinals."

"Yes, it ruins the taste," said Kieran.

Oliver was pretty sure that he was joking, but young boys were rarely noted for their cleanliness. It would certainly be hard to persuade Kieran to have a second bath inside 24 hours, but he needed one after their search.

"I'm hungry," said the youngster.

Oliver checked his wallet. He had enough money for a meal, but not enough for two. Seeing as the nearest cash point was a big walk up a small mountain, Oliver bought Kieran a bowl of soup at a nearby pub, and went hungry himself. Budgeting for two was coming as a nasty shock. Kieran had doubled Oliver's living costs, and he demonstrated little gratitude for the extra expense. It was like being married.

Oliver and Kieran were sitting outside, partly to enjoy the view, and to avoid awkward questions in the pub like 'is he old enough to be in here?' and 'what's that smell?'. As Kieran dunked his crusty bread into his nourishing soup, Oliver gazed at the river. He ran the search through his head, trying to recall if they'd missed anything. It seemed unlikely, and the possibility that someone had already found Carmel's notes could not be discounted. However, there was another explanation, and when it came to Oliver, he kicked himself.

"Of course," he groaned. "I know where we didn't look."

"Where?"

"The ladies' toilet," said Oliver, raising his arms in exasperation.

"How can we get in there?" Kieran asked, spooning another mouthful.

Oliver was about to reply, but silence drifted from his gaping mouth when he realised that he didn't have an answer. He stared at the toilet block, which suddenly looked painfully public, given that they would have to enter the forbidden side of the building. In all of Oliver's years as a crime reporter, he'd never been called upon to sneak into a ladies' toilet, and had no idea where to start.

While Kieran finished his soup, Oliver jotted some methods of sneaking into the toilet block. A sign said it was locked by the council at six o'clock every night, so he'd have to wait until October for darkness. His other ideas read: 'wear wig, dress and wig, Kieran wears dress and wig, police cordon, bomb disposal hoax, just chance it'.

Oliver eventually scrapped his initial plans, and settled on posing as a 'local authority sanitary hygiene officer', or a toilet cleaner for short. After lunch, he drove into town to buy a bucket, sponge, and pair of overalls. He also purchased a face mask, not as a disguise, but to muffle the stench in the toilet block.

Oliver returned to the riverside and squeezed into his overalls. He soon realised that he'd bought the wrong size. Convinced that his cycling must have done some good, Oliver chanced a medium pair, but the stitching was groaning and the garment felt poised to burst into shreds like a low-budget version of *The Incredible Hulk*.

"Keep watch please, Kieran."

"Your overalls are too small."

"Fancy searching the toilets yourself?"

"It fits you perfectly," said the youngster, swiftly backtracking.

Oliver trudged into the toilet block, having fixed a sheet of paper to the door advising patrons to take their business elsewhere unless they wanted to be doused in bleach.

The interior of the ladies' restroom was no better than its male equivalent. The lights were broken, so Oliver used a torch. He began by looking under the sinks, which didn't take long as there weren't any. He then checked the cubicles. The first toilet was missing its seat, the second had no cistern, and the third was just plain missing. Oliver then entered the fourth and final cubicle. He looked behind the bowl, under the cistern, but found nothing. He then stood on the seat and lifted the cistern's grimy lid. Shining his torch into the murky waters, he saw the mechanical parts, but little else. Oliver then felt the bowl creaking beneath his feet. He was about to abandon the search when a dark object in the bottom of the cistern caught his eye. With reluctance, he reached into the stagnant water. The object was made of plastic, and seemed watertight. Oliver removed it, but as he did so, the bowl he was standing on finally tore itself from the wall.

Oliver fell backwards. His back clattered into the toilet door, ramming it shut. At first he noticed the pain, then realised that he'd stopped falling. He quickly deduced that his collar was stuck on a coat hook, which explained the increasing sensation of being garrotted. He then heard a creak of metal, and his fears of being strangled were no more. As its rusty screws snapped in two, the hook shot away from the door, rebounding off Oliver's head. Now he felt pain in his back and skull. He was also falling again. Uninhibited by the hook, he slid down against the door, rapidly picking up speed. His nether regions crashed onto the sodden floor.

The pain in his skull was then reinforced when he gazed towards the ceiling, only to see the ageing hook plummeting his way. The piece of rusty metal deflected off his head and bounced into the darkness. Oliver then looked forwards, and saw the sad remains of the toilet bowl. Behind it was the outflow pipe, from which an increasingly loud grumbling sound was emanating. It climaxed in a noise similar to an ill warthog breaking wind.

The pipe deposited its contents over everything within a five metre radius. Oliver was directly in the firing line. Enough said.

Kieran snorted the air with disapproval as Oliver plodded sheepishly out of the block.

"Are you getting enough sleep?" the boy asked.

"Why do you ask?"

"Because you look like shit."

Oliver then held aloft the stained container he'd retrieved from the cistern. He then asked the youngster if he wanted to open it straight away.

"No, I can wait."

It struck Oliver that he'd won a minor victory in teaching Kieran the value of being patient. However, if he had to be drenched in effluent just to make a point, he figured that being a lousy parent would be easier.

***

Oliver stepped from the shower. He could still smell the results of the accident, but whether it was just psychological, he couldn't quite tell.

The shower block was on a campsite half a mile from the river. Oliver had tried to ask the owners of the pub near the toilets if he could have a bowl of soapy water, but the locals hastily barricaded the door. He then heard them shrieking inside about the 'abominable turdman' in the beer garden. Oliver could already imagine the headlines in the local press. Thankfully, for his sake, the campsite owner hadn't been so fussy.

Oliver peered out of the shower block. He was waiting for Kieran to return with some fresh clothes, having sent him to a nearby shop. Seeing as he'd given the youngster his wallet, there was the outside chance that Kieran would vanish to make a new life for himself. Oliver knew he should feel guilty about such a dereliction of duty, but was more preoccupied in not smelling worse than a yak's laundry basket.

Kieran reappeared with a pile of clothes. Before he was within thirty yards, Oliver realised that he'd made a dreadful mistake to bankroll the youngster. He could already see a luminous yellow garment. On closer inspection, it turned out to be a hoodie with the word 'skunk' inscribed in large lilac letters on the chest.

"I saw this and thought of you," said Kieran, still holding his nose. To accompany the deafeningly loud top, he'd purchased a pair of tragically unfashionable grey slacks.

"These are granddad trousers," said Oliver.

"That's what old people wear," protested the eleven-year-old.

Oliver retreated into the shower block and changed into the slacks. He emerged a few moments later, gripping the waistband with both hands.

"I asked for 34-inch trousers."

"I thought you said 54."

"So I gathered."

While in the shower, Oliver had also washed the box that he'd salvaged from the toilet block. Now standing in the middle of the campsite, he decided to open the container. At first glance there was nothing inside but a large stone, which had weighed the box down in the cistern. However, trapped underneath the stone were a few sheets of paper.

Oliver and Kieran decided that reading the notes should be their second priority. Their first was to burn the soiled clothing. They headed to a clearing in some woodland high above the River Tamar. Oliver placed a bucket on the ground. His old garments were inside and they were covered in petrol taken from the emergency can in the back of the Gordon Keeble. With a heavy sigh, Oliver flicked a match towards his old clothes. The contents of the metal bucket started to burn immediately.

"What's that smell?"

"My favourite jeans going up in flames," muttered Oliver.

"No, it's something worse," insisted Kieran, pinching his nose again. Oliver sniffed the air. He immediately felt the urge to be unwell. Far from consigning the dreadful stench of the overalls and the rest of his clothes to history, the fire was creating a putrid cloud of sickening smoke. Oliver responded by leaning back and thumping the metal pail with his right boot. The blazing bucket soared into the distance before plunging down to the river far below. The flame soon flickered and died in the strong currents. Kieran was laughing his head off at the spectacle. His reaction puzzled Oliver. It struck him that the youngster was putting a brave face on things, seeing as both of his parents had now kicked the bucket within a week.

***

The Gordon Keeble left the toll booths on the Tamar Bridge. Oliver and Kieran had now read the notes rescued from Saltash, and were heading to Plymouth. Their mission was to infiltrate a disued military base, and if that wasn't tricky enough, they would have to find it first.

Carmel, as ever, had left them with several unanswered questions. The paperwork came from Détente, and was relatively recent. It related to a small island in Plymouth Sound, which used to be owned by the defence firm. The notes indicated that some kind of secret experiment had taken place there, and its remnants might point Oliver in the right direction.

Thirty minutes after leaving Saltash, Oliver parked at Plymouth Hoe, half a mile from the sea. He then walked towards the coast with Kieran and soon arrived at The Promenade, a stretch of open space high above Plymouth Sound. To their left was the stark Citadel with its massive grey walls. Below them was the Tinside Lido, which was an archaic complex of diving boards and abandoned swimming pools cascading down to the sea. Underneath their feet, buried beneath The Promenade, was the Plymouth Dome, and underground museum dedicated to the history of Devon's largest city. It was in this subterranean maze that Carmel had advised them to continue their search for Detente's secret island.

Oliver was upset that he had to pay to enter the museum, seeing as he no intention of studying its exhibits. He was even more agitated about stumping up a further fiver to bring Kieran inside. Oliver was learning that parenting was not only time-consuming but irritatingly expensive. On that subject, while he'd burnt his jeans, he had remembered to salvage the number for social services in case the novelty of fatherhood wore off.

Once past the reception desk, Oliver and Kieran arrived in a darkened cavern. It was meant to resemble deprived medieval Plymouth, but wasn't scary until an actor leapt out of the darkness to welcome them to the museum. Kieran jumped in fright, quickly followed by Oliver when the youngster landed heavily on his left foot.

Oliver hobbled into the next room. With the medieval zone behind them, they arrived in a bright room with a large window offering panoramic views of Plymouth Sound. This was where they could find the island, according to Carmel's paperwork.

"What's the rest of the clue?" Kieran asked.

"Once you've found the window, look for a television screen," Oliver recited from the notes. He then spotted a large monitor, but it hardly looked promising. It displayed nothing besides gentle waves on the sea. However, there was a joystick beside the screen, which Kieran promptly commandeered.

"You can move the camera," beamed the youngster. Using the controls he began to search Plymouth Sound, using the zoom to bring distant lighthouses into focus and close up shots of unsuspecting holidaymakers strolling by the sea.

"That boy's picking his bogeys," chuckled Kieran, zooming in on the lad in question.

"Stop being nosy, we're looking for an island."

"What kind?"

"The clue says 'Nick had it, then Francis nicked it, then it was a nick'."

Kieran continued to scan the horizon, zooming in on every island he could find.

"How about this one?" he enquired, pointing to the monitor.

"Too far, it's probably the Eddystone Lighthouse," Oliver replied, glancing at the map beneath the screen with places of interest in Plymouth Sound. Kieran continued the search, zooming towards Sutton Harbour and the RAF station on the headlands near the open sea. He then turned west towards Cornwall. The River Tamar estuary was visible with a rugged coastline in the distance. In the foreground, stranded in the river channel, was a small island barely two hundred yards across. The remains of a bleak building stood in the middle of the barren rock, and there were no signs of life.

"How about this one?" Kieran asked.

"Drake's Island," stated Oliver, reading the map, "once known as St Nicholas Island."

"That must be 'Nick' from the clue."

"And 'Francis' would be Sir Francis Drake," said Oliver, who then studied the screen and deduced that the bleak building was a former prison, or 'nick'.

While Kieran and Oliver were happy that they had found the island, the youngster insisted on scanning the rest of Plymouth Sound, simply out of curiosity. Oliver indulged him, but soon regretted the decision.

"Look, there's an ice cream parlour," enthused Kieran, zooming towards a chocolate sundae on one of the tables. Oliver could already feel his wallet becoming lighter.

***

"Mice race," beamed Kieran, stabbing at the giant bowl of ice cream.

"Mice race?" said Oliver, shaking his head in confusion.

"It's like the name you write your books under."

"An anagram?"

"Yes, if you mix up 'ice cream', what do you get?"

"A mess," diagnosed Oliver, pointing at the smeared glass bowl.

"Mice race," announced Kieran, looking smug while he licked his spoon. Technically they were sharing the chocolate sundae, but the youngster had taken the lion's share and enough for the cub as well. A small outcrop of ice cream was treading water in the bowl, marooned in a sea of syrup. It reminded Oliver of the island they had just investigated.

Drake's Island was just a stone's throw from central Plymouth, but was deserted and virtually impossible to reach. They went there immediately after leaving the museum, but with no ferry service, or access to a boat, it seemed impossible to reach the barren outpost. Instead they had to make observations from the mainland, which was costly, as the coin activated telescopes on the promenade had a relentless appetite for cash.

After their reconnaissance trip, Oliver finally gave way to Kieran's requests for ice cream. The open air parlour was beside the Tinside swimming complex, with views across the sparkling sea. Around the corner of Plymouth Hoe was Drake's Island, the mysterious base once owned by Détente.

"Let's recap what we found," said Oliver, pointing at the small mound of ice cream left in the gigantic bowl. "This is Drake's Island, and the strawberry sauce around it is the river."

"Where are we now?"

"The mainland is the napkin dispenser," said Oliver, placing the shiny metal box next to the bowl. "We have to reach the island, but there's no ferry service, so we'll have to swim or hire a boat."

He then raised the issue of the security guards. While Détente had abandoned the island, which was fenced off with "danger" notices and barbed wire, the firm had retained a lookout post on the mainland. It was equipped with searchlights, and staffed by half a dozen burly-looking officers intent on stopping anyone getting anywhere near the former base.

"That means we can't risk a boat, as they'll spot it," said Oliver.

"Looks like you're swimming," chuckled Kieran.

"You could be right, but the tough security only makes me more curious about what's over there."

From their observations, they had spotted the remains of an old prison, but there was no sign of anything out of place. Carmel's notes had referred to the outpost being used to test a device called the "HD Cotton Crater Plant". Oliver had no idea what it was, but hoped that some trace of it might still be on the island.

"This is the plan," he announced, pointing his spoon at the mound of ice cream in the sundae glass that was meant to be the island. "I will swim across the river after dark and use wire cutters to get through the fence."

"Is the wafer biscuit the barbed wire?" asked Kieran, pointing at the bowl.

"Yes, and the walnut is the jail," added Oliver, gesturing towards the nutty peak of the ice cream outcrop. "I'll search the prison, then look outside if there's no sign of the device. I'll then swim back."

"Where do I come in?" asked Kieran, popping the walnut into his mouth.

"You'll wait in the car."

"I want to join in," protested the youngster, munching on part of what was supposed to be the barbed wire fence.

"It's too risky, especially the old jail. By the way, where has it gone?"

"I ate it," muttered Kieran, gesturing at the bowl.

"The biggest danger is the river," added Oliver. "The currents would sweep most people out to sea. They might even catch me, so I've come up with a secret weapon."

Instead of curiosity, Kieran greeted the news with indifference and continued his ice cream, clearly disappointed that he wouldn't be taking part. Oliver gazed along the scenic coast, and felt his heart sink as well. Not only was he apprehensive about sneaking onto the island, but in the foreground, he spotted one of his favourite bars. He remembered spending an afternoon at The New Waterfront shortly after arriving in Devon. He'd lazed by the sea all afternoon watching Royal Navy destroyers vanquish imaginary targets while he sank pints of real ale. Any chance of sloping off to the pub was limited with an eleven-year-old in tow. Life before Kieran was dull but enjoyable. Oliver's existence was rapidly becoming exciting but less fun. As the bill arrived for the ice cream, he realised that life was also becoming much more expensive.

***

Thirty minutes after nightfall, the Gordon Keeble cruised to a halt on Plymouth Hoe. Oliver and Kieran were now directly opposite Drake's Island, which was shrouded in total darkness. The searchlights bolted to Détente's building on the mainland were switched off. Oliver was initially pleased, then realised that the defence firm probably had countless other security devices that were not so obvious. All the same, he needed to know what was on the island. Above all, he had to discover why Carmel had been murdered in order to expose the killers and avoid the same fate himself.

"This will be dangerous, so stay here," ordered Oliver, as he stepped from the car. He opened the boot and removed a waterproof backpack that he'd bought after leaving the ice cream parlour. Inside was a torch, camera, trowel and watertight box. He then extracted two metal hooks from the boot, one of which he placed in the backpack, and a reel of sturdy plastic cable. The sales advisor at the hardware store promised that it would stretch to over a quarter of a mile. Oliver hoped that he was right, or part of his plan would be in jeopardy.

After closing the boot, Oliver looked around to ensure that nobody was watching. The western side of Plymouth Hoe was much quieter than the eastern and southern sides, which were often busy with visitors. Satisfied that he was not being watched, Oliver removed his outer shell of clothing to reveal a wetsuit underneath. He'd picked it up from a second-hand surf shop. However, he wasn't planning on riding any waves, but had a nasty feeling that his moonlit visit to Drake's Island was about to create some.

Oliver fixed one of the metal hooks into the grass verge near the water.

"What are you doing?"

He spun around immediately, his heart racing in panic. He then found himself eyeball to eyeball with Kieran.

"I told you to wait in the car," reminded Oliver, trying to regain his composure.

"It's boring," protested the youngster. For a moment, Oliver considered sending his pint-size accomplice across to the island while he relaxed in the driver's seat. However, he quickly realised that getting an eleven-year-old arrested or drowned wouldn't sit easily with social services. He marched Kieran back to the car.

"At least tell me what you're doing," protested the boy.

"I'm fixing the cable to the hook. When I reach the other side I can use another to secure the cable and then drag myself back."

"What if you don't make the island?"

"If the currents are too strong, I'll use the hook on this side to drag myself back. That means I won't get washed out to sea."

Kieran returned to the car looking decidedly grumpy. Oliver trudged to the water's edge, placing the backpack over his shoulders and tying the cable to his left arm. As his feet entered the water he felt a surge of adrenaline surging through his body. Even in July, the water was cold. He immediately began swimming to build up some body temperature. The currents in the River Tamar were considerable. For every metre he swam towards the island, he had to swim another upstream to avoid being carried out to sea. His diagonal trajectory was slow, but at least the security staff on the mainland seemed in the dark.

Oliver knew he wasn't an Olympic swimmer, but he could cover a mile without much trouble. However, his legs were now burning with the constant battle against the currents. He was also being buffeted by the waves, and every so often, he received a mouthful of foul tasting sea water. It was going to take most of his strength to reach the island, and even then, he would have to swim back.

When Oliver dragged himself onto dry land he felt exhausted. Looking back towards the mainland, all was still quiet at the security building. He perched on a rock to recover his breath. If swimming across to the island was risky, breaching its barbed wire fences would be even more daring. He tried to recall if he'd done anything so dangerous during his years as a crime reporter. He'd certainly interviewed lots of relatives of murder victims, which was emotionally draining, but not physically dangerous. He'd written about organised crime, but never been threatened by any mobs. On one occasion, he'd been instructed to do a feature on training police dogs, which involved him dressing as a mock gangster and being chased by the canine raw recruits. However, while the hounds bundled him over, they did not really hurt him. Although one did relieve itself on his suede shoes. This was when Oliver realised that there was a subtle difference between a Metropolitan Police Doberman peeing on your foot, and a miniature poodle, namely that you let the police dog finish.

The searchlights were still switched off, and having recovered his breath, Oliver took the wire cutters from his backpack. After a short time, he'd created a large enough hole in the fence to crawl through. Before doing so, he untied the plastic cable from his arm and fixed it to a second metal hook, which he sank into the ground. He would now have an easier trip back, assuming the guards didn't spot him and the hooks held firm.

Once through the fence, Oliver trudged up the rocky terrain towards the jail. There were no security guards on the island and it seemed deserted. In the distance, Oliver heard the traffic noise of Plymouth drifting across the pitch black water. As he entered the ruins of the prison he switched on the torch. There were no signs of it being a former jail, with no telltale bars or steel doors. It could have been an old factory or warehouse to the casual eye. However, there was something unusual in the centre of the building. Oliver walked towards it and was baffled by what he saw. There was a crater around ten metres across and several feet deep. The explosion – if that was the cause – had removed the stone flooring and uncovered the soil beneath. The crater was also covered in a fine white powder. It looked furry to the touch, but Oliver decided against finding out, just in case it reduced his fingers to a quartet of charred stumps. Using the trowel, he placed a few samples into the waterproof box. He then took pictures with the camera, but stopped when its flash seemed to be overly bright. He also switched off his torch, but the glow did not disappear.

"Searchlights," he muttered. It was unclear if he'd triggered a hidden sensor, or if the camera flash had been spotted, but Oliver knew that he had to escape. He sprinted from the building, then plunged to the ground as he emerged outside. He started to crawl towards the water between the sweeps of the searchlights. It took ages to drag himself over the jagged rocks but he gradually crept towards the barbed wire fence. Eventually he reached it, but hit a major problem. He wasn't in the same place as before, and couldn't find the original gap. He thought about cutting a fresh hole, but that would take time, and he would be nowhere near the plastic cable. He still hadn't regained his strength from the swim, and the frenzied activity at the security building across the water was not helping his heart rate to recover. Oliver wriggled along the ground and searched for the gap. He still couldn't find it and the severity of his situation was beginning to sink in. Even if he reached the mainland, he'd have to dodge the security guards. His predicament eased a little when he found the original gap in the fence. After crawling through he located the cable and scrambled into the water. He began to drag himself along, but his progress was painfully slow. It would have been faster to swim but Oliver couldn't muster the strength. The best option seemed to be the cable, but his situation was about to go from bad to worse. Despite grabbing the line with both hands, Oliver could feel himself drifting. He realised that the metal hook on Drake's Island must have given way. Owing to its barren and rocky surface, he'd struggled to find anywhere to fix the cable, and the small slither of soil near the water had proved insufficient.

Oliver was tempted to abandon the cable and swim, but he didn't have the energy to reach the mainland. Even so, he was now halfway across, and despite the intense activity at the security building, no guards had found the hook that was helping Oliver back to dry land. The searchlights were also avoiding him, presumably in their vain search for a nearby boat or intruders on the island. His plan seemed to be working, but then he saw a figure walking towards the patch of ground where his hook was fixed. For the first time Oliver felt properly afraid. At best he would be caught, at worst cut adrift. The figure reached for the cable. Oliver felt himself being pulled towards the mainland. He was now contemplating jail instead of a watery grave, which was some consolation. However, as Oliver neared the shore, he realised that the figure was not a burly guard, but a young lad.

It struck Oliver that for the first time since meeting him, he was actually pleased to see Kieran. His progress through the water was now much faster, but he was worried that the guards might become suspicious. He was tempted to wave Kieran away but his arms barely had the strength to cling to the cable. All he could do was to keep pulling himself towards the shore.

Once Oliver was within 50 yards of dry land he thought he was virtually home. However, the coast was frustratingly elusive. He almost felt that he could reach out and touch the grassy bank. He also noticed that the water was becoming brighter as he dragged himself towards the street lights on the mainland. In fact, it was so bright, that he was practically blinded. Oliver then realised that he'd been picked up by a searchlight.

Kieran was still on the bank, pulling the cable and its exhausted cargo towards safety. Oliver felt a wave of panic shoot through his body, and he dragged himself towards the shore. When he was within a few yards he tried to stretch out a leg to see if he could touch the river bed, but felt nothing. He hauled himself along for a few more agonising yards and tried again. This time he felt slippery rocks beneath him. Oliver released his desperate grip of the cable and started wading through the water with the gait of a bewildered drunk. He toppled forwards onto the bank, marvelling at the sensation of the soft grass beneath his palms. He then looked at the security building, and was blinded once more by a searchlight. He knew he wasn't safe, but he could barely force himself to stand. He was so tired that he no longer cared if he was caught.

"Hurry up," urged Kieran, tugging at his arm. Oliver then realised that he wasn't the only one in danger, and even if he wasn't bothered about saving himself, he still had to protect Kieran. He staggered towards the car, being tracked by the searchlights all the way. When he reached the vehicle he unlocked the driver's door, threw his backpack on the rear seats, then dragged himself behind the wheel. This time it came as second nature to open the passenger door and let Kieran onboard. Seeing as the youngster had saved him from being captured, he was hardly likely to forget him.

Oliver jammed the keys into the ignition and the engine fired angrily. The car tore away from the kerbside, with the screech of tyres only being drowned out by the roar of the V8 motor. Oliver then checked his mirror and saw a jet black range vehicle in pursuit. It was moving fast, but disappeared from view when Oliver veered into a side street. He then took another sharp turn in an attempt to shake them off. He checked the mirror again and saw nothing. He then looked forwards and noticed that the narrow road was deserted. Oliver flicked a switch and turned off the headlights, creeping forwards at walking pace. He gazed at the mirror once more and saw the range vehicle flash past. It had missed the turning and was charging off in the wrong direction. Oliver breathed a sigh of relief, but then realised that he was utterly lost. He reached for his Devon road atlas in the glove box, but Kieran had already taken the book.

"Turn left," he instructed.

"If you insist."

"Headlights," reminded the youngster.

"Wise guy."

***

Oliver closed the garage door at Edenhurst Court. He was home in one piece, but thought it wise to keep his car out of sight for a while in case the security guards had noted its description.

When Oliver returned to his apartment he just wanted to collapse onto his bed. But then he remembered why he'd fled in the first place. His normally tranquil and well-ordered sanctuary was an unmitigated mess of Kieran's belongings.

"Could we leave this lot until morning?" sighed Oliver, gesturing towards the rickety skyscrapers of toys and clothes. Kieran nodded in reply.

"Good, let's get some sleep," said Oliver.

"I can't go to bed."

"Why not?"

"Mine's in pieces."

Five minutes later Oliver was still struggling to find sheets and pillows. He was also trying to decide if parenting was harder than infiltrating a global defence firm. The former suggested itself as he battled to clear a space in his study for the frame of Kieran's bed. He then heaved the mattress into place and wrestled the sheets and blankets into submission. His arm muscles were burning after his trip to Drake's Island, and while he toiled in silence, Kieran was sitting comfortably, waiting impatiently for his bed.

"It's ready, time for lights out."

Kieran left the sofa and picked a path through the awkward towers of his belongings.

"Where are we going tomorrow?" he asked.

"Nowhere I hope, this mess needs tidying."

"That'll take you hours."

"You're helping too," said Oliver. The youngster looked unimpressed. Not only would the following day be unexciting, but he might have to do some work. Oliver closed the door and headed into the kitchen. He then noticed a light blinking on his answer phone to indicate there was a message. He pushed the button, expecting a cold call from someone offering a useless product. Given his sixth floor existence, a potting shed sprang instantly to mind.

"Mr Dart, this is Mrs Lightbody," the message announced. Oliver now wished that it had been a sales call. He didn't need a shed, but would have happily bought one to avoid Kieran's larger-than-life social worker.

"I was ringing to say that I'm visiting you tomorrow."

Oliver was now prepared to buy a shed, picnic table and set of garden chairs.

"I want to ensure Kieran is settling in, so I'll drop by at eleven o'clock. Unless I hear from you. I'll assume that's convenient."

The message ended. Oliver felt drained. It was not too late to ask social services to take Kieran back, but he couldn't consider it after the youngster had saved him at Drake's Island. He couldn't turn him away, but Mrs Lightbody's visit was still filling Oliver with fear. Not only did she have the ability to inflict children on him at a moment's notice, but she could also take them away.

***

"Where does your wardrobe go?" asked Oliver. Having emptied the study of his furniture, and filled the rest of the apartment with it, there was now space for Kieran's things. Oliver was now moving the items around to the personal taste of his new flatmate.

"In the corner beside the television," said Kieran.

Oliver was shocked by how many gadgets had appeared in his flat. Kieran had a computer, television, mobile phone, music system and games console. It struck Oliver that children now came with more hi-tech equipment than a motorised nuclear missile launcher. When he was a child, a ghetto blaster seemed impressive, but it was now a museum piece.

The doorbell excused Oliver from his removal duties, and he left the room. It was exactly eleven o'clock and Mrs Lightbody was lurking in the hall. Oliver opened the door and was poised to invite her in, but she immediately marched inside before he could do so.

"Coffee?"

"Yes please," she replied. "Skimmed milk, decaffeinated, four sugars."

"White or brown sugar?"

"Either, I'm not fussy," she insisted, setting her oversized bag onto an unsuspecting kitchen work top. "How is Kieran getting on with you?"

"Okay."

"Excellent, now where is the little cherub?"

Oliver replied that Kieran was tidying his room, and asked if he should call him.

"No, I want to speak to him alone," said the social worker, marching towards Kieran's new quarters. "I'll have the coffee when I cross-examine you later."

The study door slammed shut. Oliver was starting to feel like a second class citizen in his own home. He plodded towards the sofa and collided with the writing desk from his study that was seeking asylum in the lounge. He hobbled awkwardly to the coffee table and picked up the *Herald Express*. As he sat down to read it he glanced at the balcony windows. His sea view was obscured by seven boxes of toys and a mound of clothes. He flopped the newspaper over his head in resignation and waited for somebody to wake him.

Some time later, Mrs Lightbody emerged from Kieran's room.

"Coffee?"

"It got cold," burbled Oliver, trying to think fast, "so I poured it away."

"You could have microwaved it. I'm not that hard to please." she snorted, lifting the newspaper from Oliver's forehead. "Now we have some sensitive issues to address."

"It's about those fifty-eight people I chain-sawed, isn't it?"

"No need for sarcasm, the children are always better at it anyway. Besides, we never leave youngsters with serial killers. It annoys them."

"The kids or the murderers?"

"Both. Now we need to discuss Ms Rawlings' funeral."

Oliver was shaken from his sarcastic slumber and found himself neck-deep in yet another crisis. He expressed his surprise that the burial hadn't already taken place.

"She only died earlier this week," reminded the social worker. "Kieran only stopped crying shortly before he arrived here."

If the youngster had spent any length of time with Mrs Lightbody, Oliver could easily understand his reaction. If he hadn't felt sorry for Kieran before, he certainly did now.

"You can hold the funeral when detectives release the body," she explained. "Given Ms Rawlings' lack of close family, the arrangements are up to you."

Oliver's heart sank. He had no idea how to organise a funeral. He guessed that a church or crematorium would feature somewhere along the line, but the process of booking one was totally alien. He also had no idea who to invite.

"The police family liaison officer will offer some help," clarified Mrs Lightbody. "What you must decide is whether Kieran should attend."

When it came to tricky situations, it was a case of 'out of the frying pan and into the vat of nuclear waste' as far as Oliver was concerned. He could only see one solution.

"I'll ask him."

"He is only eleven," reminded the social worker.

"He's strong, and grown up for his age."

"Yes, I suppose he is," reflected Mrs Lightbody. "Kieran is certainly an intelligent boy. I could tell that from speaking to him."

Oliver was impressed that Kieran had managed to slide a word in edgeways. Then again, perhaps he just seemed like an attentive listener.

"He said he enjoyed the last two days with you."

"Really?" asked Oliver, failing to mask his surprise.

"He told me you spent a day at the beach in Cornwall. He also said you'd shown him the Tamar Bridge and the Plymouth Dome, and gone swimming."

It wasn't quite accurate to imply that Kieran had taken a dip as well, but the story had certainly saved Oliver from deep water.

"I'm glad he's having fun."

"Yes, he says he enjoys your 'little adventures'. It's certainly a good idea to keep him occupied for now. These daytrips will take his mind off his mother's accident."

"She was murdered, you do realise that?"

"Indeed, but I don't like using such brutal language in these cases. Anyway, I'll return to check on Kieran next week."

"Drive carefully, you wouldn't want an 'accident'," muttered Oliver.

"I'm a very safe driver," retorted Mrs Lightbody, marching towards the door. After it slammed behind her, Oliver dragged himself from the sofa towards the study, clattering immediately into a bookcase that used to reside there. The social worker's visit had left him shaken, but one part of her bossy rhetoric seemed to contain some good advice. All the time that Kieran was occupied, he was unlikely to dwell on his mother's death. Oliver approached the door to his room.

"Can I come out now?" the youngster asked.

"Yes, and bring a small travel bag. We're going on another adventure."

***

Kieran seemed in buoyant mood as they headed towards the railway station. Oliver wanted to travel by train in case Détente – or anyone else with weapons of mass destruction – was looking for his car. He needed to know more about the company. In particular, the soil samples from Drake's Island required an expert eye, which was the main purpose of the trip. However, there was a second reason, which Oliver kept to himself.

It took around twenty minutes to walk from the apartment to Torquay station. It was a scenic route, and once they'd sauntered down to the marina, it was virtually flat, which was a rare comfort in the resort. The sea was lapping at the sandy beach, making ideal conditions for the bucket and spade brigade. However, Oliver and Kieran had more important things on their mind than ice creams and sandcastles.

The ticket clerk at the the station belly-laughed when Oliver asked if children went free on the railways.

"Okay, I haven't travelled with a kid before," he explained.

"Bit old for his first trip, isn't he?" said the clerk.

"His mum normally takes him," Oliver replied, handing over a painfully large amount of cash for the tickets. They then meandered onto the platform and kicked their heels waiting for the next train.

"You don't smile much," said Kieran.

The remark caught Oliver off guard. He was upset about the price of the tickets, but wasn't suicidal. He was a little reclusive, but wouldn't describe himself as depressed.

"I smile sometimes," he replied.

"I've never seen it."

"Well, I don't always smile, but I enjoy things."

"Like what?"

"Classic cars," shrugged Oliver, scrutinising the cost of his train tickets.

"And?"

"Good food, cycling, loads of stuff."

"But they don't make you smile."

"You don't have to smile to enjoy yourself."

"Are you afraid to?"

"No, I just don't see the need."

The train wheezed to a halt, allowing Oliver to excuse himself from the conversation and lead Kieran into the nearest carriage.

"Where are we going?" asked the youngster.

"Exeter."

"I know that, you told the ticket office man," groaned the youngster. "I meant where are we going once we arrive?"

"The exit," retorted Oliver.

"After that?"

"Outside."

"Then where?" demanded Kieran, becoming frustrated.

"You'll see."

The train pulled out of Torquay station and headed north. Kieran was silent once they were in motion. His eyes were glued to the window, soaking up the scenery like a sponge as if he was trying to memorise every last farm, haystack, hill and stream.

After an hour they arrived in Exeter. It was smaller than Torquay, and microscopic compared with London. However, it was the county town of Devon, and its main station – St David's – was impressive. Given the city's position, virtually everyone in Cornwall and Devon who wanted to go elsewhere in Britain went through Exeter. However, for Kieran and Oliver, their journey was complete.

The Streatham Campus of Exeter University was only half a mile from the station but was perched on a steep hill. The trees hanging over the paths provided some shade, but the day was still uncomfortably sultry. When Oliver arrived at the biosciences building there was hardly anyone there, given that it was the summer break. However, he'd phoned ahead to check that the person he wanted to visit was there. His name was Lucas – a lab technician who needed to join workaholics anonymous. He met Oliver at the faculty door, resplendent in rubber gloves and a fraying lab coat that was just about white enough to mask his dandruff.

"Hello Dart," he said, squinting as he lifted his safety goggles. He then offered his right glove to shake, but Oliver declined when he saw that it was covered in smoking slime.

"Sorry, I'm halfway through an experiment," he clarified.

"You haven't been eating uranium again?"

"Not since the professor's memo."

"The one entitled 'the periodic table is not food'?"

"It's framed on my wall," he reflected with a smile. "So what brings you here?"

"Remember our graduation?" posed Oliver, removing his sunglasses.

"That was over twelve years ago, the Third Reich came and went in less time."

"Fair point, but I've kept my promise to visit."

"Which you made after five pints of snakebite and tomato juice."

"Horrid stuff," muttered Oliver, recalling the taste. Lucas had dared him to tackle the concoction on their last night on campus. Seeing as tomato juice was a major ingredient in a Bloody Mary, the snakebite version was nicknamed the Bloody Horrendous. It was the most feared tipple in the student house that Lucas and Oliver had shared with six other people for nearly two years. They barely knew each other when they moved into the dilapidated hovel, but became friends. However, they drifted apart after entering the working world. Oliver had now decided to track down his former housemate, who was understandably cynical.

"So, Dart, what do you want?"

"We've got a soil sample," announced Kieran. Lucas suddenly switched his gaze to the youngster, having previously ignored him.

"So, is this your…"

"…faithful assistant, yes," interrupted Oliver, before Lucas could ask if Kieran was his son. The lab technician invited his guests inside, and they negotiated a network of stairwells before reaching a storeroom cluttered with Bunsen burners and bottles of acid.

"So where's this sample?" asked Lucas.

"In here," said Oliver, holding up the waterproof box from Drake's Island.

"Looking for anything in particular?"

"Dangerous chemicals, or signs of a military test," said Oliver.

"Oh, been digging the garden, have we?" muttered the technician. He then opened a cupboard and took out a gargantuan pair of tongs. He used them to grab the container and lowered it carefully inside a steel chest which he immediately padlocked.

"Can't you do a quick test to determine what's in the sample?" asked Oliver.

"Not really, if the soil is contaminated then I'll need specialist equipment. It might be days before the right laboratory comes free."

"Who's in there at the moment?"

"The professor – he's brewing nettle Champagne for his daughter's wedding."

Kieran then asked, for the fifth time in half an hour, if he could visit the toilet. Oliver had refused on the previous four occasions, urging him to wait until they reached the faculty. Now he relented, and allowed Kieran to scurry off down the corridor.

"I hoped he'd disappear for a while. I have something awkward to discuss."

"Go on," muttered Lucas, fixing an 'extreme danger' notice to the steel chest.

"While I'm here, I wondered if anyone on the campus did these things," said Oliver, handing the technician a piece of paper.

"You want a 'pat-a-cake taste'?"

"No," whispered Oliver, "a paternity test."

"It's your awful handwriting again. Remember that list of chores from university?"

"My note said 'blow dry sheets'."

"Fair enough, but you must admit, it looked like 'blow up shed'."

"I was picking splinters out of the gnomes for months."

"It went with a bang," chuckled the technician. "When that lawnmower flew over the fence and set next door's washing alight, I knew science was fun."

"What did you brew up to obliterate that shed anyway?"

"Hopefully not the same stuff as your sample. I must say Dart, tests for weapons of mass destruction and love children; your life sounds interesting."

"It didn't used to be," Oliver sighed.

Lucas then opened a drawer and removed a business card, which had the name of someone in the medicine faculty.

"This guy is a friend," he said. "He'll do your Darth Vader test."

"My what?"

"'Luke, I am your father'," sniggered the technician, cupping his hands to perform the ham-fisted impression.

"Here's my details," said Oliver, passing Lucas his phone number. "Call me after the soil tests and I'll stand you a pint."

"Okay, so long as it's not a Bloody Horrendous."

***

The medicine faculty was one mile across town at the St Luke's Campus. Oliver and Kieran walked through the city centre and into the cathedral close. Fashion-conscious diners were posing outside the chic bars and restaurants nibbling lunches which all featured pesto, salsa, watercress, rocket, and no chips. Oliver kept walking, carefully negotiating the cobbles outside Exeter Cathedral. Kieran was complaining about sore feet, but Oliver was facing a bigger problem. He had to convince the youngster to take a DNA test, and was unsure if he should come clean about it, or trick him. Neither seemed ideal, as Oliver didn't want to dupe Kieran, but admitting that he was uncertain if they were related sounded even worse.

On arriving at the medicine faculty, Oliver presented the card that Lucas had given him to the receptionist. A phone call was made and before long a small furry creature answering to the name of Bertie scurried into view.

"Lucas said you were coming," he chirped.

"Did he explain why we're here?"

"Indeed," said Bertie, scrutinising his visitors for any family resemblance.

"What are we doing?" asked Kieran.

"Another test," shrugged Oliver. "We need to see if the soil sample has any effect on humans. Isn't that right, doctor?"

"It is?" he muttered, failing to notice that the other grown up was winking wildly.

"Yes, it's just routine," said Oliver, now nodding for good measure.

"Of course, what was I thinking?" Laughed Bertie, finally catching on. He ushered his two visitors into a side room and seated them before asking which one would go first. Oliver volunteered and went into a small office where Bertie took swabs of his mouth.

"What will this cost?" mumbled Oliver, as the cotton bud tickled his gums.

"Don't worry, it's free. I need the experience."

"Pardon?"

"I haven't done this on humans before, I normally get sheep."

"You're not a vet, are you?" asked Oliver.

"No, a medical student, but my tutor won't let me tamper with people."

Oliver sighed in resignation, knowing that he could hardly complain given that the test was free. However, he had a nasty feeling that the results would indicate that he was second cousin to Baa Baa Black Sheep. He left the office and returned to the side room.

"Nothing to worry about," Oliver said to Kieran, "he just puts a cotton bud in your mouth, so there's nothing nasty."

The youngster dragged his feet as Oliver manoeuvred him into the office. Bertie then took swabs of Kieran's mouth, instantly doubling his experience of DNA testing on non-ovine subjects.

The medical student added that the results would be available within a week.

Oliver led Kieran from the building. The youngster seemed quiet, as if concerned by the medical tests.

"You're not worried about the results, are you?"

"What if the soil gives us cancer?" Kieran muttered.

"It won't," chuckled Oliver, but his mirth soon evaporated when he realised that the idea wasn't completely ridiculous. He hadn't a clue what Détente had unleashed on Drake's Island, and breaking into the test site suddenly didn't look so clever. Now Oliver was equally worried, but he had to stay calm for Kieran's sake.

"The doctor said the tests might have side effects."

"Like what?" asked Kieran, clearly on edge. Oliver's response was calculated to take the youngster's mind off Drake's Island. He replied that their blood sugar would be low, and they would need to eat quickly.

"They say chocolate and ice cream is good for kids," he added. "I think burgers and pizzas are recommended too."

"Brilliant," enthused the youngster, "can we have another test later?"

"Sadly not, but you must eat immediately."

"Do you need burgers and chocolate too?"

"No, the medication for grown-ups is different. In fact, the doctor said cold beer would do nicely."

***

Kieran devoured the pizza as if it might save his life. Oliver put the gorging down to hunger, seeing as the youngster seemed calmer about the university tests. They caught a bus from there to the historic waterfront beside the River Exe. The afternoon was warm, and several boats were nudging past towards the coast a few miles south. Oliver spotted a table outside a bar, and was soon sipping a beer while Kieran dispatched a pizza.

"Are you old enough to drink alcohol, sir?"

Oliver found himself staring at a policeman. Thankfully, he was on good terms with this particular flatfoot. Dressed in a blue shirt and wearing brogues that were polished to the point of absurdity, there was no mistaking Detective Sergeant Kwame Ebwelle.

"I got your message," he added, assuming a seat. Oliver then asked his best – and indeed only – friend in Devon and Cornwall Constabulary if he fancied a drink.

"You read my mind."

"Mineral water as you're on duty?"

"No, I've just finished, so I'll have a large scotch."

"Great," said Oliver.

"Bollocks," thought Oliver, plodding mournfully into the nearby pub. On reaching the bar he sensed that he was being followed.

"Who's the nipper?" asked the detective, who was hovering at Oliver's shoulder like a bored wasp. While buying the drinks, he explained that Kieran was allegedly his son, and that his mother was Carmel Rawlings.

"I never knew you had a kid," said Kwame.

"Nor me," muttered Oliver, trying to muster enough coins from his wallet to cover the round. "He arrived on my doorstep after Carmel's murder."

"Poor lad," sighed Kwame, adding that he'd investigated her shooting, but forensic experts had not matched the bullet to any known source.

"It was fired from distance though, which suggests a professional," he said.

"But who hired them?"

"Somebody rich that wants to stay that way."

He then explained that lengthy inquiries had been made in Perranporth, but without success. None of the hotel owners had seen anything suspicious, making it hard to tell if the assassin was lying in wait, or simply drove to Cornwall for the day.

"It would be useful to know whom Carmel was investigating," the officer added.

"That's what I'm trying to find out."

"Any luck?"

"Nothing yet, but there's some paperwork you'll want to see."

Oliver and Kwame returned outside. The youngster was thumbing through the folder of documents left by his mother. When asked, he handed them to the officer. Kwame flicked through the pages, but his look of expectation turned to confusion. As he wrestled with the Royal Navy documents and those from Détente, he shook his head.

"Is this a dodgy defence deal?" he asked. Oliver replied that Détente was building something called the 'HD Cotton Crater Plant', which was apparently in Plymouth.

"Shame it didn't go off," cackled the flatfoot.

"I reckon it did," replied Oliver, "I've seen the crater it left behind." He then recounted the story about Drake's Island, and giving the test samples to the university.

"Why didn't you bring them to us?" whined the policeman. Oliver asked where they would have been sent.

"To the specialist lab."

"Which is where?"

"The university," conceded the officer.

"See, we saved you a trip," chirped Kieran.

Oliver then returned to the issue of the HD Cotton Crater Plant. Until the test results arrived, the only line of investigation was Détente's dossier and the Royal Navy papers.

"The key question is what connects them," he added.

"Is the navy trying to buy this weapon?" Kieran asked.

"Possibly," shrugged Kwame, "they could even be funding its research."

"I'm not so sure," muttered Oliver, adding that the prototype weapon was not tested at sea, suggesting that the army or air force were more likely customers.

"So if the navy isn't buying, why are they involved?" asked Kieran.

"Perhaps they're flogging redundant bases to Détente for military tests," speculated the detective.

Oliver replied that it was plausible, but the naval papers were disciplinary reports and not property documents.

"That suggests Carmel was checking people instead of places," he added.

The policeman asked who was named in the reports. Oliver replied that the identities were obscured, and given that they were copies, the files were probably censored by naval chiefs. However, it appeared that five sailors were involved. Four were charged with bullying the fifth, and they were all new recruits based at Portland in Dorset. The quartet were found guilty, and court-martialled, while the fifth one left the service.

"They must have done something awful to him," he added.

"You virtually had to kill someone to get court-martialled 30 years ago," said Kwame. "These days you only need to break wind without apologising."

Oliver knew Kwame had been in the army for several years before joining the police. The officer had often joked that patrolling war-torn countries was ideal training for working at Scotland Yard. After drinking his whisky, the detective produced his notebook and took down the main details from the naval papers.

"Any idea what became of these sailors?" he asked.

"No, but it would be useful to know," said Oliver.

"I'll try to find out," said the detective, who closed his notebook. He then rose from the table and strolled off, but Oliver caught him a few paces later out of Kieran's earshot.

"You'll keep this between us, okay?" he muttered.

"Still hungry for the scoop," observed Kwame.

"I just need to know if I'm in danger."

"What about the kid?"

"He wants to know who killed his mother."

"You might be safer not finding out," warned Kwame.

***

The shadows were growing long as Kieran and Oliver returned to Torquay. The bucket and spade brigade had left the beach, driven away by the sinking sun and rising tide. The couples, friends and stag parties that would usurp the town later were yet to arrive. Most of the commuters were now home, leaving only a handful of people on the streets.

As they walked along the seafront, Oliver began to worry about Kieran. Since they had met, they had dashed from place to place, but their investigation was beginning to stall. They needed the test results back from the university, but that would take time. Oliver knew that he couldn't sit around and wait, as Carmel's killer might be hunting him. With the police drawing a blank over her shooting, it was vital to find the culprit before the assassin caught him, and also found Kieran.

For a while, as they walked past the harbour, Oliver considered the idea of running away. He tried to think of where he could lie low, but then remembered what happened to Carmel. She fled London and went to ground in a remote Cornish resort. Despite being a stranger there, she had still been found. Oliver now realised that it was pointless to play hide and seek with her killer, unless he could be the seeker.

On returning home, Oliver expected to find his furniture tipped over and documents scattered across the floor. The actual scene was pretty close, but only because he'd left it that way.

"I'd forgotten what a mess this place was in," he groaned.

Kieran then inquired what was for dinner. Oliver's heart sank, realising that the boy hadn't eaten for three hours and would become riotous without a prompt infusion of calories. The only consolation was that Kieran was now old enough so that nobody needed to change his nappy.

Within a few minutes the Bolognese sauce was starting to look like something out of a horror movie. Oliver was stirring it unconsciously while slouched in front of the cooker. His gaze was focused on the Royal Navy paperwork beside the hobs. Every so often the motion of his wooden spoon would slow down and the sauce would begin to spit. A few red dots would then appear on the reports, and Oliver would start to stir more vigorously again. Meanwhile, the saucepan of Penne pasta was boiling with the violence of a small nuclear reactor. It barely registered with the chef, who was determined to find out what linked the five sailors with Détente and the HD Cotton Crater Plant.

"Art sun bap," announced Kieran, waiting impatiently at the table.

"What's that?"

"An anagram."

"Of what?"

"Burnt pasta."

"Damn," muttered the grown up, switching off the gas. He strained the mushy Penne and promptly drowned the evidence in his mediocre Bolognese sauce. He then deposited the plates on the table with all the grace of a drunken walrus. Kieran then started to eat the meal, but without any obvious sign of appreciation.

"I need to ask a tough question," said Oliver.

"It's okay, I don't want Parmesan cheese."

Strangely enough, this wasn't the line of inquiry that Oliver had in mind.

"It's about your mother."

Kieran stopped eating immediately and stared across the table.

"There's going to be a funeral," Oliver continued. "Now some people would order you to attend or stay home, but I think you're old enough to decide for yourself."

Kieran reflected on the bombshell in silence.

"It's your call, I'm not going to pressure you," said the grown up, although he realised that he was placing him under huge strain.

"I don't know," he muttered, slowly pushing his burnt pasta around the plate. Oliver remained quiet, hoping that Kieran might come to a decision, but none seemed likely.

"Okay, do you think your mum would want you to be there?" he posed.

Kieran nodded, his gaze fixed downwards.

"Then we'll go together," Oliver resolved.

***

The clothes in the wardrobe were presented with military precision. First in line were the casual tops, followed by the sportswear and the jeans. Later on came the suits, the shirts and finally the ties. Oliver hated ties. They reminded him of school and countless thankless days at work. His least favourite was the black one, because there was only one occasion when he ever needed to wear it.

Carmel's body was released soon after Kieran's agreement to attend the funeral. Oliver arranged it quickly. He rang her old newspaper to see if anyone could attend, but most didn't know her, and the rest couldn't spare the time. Carmel had no close family, which had been underlined by Kieran's arrival on Oliver's doorstep. It was difficult to contact any friends because Carmel left no address book. Oliver had asked Kieran if he could think of anyone to invite. He mentioned a distant cousin in Australia, and another in Canada, but otherwise drew a blank.

Given Carmel's lack of relatives, Oliver started to wonder who identified her body. A dreadful thought crossed his mind that it might have fallen to Kieran. It then struck Oliver that if the most traumatic thing facing him was to organise a funeral, then he'd escaped lightly.

Given that Carmel had never struck Oliver as religious, he organised a simple service at a crematorium. As he arrived, he felt incredibly low. Barring the vicar, the chapel was completely empty. The clergyman asked if they wanted to wait a few minutes in case anyone else might arrive. Oliver declined the offer; his priority was to lay the issue to rest as quickly and painlessly as possible.

The vicar breezed through the service with the efficiency of a crematorium veteran. Oliver wondered how many funerals the clergyman had conducted. Hundreds seemed likely and thousands were possible. Kieran remained silent for most of the service, and only began to weep when the coffin was taken away. Oliver felt like joining in, but not because he'd lost somebody dear to him. He was upset that a human being had been murdered, and only two people had recognised the fact.

***

After returning from the funeral, Oliver made Kieran a meal and put him to bed. It had been an emotionally draining day, and the boy was soon asleep. Oliver opened a bottle of ale and walked to the window. The clutter in his lounge had been removed, and his excess furniture slotted into the most inconspicuous corners that he could find. He gazed towards the marina and its bars and restaurants, which were becoming busy. Dressed in his black tie, and with a youngster to look after, Oliver was totally isolated from the fun outside. He felt taunted by the distant laughter and muffled cheers.

The curtains were closed and Oliver retreated to the sofa. Carmel's paperwork was strewn across the coffee table, waiting to be pieced together. There was another item there, which now presented a further problem. It was the casket containing Carmel's ashes. Oliver stared at the shiny metal cylinder. He hadn't a clue what to do with it. Letting it gather dust in a drawer was disrespectful, and putting it on display seemed morbid. Giving it to Kieran would be awkward and put the youngster under greater strain. Oliver wondered if he should scatter the ashes somewhere. Carmel liked Cornwall, but as she was murdered there, it wasn't ideal. Fleet Street briefly occurred, but seeing her ashes drift into the London bustle to be whipped up by taxis and inhaled by overweight tourists was a non-starter.

"What am I going to do with you?" he muttered to the casket.

Oliver swapped his bottle of ale for some paperwork. He studied the Royal Navy documents. He wished he could uncover the identities of the five sailors in the disciplinary reports. He wondered what had become of them.

***

"Where's my Cortina?"

"In the harbour," cackled the first sailor.

"It's brand new!" the new recruit screamed.

It was 1979, and a spotless Ford Cortina Mk.4 was just starting to rust at the bottom of the English Channel near Portland naval base.

"We had to dump it in the drink to put the fire out," added the second sailor.

"It went up a treat," cackled the third.

"Sorry, I shouldn't have been smoking those fags," taunted the fourth

"You've stolen my money, my cigarettes, and now my bloody car."

The sailors had always resented the new recruit's privileged background. He was the only one at their base with a new car, or at least had been. It was the straw that broke the camel's back, or more accurately, the outrage that made the rich boy flip and lunge for his tormentors with a pair of scissors. He jabbed the first in the arm, and was about to attack the second, when the third and fourth rushed him from behind.

Sixty seconds later, the scissors were on the floor. The new recruit was lying next to them and he was soaked in blood. His chest was covered in cuts, administered by the weapon he'd used to attack the four sailors. As they left the room laughing, he passed out.

Soon after, the sailors were discharged from the Royal Navy. The recruit left hospital at roughly the same time. The cuts eventually healed, but the scars never did, and it wasn't just the marks on his chest. The mental scars would always be there, and he would never forget his time at Portland naval base.

***

Oliver read the Royal Navy documents again and pieced together what events had taken place. He felt sorry for the recruit. Oliver knew that if he could find him, then Carmel's investigation might receive the breakthrough that it needed.

He stared at the casket once more. He wanted to feel upset, but it was hard to grieve for someone that had drifted so far away. It was certainly less painful than the last time he'd lost somebody close to him.

Michelle was her name. Oliver tried not to think about her, but it often proved too difficult. She was the only woman he'd ever loved, and she had loved him back. They spent fourteen months together and were poised to buy a flat. Then fate intervened.

Oliver had written countless newspaper stories about people dying in car accidents. They were depressingly frequent, but he managed to detach himself from the raw tragedy. 'Never met them' he would remind himself as he wrote the articles. But then one day it was somebody he knew.

It would have been impossible for Oliver to write about Michelle's death. It took him several days to summon the courage to read the story, but he needed to know how she was killed. Michelle had been the only passenger in the car, and it was driven by her father. He had survived, but Oliver had not spoken to him since that day. Even though the crash was caused by a mechanical defect, he'd always been worried that he drove too fast.

There had been three lasting impacts about Michelle's death. First, Oliver didn't trust modern cars, as her father's vehicle suffered brake failure due to an onboard computer fault. The second was that Oliver always obeyed the speed limit. The final consequence was that he expected that he would never fall in love again.

Carmel, by comparison, was a ship that passed in the night. Oliver was on the rebound, and trying to convince himself that he could forget Michelle. In the end, the only way to move on was to move away, and he'd been hiding in the West County ever since. Now Carmel had returned, but not in the way he would have predicted.

"You've no idea how much trouble you've caused," he muttered to the casket. It failed to reply. Oliver realised that Carmel couldn't answer his questions from beyond the grave. While she'd found the pieces of the jigsaw, it was his job to fit them together, and he couldn't help thinking that several bits were missing.

***

The trail of seagulls followed the boat like a heat-seeking missile. The vessel was one of several in Torbay, taking in the sights of Brixham and Paignton. Most departed from the marina in Torquay, which was a short walk from Oliver's apartment. Buying two tickets seemed a sensible, albeit costly, way to keep Kieran occupied for two hours.

The youngster was increasingly restless. It had been several days since the Exeter University trip, and the only journey since then was to the funeral. Kieran spent most of his time watching films and playing computer games, while Oliver tried to produce another Spib adventure. However, it was hard to write anything, as his mind was focused on Carmel's investigation. Until the test results arrived, or his police contact came back with something, it was in total limbo. He phoned for updates every day, but nothing happened.

The boat headed along the northern edge of Torbay, past the rugged cliffs with their distinctive red rocks. It was a beautiful scene, but Oliver's thoughts were elsewhere. It was hard to relax with a former girlfriend dead, an alleged son appearing from nowhere, and possible death threats. His attention only returned to the voyage when some mouldy bread was thrust under his nose. Oliver saw that the other seventeen people on the boat, including Kieran, were identically armed with three slices of malted brown.

"We're feeding the birds," chirped the youngster. Oliver glanced to his left and saw the swarm of seagulls converging on the boat. Some passengers began ripping their bread into chunks and hurling them at the flock. Several pieces were caught in mid air, while others were scooped off the sea. Oliver could barely hear himself think, but amongst all the engine noise, coastal breezes and baying seagulls, he detected that his phone was ringing.

"Hello Dart, it's Lucas here, I have your test results."

Oliver was momentarily silent. He looked at Kieran, who was flinging bread with total abandon. This phone call could be the moment that he discovered if the child was his son.

"Go ahead."

Lucas then replied, but Oliver couldn't hear with all the background noise.

"What did you say?"

The technician repeated the statement, but without success.

"Look, you'll need to speak up. I have to know if he's mine."

Lucas heard what he said, as did most of the passengers. Kieran was among them. He stopped throwing bread to the gulls, and stared at Oliver.

"Sorry, I'll have to ring back," he added, hastily finishing the call. The youngster was glaring at him.

"Do you want the rest of my bread?" he asked. The youngster ignored the pathetic attempt to brush the matter under the carpet. Oliver walked to him as the boat turned back to port and the trail of seagulls disappeared.

"Kieran, you're a smart kid, so I'll be straight with you."

"You don't think I'm your son," he interrupted.

"I'd like to think you were," Oliver replied, but with scant conviction. "I just want some proof."

"Mum said you were my father."

"She might have said that, but never told me."

Oliver then explained about the DNA test at Exeter University, and that he expected the results back soon.

"What if we aren't related?" Kieran asked nervously. Oliver knew the answer, and it involved a swift call to social services and the reinstatement of his previous existence. The question that Oliver was frightened to ask was whether they were father and son.

"We'll figure it out," he replied. Kieran looked unconvinced and Oliver didn't blame him. He'd hoped that the tests could be performed without his knowledge, but that idea was dead in the water. As the boat continued its journey, Oliver thought about how to win back Kieran's trust. At best it would be difficult and at worst impossible.

The vessel returned to the marina and Oliver led Kieran ashore in silence. They took a short walk along the seaside to The Pavilion. With its ornate architecture and domes, it had been built in 1912 to hold music concerts. It was now a labyrinth of quirky shops along with a café. Oliver offered to buy Kieran whatever he liked, but his peace offering was rebuffed with a shrug of the shoulders. He bought him a soda anyway, and they took a table. Kieran declined to make conversation, and Oliver had no idea what to say. He'd only been a father, or allegedly, for a few days, and was totally out of his depth.

Oliver then recalled Mrs Lightbody's advice on keeping Kieran occupied. At first the aim was to prevent him dwelling on his mother's death but now there was a DNA test to distract him from as well. Oliver then realised that the very thing that plunged him into trouble could extract him from it – the test results from Lucas. He dialled the number at once.

"Hello, Dart here, sorry I hung up."

"No bother, it sounded noisy. Were you in a shopping centre?"

"No, a Torbay pleasure boat being chased by seagulls."

The technician replied that it sounded identical. He then asked if Oliver was ready for the test results.

"I don't think I'll ever be ready," he muttered.

"You don't sound very excited."

"I'm petrified because this could affect my whole life."

"I had no idea your soil samples were so important."

"What?"

"Hang on," he sniggered, "did you think I had your paternity results?"

Oliver fell silent, feeling hideously embarrassed. Lucas informed him that DNA tests were sent by post, and required a signature.

"We don't reveal that stuff over the phone."

Oliver asked when the letter might arrive, and heard that it would turn up within a few days. The technician then asked if he still wanted the soil sample results. Oliver produced a notebook from his jeans – a throwback to his journalism days – and prepared to take notes. Lucas stated that he performed lengthy tests on the waterproof box and its contents.

"What did you find?"

"The container had faint traces of human waste."

Oliver suddenly recalled that he'd used the same container for the samples that he found in the Saltash toilets. However, he was more interested in the contents of the box.

"Okay, Dart, first of all I need a new Geiger counter."

"Why?"

"You blew mine up."

Realising that the samples were highly radioactive, he asked if there was any risk of contamination. The technician said the dose was small, so the impact would be fairly low.

"It should only take a couple of years off your life," he added.

"I hope you're joking."

"That's only the worst case scenario. However, you might want to think twice before having children."

Oliver remained silent and shot a glance across to Kieran.

"Sorry," added Lucas, "I forgot that fatherhood was a sore point."

Oliver asked if the technician could list the elements and compounds in the sample and the technician recited them down the line.

"What do these add up to?" he asked while scribbling the names.

"Soil."

Oliver informed his colleague in the nicest possible way that he was interested in the radioactive part of the sample, and not the clod of earth.

"Okay, do you have a dictionary handy?" asked Lucas, who then reeled off a series of polysyllabic tongue twisters from the business end of the periodic table.

"A couple of those they only discovered when they detonated the first atomic bombs."

"So is the HD Cotton Crater Plant a nuclear device?" asked Oliver.

"Lord knows, I'm not an atomic fusion expert."

"I wouldn't say that, I've seen you cook."

"Just because I blow things up occasionally, it doesn't mean I'm an authority on 'genocide from above'."

Oliver enquired if anyone at the university might know what the cocktail of chemicals meant, and its destructive potential.

"The professor likes to think that he's a weapon of mass destruction, but this place is too crammed with hippies to produce anything dangerous. You'll need to look elsewhere for an expert that glows in the dark."

Oliver expressed his thanks and apologised about the Geiger counter.

"Don't worry," said Lucas, "I gave it to a first-year engineering student to repair it for his coursework."

The call ended and Oliver told Kieran what he'd learned about the samples, leaving out the possible side effects that he might have suffered. The youngster wasn't interested and continued to dwell on the revelation about the DNA tests. Oliver persisted in trying to switch his attention away from the subject.

"We need to make another trip."

"Where to?" the youngster asked, showing a brief glint of enthusiasm.

"First to see a friend, and then we might need a nuclear scientist."

"Do you know any?"

"Yes, one, but I wish that I didn't."

***

Exeter St David's station was packed with families on daytrips and sweltering office workers in oppressive formal dress. Oliver and Kieran left the Torquay service and passed through the ticket hall and into the scorching street outside.

Oliver led them towards the university, but stopped short of the campus. Instead, they passed through some ornate gates and began walking up a steep drive towards a hilltop mansion. It was the sort of residence that would have benefited from peacocks on the lawns. Instead, they were adorned with inebriated students.

The Imperial House was one of the strangest pubs that Oliver had visited. Once an elegant stately home complete with ballroom, its regal chambers had been converted into a watering hole of planetary proportions. Oliver took Kieran along the corridor, passing several rooms which boasted their own bars. Once through the passage they arrived in the modern part of the venue. The roof was a glass arch, taking its lead from a Victorian railway station. The furniture was brightly coloured, and while it was early, the atmosphere was buzzing.

"What's an orangery?" Kieran asked, spying the name on the wall. Oliver replied that it was a needlessly complex word for a conservatory.

"Conservatory is longer," the youngster pointed out.

They walked through the orangery and found a table overlooking the lawns with its decorative boozy undergraduates. As Oliver studied the menu, he became aware of a large man hovering at his shoulder.

"Hello Kwame," he muttered, without lifting his gaze from the lunchtime specials. The detective assumed a vacant seat and thumped a hefty bag on the table.

"How's the conspiracy theory going?" the officer asked.

"It's a nuclear bomb," said Kieran.

Kwame looked at the youngster and smiled, but then spotted that Oliver was making no effort to correct him.

"Are you serious?"

"Détente is developing an atomic device known as the HD Cotton Crater Plant."

"I know, you told me last time," sighed the officer, "but I can't arrest a defence firm for building weapons. That's like nicking the Spice Girls for singing."

"Sounds a good idea," said Kieran. Oliver nodded in agreement, impressed that the youngster was first to the punch line. He then explained that the soil samples suggested that Détente had developed a new weapon of mass destruction. Oliver then handed Kwame a list of the elements and compounds involved.

"This could be a toothpaste recipe for all I know," the policeman admitted. Oliver said he was none the wiser, and asked if anyone at the constabulary could decipher the list.

"Possibly, but sticking our nose into nuclear tests might raise too many eyebrows. I'd also need some justification to look into Détente further."

The detective produced a bundle of paperwork from his bag, which Oliver recognised as the Royal Navy reports and the Détente personnel documents. He added that he'd spoken to a colleague at Plymouth naval dockyard about the archive paperwork.

"We met in Iraq during my army days," said the policeman.

"Are you good friends?" asked Kieran.

"Not at first, he shot me," Kwame recalled, "he thought I was one of the other lot."

"What gave him that idea?"

"Some business about stealing fags from a cargo container."

Oliver recalled that Kwame smoked thirty a day until it was banned in pubs. He asked if there was any truth in the accusation. The policeman denied it, and said he wanted to buy some duty free packs.

"When I reached for my cash, little boy blue thought I was going for a gun."

Kieran asked why the naval guard didn't recognise his uniform.

"It was a bit worse for wear, and I'd lost the trousers in a bet. Anyway, he put a bullet in my left arm."

"You're lucky his aim wasn't better," said Kieran.

"Not exactly, it was supposed to be a warning shot," groaned the detective. He added that the naval guard was very apologetic after the 'misunderstanding' was resolved.

"He even brought me some grapes in hospital," said Kwame.

"He probably owed you one," chuckled Oliver.

"We patched things up, at least after the medics patched my arm, and we've been mates ever since. Needless to say, he doesn't mind when I call in a favour."

The detective revealed that he'd uncovered the identities of the four bullies who were thrown out of the navy.

"It's a small world, they're still at Portland," he added.

Kieran asked if they were allowed back into the navy.

"No, they're employed by our old friends, Détente," said Kwame.

"Perhaps they're working on the HD Cotton Crater Plant," speculated Oliver.

"You're getting too many pages ahead," said the policeman, adding that the bullies were 'unlikely' to be on the nuclear project. "That's unless Détente encourages its security guards to conduct atomic research in their fag breaks."

"What about the other guy in the naval papers?" Oliver asked. The detective replied that he couldn't uncover the victim's identity. He added that the navy's personnel files were also censored to keep him anonymous.

"Could it be someone powerful?" Kieran asked. It would certainly take some influence to amend Royal Navy papers, which left Oliver with two theories. Either the victim was well connected, or the key to opening a can of worms.

***

With his police contact unable to help in probing the HD Cotton Crater Plant further, Oliver had to make his own arrangements. He did know one atomic weapons expert, but hadn't seen him for years. He'd also pledged never to speak to the scientist again.

Making the phone call was hard, but after a few stunted words, the ice began to thaw and they agreed to meet. Oliver then replaced the receiver, walked across the lounge, and knocked on Kieran's door.

"He'll see us."

"Cool," replied the youngster. He then asked why Oliver had been reluctant to call the scientist. Oliver shrugged his shoulders and replied that it was a complicated story.

"Then again, it's a long drive, so I'll explain on the way," he added.

Oliver decided to take the Gordon Keeble out of mothballs for the trip. It needed a run and he was certain that nobody was bothering to follow him. Another reason was that their destination lacked a railway station.

Oliver left Edenhurst Court and drove through Torquay towards the outskirts. He liked being behind the wheel again, but knew that the journey would be difficult. Clouds were looming on the northern horizon, and he was driving right towards them.

Once past Exeter, the Gordon Keeble headed west towards Dartmoor. By now it was raining and the higher peaks were obscured by menacing clouds. Oliver left the A30 – the main road towards Cornwall – and headed further north. Their destination was Bideford.

"It's a small coastal town," said Oliver. Kieran asked if he'd been there before.

"Only once," he replied, "for a funeral."

The A386 to Bideford was a winding road peppered with villages, steep curves and hairpins. Rain was hammering on the windscreen. When they were a couple of miles outside the town, Oliver stopped the Gordon Keeble beside the road. Kieran asked if the weather was too bad to continue.

"No, there's something I must do," he muttered. Oliver stepped from the car, leaving Kieran inside in the dry. He opened the boot and took out an umbrella along with a bunch of flowers he'd purchased that morning. He admired the petals for a moment. His gaze then turned to the nearby road sign, which stated they were in Landcross. Oliver could have spent his whole life unaware of the tiny village, but fate had carved its name into his mind. He took a few paces along the grass verge until he found the spot. The last traces of the flowers he'd left there in the past were long gone, apart from the forlorn little cards that went with them. Despite being weathered by the rain, Oliver could still read his handwriting on the paper.

"To Michelle, always thinking of you, this day and forever," he said to himself, staring at the previous card.

"Who was she?" asked Kieran. Oliver was shocked to find the youngster by his side.

"You should have stayed in the car, this road is dangerous."

"Sorry."

"You weren't to know," sighed Oliver. "Michelle was my former girlfriend."

He then explained how the two of them were poised to live together in London. Then her parents moved to north Devon and she went to visit them.

"Michelle didn't drive, so her father collected her from Exeter St David's and took her along this road," he said.

Kieran asked when it happened. After checking the date on his watch, Oliver replied that it was twelve years, seven months and fourteen days.

"About the time you were seeing mum."

"Just before," conceded Oliver. He then revealed that Michelle's father had bought a new car, but the computer system controlling the brakes stuttered for a moment.

"He always drove too fast, so there was no time to react," he added. Oliver then looked at the wall on the opposite side of the road. Most of the stones were old, but several were more recent and brighter in colour. Until the accident, he'd never noticed walls that had been replaced or crash barriers where the metal was shiny and new. He now understood that these were the scars of severe accidents in the past, and often fatalities or serious injuries.

"The vehicle rolled several times and fell down this embankment," he added, pointing into the valley beyond the narrow verge. Oliver then placed the flowers next to the road. He noted that nobody else had left anything since his last visit. He wondered why Michelle's parents had not been to the spot. Oliver knew it would be emotionally draining for them, but her memory ought to live on.

"Did her dad survive?" Kieran asked.

"Yes, and we're going to see him."

"Is he the nuclear scientist?"

Oliver nodded and smiled at the youngster, impressed that he'd fitted the pieces together without any help.

"You'd make a good reporter," he added.

***

The Gordon Keeble lazily rolled into Bideford along the valley road beside the River Torridge. The town was one of Britain's busiest ports until the railways arrived, or in the case of Bideford, did not. During the previous two centuries, the transatlantic clippers had ceased to visit, and now the historic quay was populated by fish and chip parlours.

Oliver found a space near the old bridge, which was one of two that crossed the river. The other was the new bridge, which carried the A39, also known as the Atlantic Highway. The old one was much smaller, but an engineering marvel in its day. Countless stone arches spanned the fast-flowing Torridge as it raced towards the open sea.

Michelle's parents lived on the northern side of town, but Oliver wanted to meet on neutral territory. He dialled their number and her father, Graeme, answered the call.

"I'm at the quay."

"I'll meet you there."

Several minutes passed as Kieran and Oliver sheltered in the car. The rain started to ease and visibility improved. Oliver then saw Graeme in the distance, walking across the old bridge. He stepped from the car, followed eagerly by the youngster. They began to cross the river and met the retired scientist halfway across the bridge. He was a sorry sight, shuffling along in old brown shoes and a cheap grey anorak. They hadn't met in a decade, but the old man looked centuries older. It was strange to think that he'd once been a respected authority on nuclear science, and was now just an anonymous face on the street.

"Long time no see, Oliver."

"Indeed, this is Kieran."

"Hello sir," the youngster replied, opting for politeness to ease the tension.

"I met his mother after Michelle," Oliver explained.

"The years go quickly," said the scientist, running his fingers through his thinning hair, which was flapping in the soggy breeze. He then inquired about the atomic test results that had disturbed his hibernation. Oliver handed over a sheet of paper and the old man clasped it with his pale fingers. The colour soon returned to them once he'd read the text.

"This reads like the aftermath of a nuclear explosion."

"I thought you'd recognise it," Oliver replied.

"The samples are from Drake's Island," added Kieran.

"I've never heard of that testing site."

Oliver replied that it was in the Tamar estuary at Plymouth.

"They detonated this bomb in a city?" the scientist gasped.

"The crater's certainly there, but nobody seems to have noticed," said Oliver. He then described the scene on Drake's Island and what he'd discovered about the HD Cotton Crater Plant. He also told the scientist about the mysterious white residue at the scene.

"And the crater was only a few feet wide?" the pensioner asked.

"No larger than a car," said Oliver. He then asked if Détente might have constructed a miniature device to conduct a test.

"There's no such thing as a small atomic bomb," said the scientist. "Even the tiniest one will cause devastation. You certainly can't detonate them in a city without being noticed."

"Until now," said Kieran.

"It has all the symptoms of an atomic blast without the explosion," muttered Graeme, shaking his head as he studied the results. Kieran asked if he had any idea what Détente was developing.

"No," he sighed, "who'd want to build a nuclear weapon that doesn't detonate?"

A thought then crossed Oliver's mind that the test might have failed. However, if an atomic explosion wiped Plymouth off the map, he realised that Détente would have struggled to hush it up. Demonstrating a weapon was one thing, but incinerating thousands of people was a poor move in public relations terms. All he could assume was that the firm wanted a dud, and the HD Cotton Crater Plant had delivered.

"Maybe it's supposed to be quiet, like a silencer on a gun," Kieran suggested.

"Possibly," shrugged the scientist, adding that a nuclear weapon that made no noise could be useful in a sneak attack.

"But it doesn't do any damage," Oliver reminded, "it just left behind a crater and some odd powder."

As the three of them struggled to interpret the results, the conversation stalled. The rain was refusing to stop and the Torridge was flowing ever more quickly beneath them. With the silence, Oliver's mind turned to his other trip to Bideford. He hadn't spoken to Graeme at the funeral and only exchanged a few words with Michelle's mother. Most of the family ignored him that day, assuming that Oliver would drift into obscurity after the accident. It was painful to admit it, but they were right. However, another tragedy, this time on a Cornish beach, had unexpectedly thrown him back into the fold.

"How's the family?" he asked, knowing it was a risky question.

"Fine," muttered the scientist. By the lacklustre reply, Oliver could tell that things were awkward at home. Michelle was their only daughter, and their large house probably seemed very empty with just the two of them. It was also unlikely that they received many visitors, as they no longer had any close relatives. With that in mind, Graeme had ample time to contemplate his daughter's death. Judging by his appearance, the accident had taken its toll.

At the time of the crash, Oliver was initially devastated, but that soon fermented into bitterness. He didn't want to exchange another word with the old man ever again, but looking at him now, it was obvious just how much he'd suffered. With Michelle gone, Graeme had been reduced to a lonely life on the Devon coast. His fate had been remarkably similar to Oliver, except that he now had Kieran for company.

"I can't figure out these results," sighed the scientist.

"I don't know anybody else who can, and they're obviously vital, as somebody was killed for looking into this," said Oliver.

"Who?"

"My mum," said Kieran, staring the old man right in the eye.

"She died in Cornwall," added Oliver, who told the scientist about her investigation, her murder, and Kieran arriving on his doorstep in Torquay.

"And now you've involved me with it," sighed the old man.

"Look, after what happened a few years ago, I wouldn't have called you unless it was a matter of life and death. At least give it some thought," said Oliver.

The old man looked glumly at the paperwork in his pale hands.

"I guess I don't have much to lose now," he muttered. "I'll call you in a few days."

Oliver did not have a few days to wait around. He was convinced that whoever killed Carmel would soon find him, if they hadn't already and were just lying in wait.

As soon as they were home, Oliver and Kieran started to check the paperwork once more, searching for any clues that had previously eluded them.

"So the trail has gone cold," Kieran sighed.

"Not completely," said Oliver, nosing through the sheets of paper on his coffee table. "We need to find those security guards working at Détente."

With the atomic side of the inquiry on ice until Graeme had a spark of inspiration, all eyes turned to Portland. It seemed unlikely that the security guards would know much about the HD Cotton Crater Plant. However, anything they could divulge about Détente would be useful.

"What about their victim?" Kieran asked.

"I'd be amazed if the guards talked about it, and first we need to find them."

Oliver heard a knock at the door. His first reaction was to panic, fearing that it was a snap inspection from Mrs Lightbody. He shuffled across the room like a condemned man. He opened the door, but instead of being confronted by a monolithic social worker, he found a postman skulking on his doorstep.

"Need a signature," it grunted, waving a clipboard under Oliver's nose.

"Is it a ticking parcel?"

"No, it's a letter."

Oliver immediately spotted the recorded delivery sticker, partly covering the University of Exeter logo. The DNA results had arrived. His pulse raced and he scrawled a signature into the wrong box, snatched the letter, and sent the postman packing. He closed the door and looked across towards Kieran. The youngster was scribbling notes at the coffee table, unaware of the letter and its importance. Oliver stared at the envelope, but couldn't summon the courage to open it.

"Eat off cable," announced Kieran.

"Is that another anagram?"

"Yes, coffee table."

"We'll need to find a school for those language skills," said Oliver. He then looked at the letter again, and left it beside the telephone. He couldn't face knowing the truth. He also had no idea how to find a school for Kieran. He didn't even know where the nearest one was, let alone whether it was any good. He would also have to buy a uniform for Kieran and textbooks, and provide a packed lunch each day. It seemed that even if the youngster was at school, he'd still take up plenty of Oliver's time. The prospect wasn't appealing, but showing the door to Kieran would be equally tough. The DNA letter would resolve the issue, but Oliver wasn't ready to face the consequences of opening the envelope. He also had other things on his mind, namely why Carmel was dead, and if he would be next.

***

Before leaving for Portland, Oliver checked the names of the security guards on the internet to see if they were listed. Unfortunately their names were so common that he could not find anything.

"Smith, Roberts, White and Thompson," he groaned. "Why couldn't one of them be called something unusual?"

The online phone books found dozens of matches in Dorset and that was assuming the guards lived within thirty miles of Portland and were not unlisted. There was also no mention on the Détente website, which Oliver had already established was equally the case with the HD Cotton Crater Plant.

"Now what?" Kieran asked.

"If the information won't come to us, we'll have to go to the information."

The Gordon Keeble rolled away from Edenhurst Court with Oliver behind the wheel and Kieran riding shotgun. The vehicle had already tackled a run to North Devon earlier that day but now it was being pressed into service for an urgent mission to Portland.

Oliver asked the youngster if he'd packed for several days on the road.

"You told me to bring an overnight bag."

"Yes, but a thought has struck me," said Oliver, as he left the A30 at Honiton and took the Dorchester road towards Dorset. "It might take a while to find these guards, and I'm not leaving until we do."

"I've only got six computer games and four bars of chocolate," warned the boy.

"How about clothes?"

"Oh," muttered Kieran, who checked what he was wearing, "this lot."

"So you have six times more computer games than clean pants?"

Oliver found the youngster's priorities hard to fathom, though it had been many years since he was also eleven. It then struck him that if Kieran rarely changed his clothes then at least laundry days would be lighter. In fact, Oliver hadn't noticed any difference at all.

"Kieran, what are you doing with your dirty clothes?" he asked, dreading the answer. The youngster replied that he was putting them in the laundry basket.

"I don't have one," said Oliver, adding that his laundry was stored in separate airtight containers for light and dark washes underneath the sink.

"What's that wicker basket outside your room then?"

"The bin."

"You put rubbish in there?" gasped Kieran. "My clothes will stink."

"What's new?" Oliver sniggered. "Although the basket rarely smells bad as I empty it regularly."

"How often?"

"The last time was yesterday," chirped Oliver, who suddenly realised what he'd done. "Don't worry, we'll buy you some new clothes this evening."

The rush hour was starting to build when the Gordon Keeble reached the twisty road to Weymouth. Portland was perched on the southern tip of Dorset, and there was only one route onto the island. It extended across from Weymouth on a narrow mile-long shingle causeway, surrounded by the sea on both sides.

"My England shirt was in that bin."

"I said sorry," Oliver repeated, "but that was probably the best place for it, given how badly they're doing."

The peak of Portland was now clearly visible. It rose out of the English Channel like a freak of nature, and dwarfed the hills on the mainland. Even from a distance on a summer afternoon, the landscape looked windswept and hostile. A few shops and houses clung to the lower slopes, fighting a non-stop battle to avoid slipping into the sea. Further up the hill there was a jumble of old military installations and Victorian prisons. The old buildings were sunk into the rocky ground, and perched so high that it looked like a giant bird of prey had snatched them up and abandoned them there.

"Is that Détente's base?"

"One of several in Britain," Oliver replied. "Let's do some snooping."

They left the causeway and arrived in Fortuneswell, the village on the northern tip of Portland. It was the only community of any size, and Détente's base was signposted from Victoria Square, the green in the middle of the village. Oliver drove straight past it though, and across the junction.

"I thought we were taking a closer look?" Kieran asked. Oliver replied that he'd been to Portland before and knew a better place to observe the base. He drove through the outskirts of the village and the road climbed towards the summit of Portland. The route was treacherous with many tight bends. On the way they passed the gloomy entrance to HM Prison, The Verne. Further up there was a monument to Portland stone. It was a regular sight in many towns, having been used to construct countless buildings. Much of central Plymouth had been rebuilt from it after the Second World War. Had the HD Cotton Crater Plant exploded on Drake's Island, another bulk order for it would surely have followed.

Oliver brought the Gordon Keeble to a halt at the summit. On stepping from the car, he noticed that the wind was fresher. Storm clouds were converging on the northern horizon, rolling off the mainland hills. There was a sinister feeling in the air, as if something evil was about to happen.

"Burp."

"You rushed that lemonade," muttered Oliver. His accomplice scampered across the car park to a viewpoint overlooking the causeway linking Weymouth to Portland. To the west the narrow shingle barrier that made up Chesil Beach stretched into the distance. They could see for miles, but one thing in particular had caught their attention.

"That must be Détente's base," said Kieran, pointing to a line of warehouses several hundred feet below at the water's edge. There was nothing remarkable about the site, and it could have passed for a factory or transport depot to the casual eye. However, the buildings were teeming with security cameras and the steel perimeter fence was topped with razor wire.

"Are you going to break in?"

"I hope it won't come to that," Oliver replied, although he knew that strolling through the front gate and charming his way past the armed guards would be equally tough. His only comfort was that entering the base might not be necessary. If he found one of the guards in the navy reports then he wouldn't need to go beyond the checkpoint at the main entrance. If not, he'd need to confront the razor wire.

"Panic, I care," said Kieran.

Oliver asked if the sudden outburst was another spontaneous anagram. In reply, the youngster pointed proudly to a bright yellow sign that read 'picnic area'. It was certainly a scenic spot for a sandwich, but Oliver knew there was no time to waste. It was 5pm and the daytime shift at Détente's depot would soon be departing. He reckoned that some of the guards could be among their number, and he needed to intercept them.

Oliver drove back to Fortuneswell, the village beside the base, and parked in Victoria Square. He asked Kieran to open the glove box and pass the envelope that was inside.

"It's some junk mail that arrived this morning."

"What are you going to do with it?" the youngster asked. As he posed the question, Oliver carefully opened the envelope and removed the glossy marketing material that came from a dodgy-looking credit card firm. He detached the covering letter before taking a sheet of paper from his overnight bag.

"Here's one I made earlier," he said, showing Kieran a bogus covering letter addressed to an employee at Détente's base.

"So that's what you printed on the computer before we left."

"It's for one of the guards we need to contact. If we're lucky, we'll be able to give it to him personally."

"If not, at least we'll lose some junk mail," added Kieran.

Oliver sealed the envelope and stepped from the vehicle with Kieran in tow. They marched towards the depot, which even from a distance looked threatening. A huge sign with Détente's logo, an archer in Union Jack colours, towered behind the steel fences and warned visitors to keep away.

"Let me do the talking," Oliver whispered as they neared the main gate. The base was heavily protected. Instead of flimsy barriers across the road, bulky metal barricades were sunk into the tarmac. They only lowered to allow friendly vehicles to pass and were otherwise locked in place. The checkpoint was also on a tight corner, making it impossible to break through at speed. A tank would struggle to breach the perimeter, but Oliver hoped to succeed with a flimsy piece of fraudulent junk mail.

Once they were within twenty yards of the security hut, the door flew open. A large haggard man appeared whose unkempt grey hair was trying to escape from the confines of his small peaked cap.

"Hey mate," blurted Oliver, trying to sound like a 21st century yokel. "Postman left this at my place by mistake."

The guard scrutinised the letter and furrowed his brow as if having to read was physically painful.

"It's for Frank," he wheezed after conquering the first line of the address, "he's on two weeks' holiday."

Oliver enquired if he should take the 'bloody letter' elsewhere or leave it at the security hut. The guard took it reluctantly and returned to his seventeenth mug of tea since breakfast. Oliver led Kieran back to the car.

"So that guard is away for a fortnight?"

"You were listening and not watching," said Oliver.

"What was I supposed to see?"

"Did you read the identification pass on that guy's lapel?"

Kieran asked what was significant about it, and Oliver replied that along with his photograph, it listed his name.

"He's one of the four we need to find," he added.

When they returned to the car, Oliver drifted a few yards forward for a better view of the traffic leaving the depot.

"Are we going to follow him?"

"We'll have to," sighed Oliver, glancing at his watch. He added that the guards were unlikely to reveal much about Détente while on duty, so he needed to intercept them away from the base. Kieran then asked if they were going to tail the guard back to his home.

"It depends where he goes," Oliver replied. They waited for some time, trying to spot the guard in his car. Kieran voiced concerns that he might ride a motorbike and slip through unnoticed. However, his fears were unfounded.

"That's him," said Oliver, pointing at the slovenly giant. Instead of driving from the base, he was slouching along the pavement, until halting at a bus stop. He leant against the pole, which just about took his weight, and expelled a yawn that could have triggered an avalanche.

"Now we're all waiting for his bus," Oliver groaned. The minutes ticked by and the steady stream of vehicles became a trickle as the day shift disappeared. Only two employees at the base travelled by bus, and one of them was the guard.

Eventually the X7 service spluttered into view, which listed Dorchester as its destination. After picking up the passengers, the blue and white minibus shuddered away from the stop and left Victoria Square. The large tyres of the Gordon Keeble started rolling and the vehicle crept forwards like a tiger hidden in long grass. Oliver waited for one car to pass him to make it less obvious that he was tailing the bus.

The number X7 made steady progress along the causeway to the mainland. Oliver asked Kieran to watch the left side of the bus when it started to slow in case the guard disembarked. However, he remained onboard at the first stop when they reached dry land, and the car in front of Oliver managed to pull out and overtake.

"So much for keeping a low profile," he sighed. The pursuit continued as the minibus rumbled into Wyke Regis, halfway between Portland and Weymouth. The vehicle then pulled into a lay-by to take on more passengers. Oliver then panicked as he realised that he couldn't stop and block the road, or pull into the bus stop. Instead, he cruised straight past the vehicle.

"He's still onboard," said Kieran, craning his neck to see if anyone had left the number X7. Oliver looked for a side road and dived into the next turning. He then executed a hurried three-point turn, mounting the pavement, and raced back to the junction. The bus wheezed past as he arrived and the Gordon Keeble slid back into line behind it once more. The service then missed a couple of stops before grinding to a halt in the outskirts of Weymouth. A couple of Vauxhalls filed past the bus and Oliver's classic GT was then leading the queue. He didn't want to overtake but the road was clear. An impatient driver behind him then blasted his horn in frustration but Oliver refused to move. He stared at the number X7's indicator bulb, and for the first time in his life, longed for a bus to pull out in front of him.

"Two old ladies stepped off, so the guard's still onboard," said Kieran.

"Won't this bus ever leave?" Oliver sighed as the vehicle behind him blared its horn again. Finally the minibus chugged away from the stop and headed towards the centre of Weymouth. However, before it reached the shopping district, it slouched into another lay-by.

"Not again," Oliver groaned, as the Gordon Keeble slid helplessly past the stationary number X7. It struck him that tailing a bus was not as simple as it sounded. While the vehicle would never outpace his V8-powered machine, overtaking it was becoming a frequent hazard.

The classic car lurched into a side street and Oliver rammed its nose into someone's drive. He then reversed, engaged forward gear and shot towards the main road. However, before reaching it, he saw the number X7 trundle by, pursued by a mob of cars jostling for position. When Oliver rejoined the pursuit he was several vehicles behind in the line. Then matters became a whole lot worse.

"Not now!" Oliver pleaded, as the upcoming traffic lights changed colour just as the bus squeezed through the crossroads. The line of cars grounds to a halt and the number X7 vanished around the corner.

"Don't be shy, you can change in front of me," muttered Oliver, trying to will the lights to go green. He then embarked on a petulant diatribe of 'bored with this colour' until his morale was rescued by the belated illumination of the amber bulb.

"Why didn't you run the red light?" Kieran asked.

"Because it's dangerous," said Oliver, adding that he hoped he'd never have to take the risk. Unfortunately the bus was pulling further away by the second, and some swift driving would be needed to close the gap. It was made harder by the fact that none of the cars ahead seemed in any rush to use the green light that had just appeared. Just as he'd been beeped for holding everyone up, Oliver was tempted to return the compliment. The cars finally began to move and having driven intentionally slowly since Portland, he was now looking for any chance to overtake the vehicles in pursuit of the bus. To his frustration, there were no opportunities as they entered the narrow streets of central Weymouth.

Oliver was beginning to lose hope as the road wound its way into the old part of the resort. They were on the southern side of the marina which was surrounded by historical buildings on each bank of the inlet. The Gordon Keeble was still stranded in traffic. Oliver glanced across to the northern side of the Town Bridge, and could see the bus pulling into the distance. He kept sticking the nose of his car into the middle of the road like a hungry bully trying to jump the school dinner queue. Despite all his efforts, he was powerless to stop the blue and white minibus drifting out of view.

"He's getting away," Oliver seethed as they drove across the bridge. The road then turned left, and he was uncertain whether to follow the traffic.

"Stop the car!" Kieran bleated. Oliver applied the brakes and the car came to a halt on the quayside. The youngster pointed ahead at a figure matching the guard's description walking down a quiet street beside the marina. Wrenching the steering wheel, Oliver turned into the road and pulled within thirty yards of the man. He then applied the brakes and the car crept forwards at walking pace, maintaining the gap to the rotund monolith in the security uniform.

"This looks really dodgy," said Kieran, as two joggers overtook their vehicle. Oliver was just grateful that the road was quiet and no other cars were around. He couldn't be certain that the large man was the guard they were tailing, but the uniform looked identical. The figure then disappeared into The Sailor's Return, an old pub with white walls on a street corner beside the quay. Oliver drove past and found a parking space sixty yards down the road.

"Now we buy him a beer," said Oliver, stepping from the car. He opened the boot and extracted a Hawaiian shirt and gold-rimmed sunglasses. He began walking to the pub but then realised that somebody was following him.

"You'll have to wait in the car, Kieran."

"You said 'we' were buying him a beer," reminded the youngster.

"They don't serve eleven-year-olds," said Oliver. He added that he didn't want the guard to recognise him from the depot, so he'd changed his appearance. He would also drop the yokel accent, but another change was required.

"It's possible he'll remember you," said Oliver.

Kieran trudged back to the car in silence, locking himself in the vehicle. Oliver was tempted to change his mind, but knew that bringing the youngster was too risky.

The interior of the pub was adorned with fishing memorabilia, thanks to being a haunt of the deep sea angling fraternity. The walls were also sprinkled with pictures of bygone Weymouth. The woman standing behind the bar gazed at Oliver's shirt in disbelief.

"Gay night was Tuesday," she muttered.

Oliver bought a non-alcoholic beer, wary of driving under the influence, and poured it into a glass. In the corner he spotted a man in a security uniform, who had a pint of lager and a copy of the *Dorset Echo* for company. Oliver tried to summon the courage to approach him. He felt nervous, like he was asking someone for a date. In fact, he was hoping to question somebody about weapons of mass destruction and a possible threat to his life. The stark situation focused his mind and Oliver sidled over to the lonesome guard.

"What's in the *'Echo*?"

"News," muttered the housetrained ogre, eyeing his visitor with suspicion.

"A friend of mine used to write for that paper," said Oliver. It wasn't strictly true as the journalist he had in mind worked at the *Bournemouth Echo* and was no friend. However, he was confident that he could piece together enough anecdotes on Dorset stories if challenged.

"Did he write about that dolphin being spotted in the harbour?" the guard asked. Temporarily thrown, Oliver said it was tackled by the 'fish correspondent'.

"They ain't fish, they're mammals," reminded the guard. Oliver realised that with all the angling banter in the Sailor's Return, it was okay to confuse Brahms and Bach, but not a pike with a pollock – some things were sacred.

"The *'Echo* doesn't have a mammal reporter, so the fish guy stepped in," said Oliver, trying to cover his gaffe.

"So what did your mate cover, invertebrates?" chuckled the guard. Oliver was stunned that he knew such a long word. Sensing that the ice was thawing, he took a seat on the next table and pursued the conversation.

"My friend was a crime reporter and also wrote their naval stories."

"Not much of the navy left round here," sighed the guard.

"True, you'll struggle to find any sailors in Portland, except retired ones."

"I was in the navy," boasted the guard, as if preparing to reel off dozens of nostalgic stories, "but that was years ago."

Oliver's hopes of finding out something useful were temporarily dashed as the former sea dog settled back into his pint. It seemed more alcohol was needed if he was to uncover any interesting facts. Thankfully the guard's glass soon ran dry and Oliver keenly volunteered to replenish the contents.

The discussion turned to football as the next pint began to vanish. It seemed like a safe subject to encourage male bonding, but Oliver soon realised that his basic knowledge was inadequate. The guard was a Weymouth FC aficionado and could name their entire squad in alphabetical order, which he did, twice. Oliver, by contrast, was barely aware of the non-league club's existence.

"What about the England side?" he asked, diverting the conversation towards more comfortable territory.

"Overpaid and lazy," scoffed the guard while patting his beer belly.

"They ought to spend some time in the Royal Navy."

"That would teach them."

"You're right."

"No, you're right."

"You're also right."

"Then we're both right," beamed the guard, clearly delighted to be right. Oliver was less cheerful though, as despite his drinking companion's increasingly inebriated state, he had uncovered nothing of any value. He went to the bar and bought another frothy lager for the security man, along with a whisky.

"I bet discipline was tough when you were in the navy."

"They'd clap you in irons if your hair was too long," replied the guard. Judging by his current 'style', which was halfway between Ken Dodd and Wurzel Gummidge, Détente was obviously a more liberal regime.

"So how was naval life?" Oliver asked, hoping that the alcohol had sunk in.

"I wasn't there long," the old man reflected, "it wasn't my thing, if you know what I mean."

Oliver replied that he did, and the guard insisted that he knew what he meant as well. They then agreed that they both knew what they meant, and concurred once more that they were both right. Sadly, the security man's warm feeling of being 'right' was now outweighed by his even warmer feeling of being pissed. Oliver was not happy that he'd invested £13.45p in loosening his tongue with no reward. The chatter then lurched towards horseracing. Oliver knew hardly anything about it, and steered the former sea dog towards motorsport, and then cars in general.

"What are you driving?"

"Nothing at the moment, the little pigs nicked my licence, didn't they?" the old soak complained. He then recounted the evening the previous Christmas when a policewoman found him intoxicated behind the wheel of a Ford Focus that disagreed with a lamppost. Soon after, the magistrates clipped his wings, which left him at the mercy of the X7 bus.

"I was fine to drive, just like now," he protested, accidentally knocking his bag of cashews onto the carpet. "I had to swerve because of the badger."

"Badger?"

"They're endangered, aren't they? So when it shuffled across the road I had to avoid it, and succeeded, which proves I was fit to drive."

"What about the lamppost?"

"You can fix them, but you can't resurrect a flat badger, and it wasn't even me that squashed it."

"Who did?"

"The police car," said the guard. Oliver then asked how much damage the Ford Focus sustained in the crash.

"Who cares, it wasn't mine," he shrugged. "If you want to know the best motor I ever bought it was a Vauxhall Chevette. No, hang on, it was an Austin Montego. The Chevette was crap; its gearbox fell out on the A303 and caused the juggernaut behind me to veer into the escape road."

"My dad used to drive a Ford Cortina Mk.4," said Oliver. Having told a minor fib about his connections with the *Dorset Echo*, he was now dabbling in fully fledged lies. He couldn't remember anything about his father, except that the brute fled while he was in nappies. However, the deceit was a desperate last attempt to extract something useful from the drunken lump opposite.

"A Cortina Mk.4," he chuckled, "I know a story about one of those. Back at the naval base, this posh mummy's boy was training with us, and his parents bought him a new car."

Oliver enquired if it was Ford Cortina.

"You heard this story before?"

"No, we've just met."

"So we have," beamed the guard, now quite drunk. "Anyway, we decided to teach this public school poof a lesson, and nicked his motor."

Oliver asked what became of the hapless Ford. The former sea dog clenched his right fist, announcing that it was the 'car', and then extended his left palm, which was the 'harbour'. The old man then punched his palm with considerable force.

"Blosh!" he proclaimed, to add the sound effects. "And you'll never guess who it belonged to."

Oliver invited the guard to continue.

"Dr Charles Moore," he revealed, with some pride.

"Oh, said Oliver, trying to sound like he recognised the name and failing dismally. He then pushed his luck and asked if the stunt had any repercussions.

"No, I'd already decided the navy wasn't for me. It's full of cissies, wimps and toffs," dismissed the guard, who then rose to his feet awkwardly before broadcasting to the entire pub that he was going home to empty his bowels. Oliver wished the old wreck farewell.

"What was your name again?" the guard asked, on reaching the door.

"Nelson," he replied.

Oliver allowed the guard a few moments' head start while he finished his fun-free lager and scribbled the name 'Dr Charles

Moore' on a convenient beer mat. He then left The Sailor's Return and plodded back to the car.

After switching on the engine, Oliver drove back along the quay towards the Town Bridge. He then detected that something was not right. At first he couldn't place it, but then glanced to his left and realised what was wrong. The seat was empty.

Oliver jammed on the brakes and brought the vehicle to a halt beside the old harbour. He looked in the rear of the car, and even under the passenger seat before realising that it wasn't a practical place to conceal an eleven-year-old. Oliver tried to recall if the youngster owned a mobile phone, but even if Kieran had one, he didn't know the number. There was no trace of him in the car. At best, he was lost in a strange town. At worst, somebody had taken him.

***

"It took ages, but we've identified that vehicle," said the young man in the limp white shirt.

"About time," muttered the stern woman in the business suit. "It isn't like I asked you to find an anonymous VW Golf with fake plates."

"But this car was very rare."

"That should make it easier."

"At first we thought it was an Aston Martin. After that we tried matching it to an Alvis, then a Bristol and finally a Jaguar, but with no luck."

"So what is it?" the manageress demanded, losing patience.

"A Gordon Keeble GK1," spluttered her minion, "only 100 were ever made."

"There'll be 99 soon."

Her subordinate said around 85 were still roadworthy, and the one they traced was registered in Torquay. The manageress snatched the paperwork and pointed him towards the door. She then punched a number into the telephone on her glass-topped executive desk.

"Give me the chief," she ordered, impatiently drumming her nails on the glass until the call was connected. "Hello, we've identified the car outside the base. What action should we take?

***

Oliver had never lost a child before. His experience of fatherhood was limited, but already he was experiencing one of its worst moments. Even if Kieran wasn't his son, he still felt responsible for him, and he'd vanished while in his care.

Everything at the old harbour in Weymouth looked normal as Oliver marched along the quay. He wanted to run but had no idea where to go. It was becoming dark, and revellers were gathering outside the cafés, restaurants and bars. Oliver was tempted to describe Kieran to some of them, but he was ashamed to ask, as it would make him look like a terrible parent. He found it hard enough to bury his pride when seeking directions, let alone admit that he'd lost an eleven-year-old boy in a strange town. Ironically, Oliver was stomping up and down the quay so much that a couple of people asked if he was lost.

"I'm looking for someone," he told the second Samaritan.

"Who?"

Oliver froze at the question, with the words 'my son' wedged in his throat. All he could manage was 'my friend'.

"What does he look like?"

"Short," said Oliver, "and quite young."

"What was he wearing?"

Oliver clammed up again, not because the question was awkward, but that he had no idea of the answer. He knew Kieran hadn't packed a change of clothes, and had lost most of his wardrobe thanks to the wicker bin debacle. However, he couldn't recall what the youngster was wearing. As it turned out, Kieran's famine of clothes was the reason for his disappearance.

Oliver trudged back to the Gordon Keeble in case his co-pilot had reappeared. Sure enough, the boy was standing impatiently beside the locked passenger door. There was also something different about him; he was sporting a baseball cap and toting a carrier bag.

"Where have you been?" Kieran demanded.

"I was about to ask that," said Oliver, who inquired if he'd been shopping. The youngster replied that he'd been forced to, having lost his clothes in the bin.

"You were gone ages," he added. "The stores were about to close, so I bought some stuff."

Oliver was stunned that the boy felt comfortable shopping alone, yet if his mother's high street habits were any gauge, Kieran had probably heard of Prada before Preston North End. One riddle remained, however.

"Where did you get the money?"

Kieran replied that there was plenty left over from the £50 he was given to buy Oliver a new outfit following the distasteful incident at the Saltash toilets. Given the nauseating selection that the youngster had chosen, it had struck Oliver that he didn't get much for his cash. In fact it was appalling value, as he'd donated every last stitch to charity the next morning.

"You shouldn't wander off," said the grown up. He found himself waggling a finger at the boy, as if it was an inbuilt response of any parent.

"Whatever," groaned the youngster, deploying the standard teenage response to underline his maturity. Oliver unlocked the passenger door and ushered the boy inside. They headed back to Torquay.

***

The internet sprang into life on the laptop. Kieran was still asleep, but Oliver woke early and was anxious to continue the investigation. With one hand he cradled the beer mat salvaged from The Sailors Return, and with the other he typed in the name that he'd scribbled on the discoloured card. He then looked up "Charles Moore" and "Détente" on his search engine, which produced hundreds of entries.

"You fool," Oliver muttered to himself, rueing that it had taken so long to reveal a glaringly large piece of the mystery. He walked across the lounge towards Kieran's room, knocked on the door, and went inside. The youngster was hibernating under a duvet the size of Corsica.

"Do you know who Charles Moore is?"

"No," replied the duvet.

"He's the chief executive of Détente."

"Great," sighed the bedding.

"Kieran, this could be the man who ordered your mother's murder."

The blunt comment triggered a lethargic twitching of the duvet. Kieran's head popped out of the covers.

"So now what?" he asked. Oliver was about to reply, but no words left his mouth. While he recognised the importance of his discovery, he had no idea what action to take. A hero would charge into Détente's HQ and string up the perpetrator before you could say 'I'll be back'. This wasn't a Hollywood blockbuster though, and writing children's books was no preparation for storming a fortress and vanquishing a bad guy. He would need a different approach.

Oliver retreated to the laptop to study the web pages on Dr Moore. He needed to know more about him to uncover whether he was the culprit. The initial research confirmed that he served with the Royal Navy, but there was no mention of why he left. His career with Détente stretched back 20 years, starting as a chemical weapons scientist before graduating to the natural habitat of mass murderers – the boardroom.

Further reading uncovered that five years had elapsed since Charles Moore became Détente's chief executive. Since taking over, the firm had decommissioned many of its sites, including three in the West Country. Despite selling much of the family silver, the firm's share price had stagnated. Several business journals were speculating that Détente was pinning its hopes on developing a new weapon, having sunk millions into extensive research. Oliver immediately wondered if the HD Cotton Crater Plant was the item in question.

"But what use is a bomb that doesn't explode?" he asked himself. Oliver then stepped away from the table and placed a phone call. Along with tracking down a weapon of mass destruction, he had another major problem to solve.

"I know it's late to find a school, but he only turned up a few days ago."

By this point, Oliver had already spent several minutes on the telephone to Devon County Council's education department. It had allocated most of its places months earlier, which meant finding a school would be tough. Oliver recounted the story of Kieran arriving on his doorstep, which the lady at the council simply adored.

"So you've just discovered that you're a father?" she asked.

"You might say that."

"Congratulations."

"Thanks," sighed Oliver.

The council official then asked if another school had accepted Kieran already, which was indeed the case.

"Couldn't you take him there?"

"It's more than 200 miles away."

"Oh dear," said the lady. "Though if it helps, he wouldn't have to walk, as he'd qualify for free bus travel."

"Whoopee," groaned Oliver. At first, he'd tried calling the local schools directly but they were closed for the summer break. On ringing the council, he'd initially been pleased to speak to a human being instead of an answer phone. He'd now decided that he preferred the machine option.

Eventually the council official agreed to check if any local schools still had vacancies. Oliver had a nasty feeling that the nearest one would be in France. It then struck him that if no places were available nearby, then Kieran might have to return to Surrey. Oliver hadn't been tempted to call Mrs Lightbody to throw in the towel for a while, but he couldn't face a 200-mile school run. He would be sorry to see the boy leave, as while he was a burden at times, he was starting to enjoy his company.

Kieran was playing computer games, having commandeered the widescreen television in the lounge. Oliver wasn't bothered as he seldom watched it anyway. The youngster was indulging in some kind of motor racing simulation, hurling a car worth more than most people's homes around a floodlit street circuit.

"You need to drive smoothly."

"I know what I'm doing," the youngster insisted, as the supercar charged into a concrete wall, flipped several times, and blew up. Oliver commented that the game wasn't very realistic, as a fresh car promptly appeared, allowing Kieran to orchestrate more havoc.

"So you're an expert, are you?" the youngster muttered.

"My car is capable of 140mph."

"Ever driven it that fast?"

"No, that's twice the speed limit."

"Then why did you buy it?" Kieran asked, as his supercar disagreed with a Ferrari, some traffic cones, a steel barrier, and finally the harbour. Oliver recognised that the youngster had a point. He never wanted to drive quickly; in fact the prospect scared him. He'd bought the car for two reasons; first to seem more interesting and second because he had nobody else on which to spend his royalties. However, that had now changed, as there were two mouths to feed in the Dart household.

"Grab your coat, we're going for a spin," he announced. Kieran asked if they were going on another adventure.

"That's a fresh way of viewing the weekly shop," Oliver conceded.

The Gordon Keeble rolled away from Edenhurst Court a few minutes later. It was a glorious morning and the marina far below was a luscious deep blue. Kieran admired the scenery while Oliver concentrated on the twisty road. There were no pavements in Parkhill Road until the right-hand hairpin into Beacon Hill. The sturdy car plodded around the acute corner without much grace, then slid down the slope towards the marina. Now Oliver was also admiring the view, which meant neither of them had spotted that a black Audi saloon, which was waiting by the roadside, had pulled away and was close behind.

A series of palm trees flashed past on the left side of Beacon Hill, followed by The Living Coast. It was home to a plethora of penguins and other birds, and was cloaked in black netting to ensure that nothing could escape except the tourists, and then only via the gift shop. Oliver then turned right as they passed the elderly edifice of the Royal Torquay Yacht Club, followed by two further bends as they reached the marina. The restaurants on the right-hand side then made way for several gift stores, arcades, and fish and chip parlours.

"What food do you like?" Oliver asked, trying to plan his shopping list.

"Crisps."

"You can't eat those every meal."

"There's plenty of flavours," Kieran reminded.

Oliver turned left at the clock tower roundabout and headed into The Strand. The Debenhams store with its intricate façade was on their right, with the marina and its fishing boats on the opposite side. The surroundings prompted Oliver to ask if the youngster ate seafood.

"I like prawn cocktail Monster Munch," he replied.

"We're on potato chips again."

"No, they're made from maize, that's different."

The Gordon Keeble glided left at the junction with Fleet Street, which was the main retail area of Torquay. Whenever Oliver browsed its stores, which wasn't often, his mind inevitably turned to its namesake in London. He'd escaped the newspaper industry and moved to Devon for a quieter life, but his past was catching up with him. The black Audi was also in close pursuit, though Oliver was yet to notice.

"What about vegetables?" he asked.

"Now you're talking. Pickled onion Monster Munch is the business."

The concept made Oliver feel queasy. The car then glided under a decorative green footbridge, while the palm trees and pampas grass in the central reservation drifted past the driver's window. Distant beeps and buzzes were audible from the amusement arcades as they neared The Pavilion with its domes and classical architecture. As he stifled a yawn, Oliver turned into

Torbay Road. He then asked Kieran to open the glove box, remove his notebook, and start a shopping list.

"Let's begin with three onions."

Kieran asked what he was making.

"I haven't the foggiest, but they're bound to figure," said Oliver, who glanced at the list to see that Kieran had only written 'CRISPS', and was underlining the word several times. After they passed the cream-coloured Torbay Hotel, both sides of the road opened out into gardens. Exotic trees and shrubs clung to the steep hill on their right, while the seafront war memorial drifted past on opposite side.

"Three plaice fillets," commanded Oliver.

"Aye, aye, captain," replied Kieran, obediently jotting it under the most recent addition, which was 'more crisps'. Oliver continued his dictation, requesting muesli and countless vegetables. The youngster scrawled 'rabbit food' in the margin. They then drove past the Princess Theatre and cruised down the coast road, with neither of them noticing the Audi close behind.

"I might bake a pie," said Oliver, before asking Kieran to add stewing steak to the list. Kieran jotted down 'dog food'.

"Actually, let's use the economy stuff."

The youngster nodded, crossed out the last entry, and simply wrote 'dog'. The Gordon Keeble then leaned to its left as the road followed the curved beach, past a white crescent-shaped building teeming with bars and cafés. Their relaxed progress came to a halt as they reached the traffic lights at The Belgrave Hotel.

"Anticipation is the key to safe driving," lectured Oliver, adding that he usually came across a red light at the junction, and slowed accordingly.

"When did you last check your rear view mirror?"

"Why do you ask?"

"That car has been tailing us since we left," said Kieran. Oliver glanced at the mirror and spotted the black Audi. His first reaction was that the youngster was being paranoid. They had followed the coast road for most of their journey, and it was quite plausible that another driver would take the same route. However, the Audi was ideal if anyone wanted to tail him, as it was anonymous and inconspicuous. The same was not true of the vehicle that Oliver had taken to Portland.

Oliver knew there was only one way to confirm if he was being followed, and it meant drastic action. He was in the left-hand lane at the lights, having intended to go straight ahead. However, if he turned right, he could see if the Audi followed suit. The Gordon Keeble was first in the queue, and the lead car in the right-hand lane was a rusty Peugeot estate. It would be no match, or so he hoped.

"Let's see if we're being followed," muttered Oliver, who then told Kieran to tighten his belt. The revs started to build as the V8 engine prepared for battle. Oliver stared at the traffic lights, watching them like a hawk.

Within a heartbeat of the amber bulb blinking into life, Oliver released the handbrake and the ageing vehicle shot forwards as if it had just left the factory. He turned sharply right, cutting across the Peugeot, and earned a shaken fist, a blare of a horn, and several Anglo Saxon monosyllabic words for his trouble. He'd expected the tyres to screech for added bravado but the car was finely balanced and mastered the corner as if on rails. The Gordon Keeble then charged up Shedden Hill, climbing away from the beach at a considerable rate of knots. Above the roar of the veteran V8, all that Oliver could hear was a distant cacophony of car horns and an even more generous sprinkling of Anglo Saxon vocabulary.

"We're being followed," Kieran confirmed, as he scrutinised his door mirror.

"Right, let's lose him," Oliver replied, as he jammed his foot further to the floor than he'd ever dared to attempt since buying the car three years earlier. He was scared of the power, yet strangely comfortable as the vehicle seemed to relish being pushed towards the limit for once. However, the black Audi was also no slouch, and remained in view.

The road levelled out and curved to the left. An imposing stone wall appeared on the right-hand side, which made Oliver feel like he was in a tunnel as the engine noise rebounded off the rugged weatherworn stone. The Gordon Keeble then swept right and over a crest. The Audi disappeared briefly from view but Oliver knew it was close behind. He was tempted to dive into a side street and hide, just like in Plymouth when the range vehicle chased him, but it was broad daylight and his car would be easy to spot. The only way to lose the Audi was to drive faster.

St Luke's Church flashed past on the right-hand side as both cars charged along Abbey Road towards the Torquay Casino and the Torhill Road junction. Given that it was mid-morning, the traffic was mercifully light, and Oliver shot through on a green light. He then willed the red bulb to appear but the Audi slid across the junction close behind. Both vehicles then swerved right, underneath the Central Church with its imposing triangular spire, made from dozens of concrete crucifixes.

The Gordon Keeble was now heading downhill again. Oliver couldn't decide where he was going, and was opting for the route of least resistance. Unfortunately this meant he was plunging headfirst into the town centre and heavier traffic.

"What's your stance on lasagne?" he enquired, trying to reduce the tension.

"Monster Munch doesn't come in that flavour," the youngster sighed, as he added crisps to the list for the seventh occasion. Oliver was too busy focusing on the heavier traffic to notice, and whenever he found a spare moment to consult the rear view mirror, the situation wasn't good. It was also about to worsen, as the lights at the Union Street junction were red.

"Change you…"

Oliver then taught Kieran a rich combination of expletives that the poor boy had never heard before. It was taking him a while to adjust to having a child around, and he wasn't adjusting at all to being in a car chase, bringing his vehicle to a smooth halt at the lights.

"Use the pavement!" Kieran urged. Still adhering to the Highway Code, albeit vaguely, Oliver indicated left as the Gordon Keeble started to rumble across the paving slabs. Several pedestrians added a few more words to Kieran's vocabulary, and they didn't hesitate to rebuke the black Audi, which resorted to similar measures.

Oliver left the pavement and blended into the traffic passing up Union Street with the grace of a hippopotamus mounting a moped. He could hear screeching tyres close behind as the Audi fought its way into the sluggish queue. The Gordon Keeble, by contrast, was in clear air and accelerated past the 1930s façade of Electric House, a grand art deco building occupied by Torbay Council.

"What about Thai vegetable curry?"

"Maybe," Kieran mused. "I could always dip Pringles in it."

Oliver drove past Upton Church and was confronted by a sharp bend into Trematon Avenue. The camber favoured him and he carried sizeable momentum around the turn. The road then plunged downhill and they roared past the bowling green towards the filter lane into Lymington Road. The wide road encouraged Oliver to keep accelerating but his confidence wavered. The car drifted lethargically around the corner as he lifted his foot. He then realised that he'd made a mistake, allowing the Audi to catch up just as he was leaving it behind.

Both cars were now motoring along a one-way street past Torquay Library. In the distance, Oliver saw the traffic slowing as it passed the town hall. On the left he spotted a sharp left turn into St Marychurch Road. He faced a difficult decision, either to charge headfirst into the traffic, or to attempt a hairpin at short notice. The Gordon Keeble's front wheels turned left, and the rest of the car followed grudgingly. Oliver heard the tyres screeching as the vehicle complained about the change of direction.

The Audi, which had longer to react, took the hairpin comfortably. It loomed large in the rear view mirror as both cars went uphill. However, it started to drift away as the ageing sports car summoned more energy on the climb. While its V8 engine was no spring chicken, it still knew how to accelerate. The speed continued to build as it tackled a right-hand bend beneath some overhanging trees. The car then left the shade and returned into sunlight as it kept accelerating up the hill. Oliver sensed a chance to lose his pursuer and dived right into Windsor Road. The terrain levelled out and then started to fall away. He took a right-hand bend and made another attempt to shake off the Audi by sprinting into Victoria Road. His plan failed, though, as he was forced to brake as they reached the Market Street junction.

As Oliver waited for a break in the traffic, he pondered his options. Calling the police would be difficult, as there was no guarantee that a squad car would come to his aid. Even if it did, it would take ages to catch up. Oliver thought about turning left and making for the suburbs, as going right would take them back into town. If he went straight on, he would face a maze of twisty residential streets and steep hills. It then struck him that the Gordon Keeble had already shown its superior speed from a standing start, especially on a sharp climb.

When the traffic in Market Street eased, Oliver dived across into Pembroke Road. The Audi had less time to wait and was in close pursuit. A four-storey terraced block loomed large at the top of the hill ahead of them, but the sports car was making better progress. It looked like the climb was prone to flash floods, judging by the huge drains on the right side of the road. As they closed in on the large and forbidding terrace, Oliver turned left into Cavern Road. They were still going uphill, past a long line of pastel-coloured houses. Another junction then appeared in the distance, which Oliver knew all too well from riding his bicycle around Torquay's toughest climbs.

"We'll need all the horsepower we can get for this one," he announced. As the Gordon Keeble turned right in Huxton Road, it faced a twenty per cent slope that was like a tarmac-covered mountain. The sports car growled up the hill, hampered by its weight, but propelled forwards by its uncompromising V8. The Audi was now falling back and had nearly disappeared from the rear view mirror. Oliver sensed that the hill was giving him a chance to escape, and he swerved into Warberry Road West. It was a narrow residential street, which was level at first, then went downhill. After they passed over the crest, Oliver came to a halt behind a line of parked cars.

"What are you doing?" Kieran asked.

"He hasn't seen us, so he should drive past," said Oliver. He studied the door mirror and saw the black Audi wheeze into the street. It then charged downhill as the driver risked everything to narrow the gap. It showed no sign of slowing and flashed past the Gordon Keeble in a heartbeat. Oliver was about to smile when he realised that his stunt could have serious consequences. The Audi driver, obviously unfamiliar with the road, made no attempt to brake. Instead, the car plunged towards the end of the road, after which there was a small strip of vegetation. The black car bounced off the end of the tarmac and onto the grass. Oliver knew what came afterwards, and the Audi driver could see it too. The driver's door flew open and the motorist, a stocky man dressed in black, threw himself from the vehicle. He rolled several times before coming to sudden halt in a large patch of brambles.

"Lucky sod," muttered Oliver.

The driverless Audi was still hurtling towards the end of the grass strip. Ahead was a sheer drop of one hundred feet. Oliver and Kieran watched in amazement as the vehicle flew into the air, its wheels helplessly rotating in the summer breeze. Its nose began to dip forwards and the underside of the doomed vehicle came into view, its exhaust pipe expelling the Audi's dying breath. Apart from the engine noise, the spectacle was completely silent. However, Oliver began to wince as the car plunged towards the trees and rocks far below.

The deafening explosion when the Audi smashed into the ground seemed to reverberate around the whole town. A huge fireball charged up the side of the hill, and torched the grass clinging to its jagged rocks. The plume was then replaced by a cloud of black smoke as the wreckage of the vehicle burned on the ground below. Even a few seconds after the impact, Oliver could still hear the din echoing through the street. It was then drowned out by a muffled creaking and groaning, as the tree that the Audi collided with on the ground below snapped in half, its branches crashing to the floor alongside the mangled and smoking remains of the car.

The motorist dragged himself to his feet and staggered away from the scene, his clothes ripped by the brambles, his arms covered in scratches.

"Let's follow him," Kieran suggested, reaching for the door handle.

"Not so fast," said Oliver, grabbing the youngster's arm before he could leave the car. "It might be dangerous, that guy could be armed."

The stocky man limped out of view, heading for the town centre. Oliver could feel the adrenaline of the chase ebbing away, which he knew would be replaced by delayed shock. While he was still composed, he placed a call on his mobile phone. He then asked the switchboard operator for Detective Sergeant Ebwelle. After a few seconds, the call was connected.

"It's Oliver here," he announced. "You're not going to believe this."

***

"So the car took off here?" the detective asked, pacing towards the edge of the grass verge. Oliver remained motionless, sitting on the kerb and staring into space. Kwame looked to Kieran instead, and the youngster nodded to confirm the scene of the accident. The detective peered over the precipice and caught sight of the smouldering remains of the Audi. By this point, several uniformed officers were sifting through the wreckage.

"It's lucky there isn't a house down there," said the detective, who asked what happened to the driver. Kieran replied that he staggered towards the town centre.

"What did he look like?" the policeman inquired.

The youngster said he was dressed in black and had a few cuts after tumbling into the brambles, but didn't get a close look.

"I wanted to follow him," he added.

"Why didn't you?" the detective asked.

"He wouldn't let me," Kieran grumbled, glaring at his supposed father.

"It was dangerous," Oliver protested, breaking his silence for the first time in minutes.

"Back with us, are you?" the detective asked.

"I've just been through a very frightening experience," Oliver complained.

"It was cool," beamed Kieran, before turning to the policeman. "Have you ever been in a car chase?"

"Some, but you adapt to them."

"That's easy for you to say, you've always done the chasing," said Oliver.

"Not always, those London estates can get frisky," replied Kwame. He then walked across to join Oliver sitting on the kerb. The policeman noticed that his old friend was clearly shaking.

"Are you okay driving home?" he asked. Oliver replied that he would take the bus, and collect the car when he was feeling better.

"I could drive," Kieran beamed.

"I think Oliver's had enough excitement," said Kwame. "So do you reckon this chase had something to do with your defence investigation?"

"It must do," he replied.

"I'm not sure, double glazing salesman can be pushy," the detective chuckled. "So what's the latest with your weapon of mass destruction?"

"Détente's made a bomb, but it didn't blow up," said Kieran. Oliver added that it was unclear if the Drake's Island device was a dud, or designed not to explode.

"You can see the test results if you like," he added.

"Okay, just as long as it doesn't result in daily car chases," replied Kwame.

"You think this is funny, don't you?" Oliver muttered.

"Look, if you're seriously spooked, I could swing you a short spell in protective custody or witness protection."

"What's the point?" Oliver sighed. "Carmel went to ground in a quiet seaside town she'd never visited and they still found her."

"So what are you going to do?"

"It's simple," he replied. "I have to expose them before they catch up with me."

"Well, before you take on half the world single-handed, you'll have to visit the station to give a statement," said the policeman.

"But we've already described the Audi driver," Kieran reminded.

"Who's talking about him?" the detective replied. "We need to chat about those five speed cameras you set off."

"I think I'm going to faint," Oliver muttered.

***

The stern woman in the business suit gazed at her victim as she paced slowly around her desk. The heels of her designer shoes sent shockwaves around the room as each brooding footstep assaulted the polished stone floor.

"What were you supposed to do?" she asked.

"To follow them," replied the man.

"And what else?"

"To keep a low profile," he added.

"Would you say indulging in a car chase satisfies that requirement?"

The businesswoman paused and hovered behind her victim. She noticed that there were still blades of grass caught in his unkempt hair from rolling out of the car.

"He was driving like a madman, I couldn't keep up," he said.

"That's no excuse," snapped the businesswoman, slapping her victim around the head. "His car belongs in a museum."

"I had to chase him," he grovelled. "What would you have done if I lost him?"

"This," she said, clouting him around the head again. She then returned to the executive chair behind her desk. "At times like this, I wish there was a pedal behind here to tip you backwards into a pool of sharks."

"Give me another chance," pleaded the henchman, "I'll find him."

"That's the problem," she snapped. "We knew his exact location until your little stunt. Now he could be anywhere."

"I won't let you down again."

The businesswoman stared at her helpless minion.

"You'd better not, as next time, I'll have the shark pedal installed."

***

Oliver scrutinised the steady stream of products sliding down the checkout. Most of them seemed to be crisps. Kieran busied himself packing his loot into a small army of shopping bags. Oliver loaded the swag into their trolley. The teenager behind the checkout muttered the total price, which sounded like the cost of a holiday.

After a few minutes the shopping bags were packed awkwardly into the car and Oliver drove away from the supermarket. He was checking his rear view mirror more often than usual, fearful that somebody else might chase them. He'd already decided against returning to Edenhurst Court, but had no idea where to go. He was reluctant to hide, as Carmel had tried to run without success. If he wanted to go to ground it would have to be somewhere spectacularly obscure like Bhutan, Honduras, Tajikistan, or Rotherham. As it happened, the decision was made for him.

"Your phone's ringing," said Kieran.

"I can't take it now, I'm driving."

The youngster spotted the obsolete and inescapably low-tech handset singing merrily to itself in the Gordon Keeble's ashtray. Kieran answered the call.

"Oliver Dart's messaging service," he announced. The caller left their details, and the youngster memorised the information.

"That was Graeme, the retired scientist," said Kieran.

"What does he want?"

"He's figured out how the bomb works."

Oliver immediately performed an emergency u-turn at a mini roundabout, and the vehicle tore back down the street in the opposite direction. They were returning to Bideford.

The ageing sports car charged away from Torquay and motored towards the North Devon coast. The road from Okehampton to Bideford was less daunting in the dry but Oliver's heart was still in his mouth as he arrived at Landcross. He glanced at the roadside when he passed the spot where his girlfriend, Michelle, was killed. The flowers he'd left on the verge a few days earlier were still there, but they were the sole tribute. Since visiting the scene, Oliver had taken part in a high-speed chase, which only underlined how treacherous the roads could be. However, it paled into insignificance compared with the risk that Détente, or whoever killed Carmel, would target him next. He had to uncover the secret of the HD Cotton Crater Plant, and he only knew one man who could help.

As the Gordon Keeble rolled into Bideford, Kieran's nose began to twitch.

"Something stinks," he complained.

Oliver sampled the air, and diagnosed that his nostrils were being assaulted by warm cheese. He then glanced behind him, and realised that in his haste to reach Graeme, he'd forgotten about the shopping.

"Oh no," he sighed, "we'll have to throw most of it away."

"Don't worry, I think the crisps are still fine," said Kieran, opening a bag of salt and vinegar. He then asked where they were meeting the scientist.

"Good question," Oliver conceded. He pulled up beside the quay and reached for his mobile phone. He called Graeme's number, but after several rings, there was no reply. The only option left was to call at his house.

The retired scientist lived on the northern side of town. His property was one of several in a middle class avenue of identical houses with well-tended gardens. At first glance, this was not the obvious retreat of a man who once developed weapons that could exterminate a city in a heartbeat.

The Gordon Keeble cruised to a halt beside the kerb. Oliver was reluctant to ring the doorbell. Meeting Graeme a few days earlier had been difficult, as it brought back so many memories of Michelle. Speaking to the scientist on neutral territory had made it easier, but now he was outside the old man's house.

"What are you waiting for?" Kieran asked, finishing his crisps.

"I'm nervous."

Oliver then jumped on hearing the explosion. Adrenaline filled his veins and his eyes darted around the street, looking for the plume of smoke. He then checked the passenger seat to make sure Kieran was unharmed. The youngster was holding the remains of his crisp packet, having inflated it and popped the bag.

"Got you," he sniggered.

Oliver left the car, frowning like a traffic warden on laxatives. The youngster trotted along behind him. As they reached the front door, Kieran rang the bell before Oliver had a chance to compose himself. Through the frosted glass, he could see somebody approaching the door. They were wearing pastel pink, which suggested it was more likely to be the scientist's wife.

"Hello?" she asked, keeping the door on the latch.

"We've come to see Graeme," said Oliver.

"He's not here at the moment."

"When will he be back?"

"I'm not sure," she said. "Who should I say called?"

Oliver was genuinely shocked that she didn't recognise him. His appearance hadn't changed much, but Michelle's mother had obviously decided to forget what he looked like. He opted not to remind her, in case it brought back sore memories.

"Don't worry, I'll speak to him later," he shrugged, and turned away.

"Tell him that Oliver called," said Kieran, remaining on the doorstep. The old woman then gasped, and called after him.

"So, you do recognise me," he said.

"I'm sorry, it's been a long time," she said. Oliver could see that the years had taken their toll on the old woman. He remembered her being smart and outgoing, but now her complexion was tired and her eyes were watery; it seemed that her life had drained away. Oliver then noticed that she was scrutinising Kieran from head to toe.

"Is this your boy?" she asked.

Oliver tried to reply, but on opening his mouth, no clever words came to his rescue. It fell to the youngster to break the silence.

"I'm Kieran," he announced, shaking hands politely with the old lady.

"I call him 'trouble on legs'," Oliver sighed.

"Oh, then he must be your son," she chuckled.

"Actually, he's doing a school science project, and that's why we're looking for Graeme," said Oliver, trying to improvise.

"What's it about?"

"Big bombs!" beamed the youngster, flailing his arms for added effect.

"Then he's your man," conceded the scientist's wife. She added that he was taking the dog for a walk, and would be home later that afternoon. Oliver recalled that Michelle's parents used to have a 13-stone bullmastiff called Thor, which never really took to him. Saying that, they only disagreed on one point, namely that Oliver thought that he should be alive, and the dog begged to differ. On hearing that Graeme was exercising his canine companion, Oliver hoped it wasn't the same one as before. If it was, they wouldn't return when Graeme specified, but when Thor dragged him home.

The old woman said the dog usually stretched its legs on the Tarka Trail, a disused railway line on the eastern side of town.

"It wouldn't be Thor, would it?" Oliver asked warily.

"No, he died many years ago," she replied, adding that the dog met its maker due to an infection contracted after gnawing something that disagreed with him.

"Was it a rabbit?" Kieran asked.

"Not exactly, it was the postman," she replied.

Oliver and Kieran headed back across town in the Gordon Keeble to pick up the Tarka Trail. They left the car at the start of the route, and began to walk along the path. The former railway line was elevated above the town, and they could see the River Torridge below them, snaking into the rugged Devonian hills to the south. The trail was named after Henry Williamson's book, *Tarka the Otter*, and it provided some magnificent views. Oliver hoped that Graeme would be returning to the car park, and they would meet him on the way. However, he soon regretted that his hunch had seemingly paid off.

"Killer, stop that!"

At this stage they could only hear the old scientist's voice, but he seemed to be coming towards them, apparently accompanied by a canine of mass destruction.

"No Killer, bad dog!"

The demon hound then appeared minus its owner. Its expression was hostile, its eyes were full of fury, and it was barking incessantly. Oliver stood firm though, in fact, he started laughing. After all, it was hard to take an agitated miniature poodle seriously. It continued yapping at him, but he glared at the dog, which yelped before scurrying back to its master in retreat. The scientist then appeared, cradling Killer in his arms.

"I guess the name is ironic," said Oliver.

"And it commands respect at the vets before they open the box," Graeme replied, as he returned the poodle to the ground. The creature then started to sniff Oliver's brogues before cocking its leg. Oliver shoved the dog aside with his other foot. While not a dog owner, he knew the difference between a bullmastiff and a poodle relieving itself on your shoes, namely that you let the bullmastiff continue.

The scientist told Oliver that his arrival in Bideford was quicker than expected, and wondered how he'd found him on the Tarka Trail.

"Your better half said you'd be here," he replied.

"You must be in a dreadful hurry to discover how this bomb works."

"Yes, can you tell us?" the youngster asked.

"I can do even better," said the scientist. "I can show you."

Graeme cajoled Killer into his estate car. Oliver then followed him back to his house, and the old man emerged a few minutes later struggling with a cardboard box stuffed with a jumble of items including kitchen cleaner, flour, and rusty saucepans. They then left the Gordon Keeble behind, and the scientist drove them out of town. Soon after passing the ovine-inspired theme park, The Big Sheep, on its northern outskirts, Graeme pulled off the A39 into a deserted field. He then removed the box of household goods, while Killer scampered away from the estate car and went to glare at some thistles.

"I was genuinely stumped about how this Cotton Crater thing of yours worked, so I decided to make one," said the scientist.

"You haven't got any nuclear fuel rods in this box, have you?" Oliver asked.

"No, self-raising flour," Graeme replied, adding that most of the elements in Détente's prototype were not available to civilians, but by using some carefully chosen household items, it was possible to construct a close, if not as potent, replica.

The scientist busied himself measuring quantities of liquids and powders into the saucepans.

"Shouldn't we be in some kind of laboratory for this?" Oliver enquired.

"Only if it needs redecorating," muttered Graeme. He then screwed a steel funnel into the earth and poured the mixture from one of the pans into it, which was gratefully absorbed by the parched soil. He then taped a coffee mug filled with clear liquid to the end of a broom handle.

"You'd better stand back," he advised, before gingerly pouring the contents of the mug down the funnel from a safe distance. Oliver and Kieran put their fingers in their ears but the result was an anticlimax. A small puff of smoke drifted away from the funnel and there was no noise.

"Is that all?" Kieran asked, clearly disappointed. The scientist paced across to the funnel and removed it from the ground. A tiny crater with a miniscule amount of white powder was left behind.

"The weapon doesn't explode, instead it implodes," revealed the scientist. "Because its payload is discharged into the earth that means it's also virtually silent."

"So what does it do?" Kieran demanded, growing impatient. The scientist led them forty yards across the field to a patch of barren grass around ten foot across.

"Here's one I made earlier," he boasted.

Oliver asked why the turf was shrivelled. Graeme replied that the ground had been contaminated, and the patch would soon be completely bare, and remain that way for several years.

"So is the weapon used for destroying crops?" Oliver enquired.

"That's one possible use, but I'd be more worried about detonating it in a built-up area," said Graeme.

The reply left Oliver alarmed but also confused. Given that major cities rarely had much vegetation, its impact sounded more annoying than apocalyptic.

"This device pollutes the ground and everything in it, including the water supply," said the scientist. "It basically makes the land uninhabitable."

"Does it kill people?" Kieran asked.

"Yes, but not immediately, judging by the ingredients," he replied. Graeme then explained that his version was relatively harmless, but the nuclear one would trigger radiation sickness within days for everyone living in the affected area. It was capable of killing thousands, or even millions, depending on its size.

"And because it's silent, nobody would realise it's been detonated until the plants start dying and people become ill," he added.

"It's the ultimate silent killer," Oliver muttered. His imagination then went into overdrive as he tried to come to terms with the implications of what he'd just heard. If the device made no noise it could be used for a sneak attack on a major city, and nobody would notice anything until it was too late. The bomb could be brought in by a truck and simply left there, with its payload being injected into the ground remotely by cowardly warlords thousands of miles away. It would also be a weapon that would delight terrorists if they could lay their hands on one. The device was clearly lethal and a blunt instrument of mass murder.

Kieran then asked how dangerous the chemicals would be if they were used above ground. The scientist dipped a piece of wood in the coffee mug and gathered a bead of the clear liquid on its end. He then threw it towards the saucepan, which had a small trace of the mixture left in the bottom, and was around ten yards away. The distance turned out to be invaluable as the piece of wood landed in the container and promptly blew it sky high. The noise of the explosion reverberated around the remote field, and the smoking remains of the saucepan landed in a nearby tree.

"Cool," grinned the youngster.

Graeme then drove them back to his house. Killer was unusually quiet on the return trip; his owner speculated that the exploding saucepan had probably given him a mild case of shock. Judging by what happened to the poodle's bowel movements immediately after the blast, it had clearly come as a surprise.

"Are you sure I can't offer you dinner?" the scientist asked, as they pulled up beside the kerb.

"That's very kind, but we need to get back," said Oliver.

"Don't worry, we've got loads of crisps," Kieran added.

The scientist headed back to his house, with Killer trotting along behind him. As he reached the door, he waved to Oliver and Kieran, who were beside their car.

"You're welcome back if you want to stay some time," he offered. Oliver was taken aback by the kind invitation.

"Sounds good," he replied, before waving the scientist farewell. It seemed that the visit with Kieran had healed the rift between himself and Michelle's parents. Now he just had to uncover why Détente had built a weapon that even a psychopath would think twice about before using, and if his life was in danger as a result.

***

The fourteen pound bowling ball slid lazily down the alley. It drifted further away from the kingpin with every rotation, until it finally slipped past and clipped three skittles in the corner. Oliver wasn't happy with the attempt, which by coincidence, also summed up his investigation into Détente. For all his efforts, he was nowhere near reaching the heart of the matter.

Oliver switched to the twelve pound ball, hoping that the lighter weight would translate into more speed, and send the skittles flying. It might have succeeded if his second attempt had been on target. Instead, the ball slipped left again, and would have taken out the three pins in the corner, if they had not already been dispatched.

"Hopeless," muttered Kieran, slurping a bottle of cola. He then took an eight pound ball and sent it purposefully down the alley. While not vanquishing all the skittles, there an impressive amount of devastation resulting from the attempt. Kieran waited for his ball to return, and when it reported for duty, he sent it back towards the defiant clutch of skittles that escaped the last onslaught. The remaining pins were then mown down, leaving the alley spotless and pristine.

"Your go," said the youngster, casually resuming his seat. Oliver was now ruing the idea of bowling. He hadn't visited an alley for years, while Kieran seemed well versed. It struck Oliver that he'd missed the golden years of fatherhood with the youngster, namely those when he could beat him at everything.

As Kieran quickly built a comfortable lead, Oliver's thoughts returned to the investigation. Following the car chase he was reluctant to return home, but fleeing overseas would also be fraught with difficulties. In a moment of paranoia, he envisaged Détente spies at every airport and ferry terminal. It would also be useless to lie low in a quiet backwater, which Carmel had attempted without success. Instead he'd chosen an option that he believed would outfox his pursuers. He'd booked into a bed and breakfast that was just a quarter of a mile from Edenhurst Court. Oliver had decided that if he was going to hide from Détente, then he would do so right under their noses.

The little hotel that he chose had a concession with the bowling alley across the street in Babbacombe Road. Eventually Kieran and Oliver tired of staying in their room watching films and reviewing the investigation notes. They opted to break cover and dart across to the bowling alley, a decision that Oliver was starting to regret.

The youngster won the first game, but Oliver had paid for two. Whether this would give him a chance to redeem some pride or just embarrass himself again was unclear. Kieran went first in the second game and made a good start but Oliver kept in touch. He even managed a strike in the fifth frame, which the youngster greeted with sarcastic applause, having bowled three already. As they entered the last frame, Kieran was on 112 points while Oliver had 101. The tension should have been high, but the youngster was so confident of victory that his mind was elsewhere.

"I think we should break into Détente," he announced, while selecting a ball.

"They'd shoot us on site," replied Oliver, hushing his voice in case the giggly girls on the next alley were actually Détente agents in disguise. "We need to uncover more about the company and the man who runs it."

Kieran stepped forwards, but with his mind not focused on the game, his ball veered left into the gutter.

"Okay, let's make a bet," he said. "If you win this game, we'll do things your way, if not, I'm in charge."

Oliver wasn't a betting man, and being eleven points in arrears, the deal was not immediately tempting. However, Kieran had wasted his first ball, which tipped the scales against the boy. Oliver saw an opportunity to silence his pint-size critic, regain control of the investigation, and redeem an ounce of sporting pride.

"You're on," he declared.

Kieran nodded and stepped towards the alley, his eight pound ball primed in his right hand. He released it swiftly but smoothly, and it rumbled ominously towards its target. Even before the impact, Oliver was already regretting the wager. The ball struck the kingpin before ripping through the skittles behind it, sending them in every direction. Once the ball had passed, all that was left in its place was a routed army of forlorn pins lying on the highly-polished battlefield.

"Drat," Oliver muttered to himself. By clearing the skittles in the last frame, the youngster had earned himself a bonus ball. Kieran sent it rolling down the alley and it knocked down seven skittles to make a final score of 129. Oliver's total of 101 now looked rather puny. Unless he bowled two strikes to earn 20 points and a bonus ball, Kieran would be certain of victory.

Oliver approached the alley with his twelve pound ball and sent it flying towards the kingpin. On reaching its target, all ten skittles fell over obediently and left the alley completely clear.

"You'll need another," warned Kieran, finishing his bottle of fizz. Oliver waited for his ball to return, but it took ages to reappear. He could feel the nerves building in his fingertips. Bowling the first strike had given him hope, but he needed a second to keep the game alive. He approached the alley and sent the ball on its way. It started to drift to the right, and Oliver anxiously watched it rotate, hoping that it would curl to the left. Halfway down the alley, it began to respond, and turned towards the kingpin. Just inches before impact, it fell into line, and the skittles tumbled like dominoes.

Oliver punched the air in triumph. His second strike had earned him an extra ball and now he was just eight points behind Kieran. When Oliver realised how close the game had become, his elation quickly returned to nerves. It would only take one decent ball to win the match, but anything less would throw it away. There was also a lot more than pride resting on the game. Oliver's cautious approach to Détente was being questioned, and he needed a firm answer.

The twelve pound ball started to roll down the alley. Oliver reduced its speed to increase accuracy, and his effort was looking good. The ball was heading straight for the kingpin and was not deviating an inch. He felt confident as it made contact, but it ripped through the middle of the skittles, and was not a third strike. Two pins, one in each corner, were left behind. One of them was rocking precariously back and forth. A small gust of air would have blown it over, but the skittle remained upright.

Oliver looked at the scoreboard. Kieran's total of 129 points was already there but his score was being calculated. Eight points then appeared beside his name, and his final position was also 129 points. The contest was drawn.

"Does that mean we break in, but cautiously?" Kieran asked.

"No, it means we investigate carefully, but more directly."

"What does that mean?"

"We're going straight after the chief executive of Détente," said Oliver.

***

Kieran gazed lazily at the signs flashing past on the roadside as they headed along the A38. They were in the shadow of Dartmoor, which even on a sunny day, rose menacingly to their right. Kieran then felt the car slowing as they passed the sign for Buckfastleigh village. The Gordon Keeble then drifted onto the slipway and came to a gradual halt at the junction.

Kieran felt his pulse starting to quicken. He'd called for the investigation to be more direct, but now he would face the consequences. He also realised that, unlike previous occasions, most of the responsibility was on his shoulders. If their plan that day was to succeed, he would have to play his part.

Two days had passed since the bowling match. Since then, Oliver and Kieran had carried out extensive internet research on Charles Moore, the chief executive of Détente, uncovering that he served briefly with the Royal Navy career at Portland. They also knew that the four bullies that hounded him out of the service were still based on the island, and ironically working for his firm. Whether the bullies had dirt on him or he wanted to bury the hatchet was unclear. The latter seemed likely after they delved deeper for more information. Away from developing instruments of death, Dr Moore raised large sums for charity by running marathons. He'd also opened the fete three times in the Devon village where he lived in a thatched cottage. It emerged that he was doing the honours for a fourth time that summer, and the event was due to be held that weekend. Oliver and Kieran knew they wouldn't have a better chance to intercept Dr Moore, and plotted a course for Buckfastleigh.

As the Gordon Keeble prowled through the outskirts of the village, Kieran felt butterflies in his stomach. He was thirty minutes away from doing something very risky, and knew that he couldn't fail. While it was a stroke of luck that Dr Moore was due to make a public appearance, there was big problem in confronting him. If Oliver made the first move then it might jeopardise the investigation. At best, he would refuse to answer his questions, and at worst, several bodyguards might appear from nowhere and launch him headfirst into the lucky dip. Oliver knew it was pointless to corner Dr Moore, as he would spot a nosy journalist from twenty paces. They would need to be subtle.

The centre of Buckfastleigh was a picturesque jumble of period cottages and pretty shops, nestling in a valley beneath the imposing shadow of Dartmoor. Oliver drove through the narrow streets to the central car park. On leaving the vehicle he was confronted by a bizarre bird, which looked like a turkey. Several were pottering beside the nearby stream. The one near the car was staring at Oliver disapprovingly.

"What?" he asked the cumbersome bird, which stood motionless. Even if the local council embraced equal opportunities, it struck Oliver that hiring a turkey as a parking attendant was going too far. He then walked with Kieran through the village centre towards Buckfastleigh Primary School where the fete was being held. It should have taken place two months earlier but was delayed due to rain, hail, gales, floods, and everything else that the British Summer could hurl in its direction.

The school was just outside the village centre. The old buildings were coated in white paint, which sparkled whenever the sunshine could be bothered to appear. The weather wasn't tropical, but at least it wasn't apocalyptic, as it had been the previous time. Oliver parted reluctantly with some coins to pay for his entry, and then a few more to cover Kieran's admission.

Around 150 people were at the fete. Judging by their appearance, many had visited the face painting stall. Most resembled the Incredible Hulk, which suggested that the artist had forgotten all their colours except green. The next stall was the human fruit machine. It comprised three pensioners clutching buckets while slumped in deckchairs. Kieran persuaded Oliver to sacrifice fifty pence to see how it worked. The old codgers fumbled lazily in their buckets, with the first producing an apple, the second a pomegranate, while a third fondled an avocado.

"You've got two more turns," wheezed the first pensioner, who then started searching for something else, and surfaced with a mango. One of his colleagues was on the same wavelength, but the other conjured up a cantaloupe.

"You can hold two items," advised the second man. Kieran kept the matching mangoes, prompting the cantaloupe brandisher to retreat to his bucket in search of something else. He emerged with a rubber chicken.

"That isn't a fruit," the youngster complained.

"A bell isn't either, but they're on the machines," he said.

"You also get one nudge," revealed the first pensioner.

"How does that work?" Oliver asked.

"Like this," said the middle man, who jabbed the chicken finder in the ribs with his elbow, "find something else you daft beggar."

"What fruit?" he complained, sifting through the bucket.

"A mango," chorused everyone within five yards.

"Oh dear, I think I got hungry and ate it."

The other two men sighed, and dipped into their buckets for rubber chickens.

"Come on Sid, we're back on poultry," said the middle man.

"That's more sensible," he agreed, producing his rubber specimen once more. Oliver asked if there was a prize for matching three items.

"Yes, you win a ruler," said the first pensioner, passing across a 12-inch piece of lurid pink plastic.

"This says 'my little fairy princess'," complained the boy.

"Sorry, we've run out of *Superman* ones," conceded the middle man.

Kieran skulked off with the ruler looking dejected and ashamed. However, he would soon face a challenge that would require nerves of steel, and he would have to conquer any fears of being embarrassed.

Half an hour passed, during which time Kieran lobbed a few darts, fired a few air gun pellets, kicked some footballs, and accidentally hurled a wellington boot at the school caretaker. Oliver sighed as he inspected his dwindling coins, which were deserting his wallet like flying ants leaving a nest. Charles Moore was due to open the fete at two o'clock, but was late. Oliver was not only worried that the delay was costing him money, but that their target might not appear.

Just as Oliver was losing hope, he noticed the crowds parting in the distance to reveal a slight figure. As the man approached, he could be seen wearing a smart pinstripe jacket and white polo neck. His hair bordered on stubble, while his designer black shoes were polished with military precision.

"Good afternoon ladies and gentlemen," he said. The announcement was met with friendly applause. Oliver was surprised; he'd imagined that Dr Moore would have the voice of a tyrannical overlord, but it was polished and quiet. His appearance was also a surprise, bordering more on Parisian poet than commercial warmonger.

"It's nice to see you again, and I'm sorry for being late. I was marooned in the holiday traffic with all those lovely people who don't live here."

The remark triggered some light laughter and gentle cheering. He was playing to the crowd and obviously knew how please them. He then talked about his cottage in Buckfastleigh and how he missed the village during overseas trips. His speech was ticking all the right boxes and he clearly would have made a good politician, especially with his comfort in dealing with weapons of mass destruction. Frustratingly for Oliver, the speech did not focus on Détente, but village life and his fund-raising efforts for local charities.

"So thank you for coming, please give generously to all the good causes here, and enjoy the afternoon," he concluded, to polite ripples of clapping. As he finished, Kieran's pulse began to quicken, because he knew what would happen next.

"It's now or never," said Oliver, handing the youngster a pen and notepad. Kieran then walked across the school grounds towards Dr Moore, who was already walking away, as if preparing to leave the fete. He caught up with him a few steps later and coughed to attract his attention.

"Excuse me Dr Moore?"

Kieran heard the multi-millionaire sigh before he turned around and flashed a sympathetic smile that wasn't totally convincing.

"Yes, how can I help?" he enquired, with the charming hostility of a restaurant manager who'd just been asked for a refund.

"I'm doing a school media project, and our teacher asked us to find a celebrity to interview."

"Well, I wouldn't say I was famous," he beamed, clearly flattered by the idea, "but I'll do what I can."

Kieran thanked him, and started by asking why he worked for Détente.

"Believe it or not, I joined the defence sector to bring about world peace," he replied. "I wanted to highlight the stupidity of war by producing weapons that were so devastating that nobody would dare to use them."

"Isn't that dangerous?" Kieran asked.

"No, the world has been much safer with nuclear weapons. You couldn't have a world war now because nobody would survive it. That's one of the reasons that I've scaled back Détente's military ventures and put more money into civilian research."

From what Kieran knew about the firm, he suspected that arms production was being scaled down because nobody was placing orders with Détente.

"Do you still create new weapons?"

"Only as instruments of peace, and I'm afraid I can't go into details."

"Are you sure sir, it would be useful to give my teacher an example," pleaded the youngster. Sadly, it did not weaken his defences. Instead, the millionaire checked his platinum Rolex and declared that he had to leave.

"Please sir, I only have a couple more questions," said Kieran.

"I tell you what, here's my personal assistant's card. If you call her, I'll make sure that your questions are answered."

After giving Kieran the card, he walked swiftly towards the car park, where he climbed into a jet black Bentley and screeched away from the school. Kieran trudged back to Oliver, who was loitering beside the beer tent with the frustrated gait of a man who needed to stay sober enough to drive.

"Any luck?"

"No, he said he builds arms to promote world peace."

"Really?" Oliver chuckled. "Remind me to quaff eight pints to crack down on drink driving. Did he say anything else?"

"No, he wouldn't tell me anything about his new weapons, and just told me to call his personal assistant."

Kieran then produced the card, and handed it across.

"You genius," beamed Oliver. "I thought you said you had no luck."

"I didn't, he would answer a thing."

"But he's told us where to find his personal assistant, and wherever she is, Dr Moore can't be far away."

"So we're going to see her?" Kieran asked.

"You bet we are."

"And then break into Dr Moore's office?"

"Ah," mused Oliver. "We'll come to that one later."

***

Dr Moore's personal assistant worked at Détente's head office in Dartmouth on the south Devon coast, around 15 miles from Buckfastleigh. The building was a stone's throw from Britannia Royal Navy College, but hardly as grand. In fact, it was a major disappointment when Oliver and Kieran pulled up outside the grey heap of bricks the morning after the fete.

"Call that a baddie's lair?" the youngster scoffed.

While Détente still boasted several large bases, its head office was miniscule, and seemed barely large enough for a dozen staff. Oliver speculated that Dr Moore didn't like surrounding himself with executives, and preferred to govern his corporate empire from an enclave away from the front line. Another possibility was that Détente was in a financial mess, and couldn't afford an imposing London HQ.

They tried the front door, but it was locked. Oliver jabbed the intercom beside it, and a crackly voice on the speaker confirmed it was the right place.

"I'm the father of Darran Kite," Oliver lied. Given that using the surname 'Dart' was probably unwise, at least in remaining covert, Kieran had chosen a pseudonym. Just like Oliver with his pen name of Trevor Dial, the youngster selected an anagram for his alias. The front door popped open.

The building had no reception area, and simply had a series of brass plaques on the wall beside the staircase. Most seemed to advertise accountants, who judging by the grim property, were not very talented in their field. Détente occupied the top floor, and Oliver led the youngster up the stairs.

Ms Potter, who was Dr Moore's personal assistant, had agreed to meet them at once. It struck Oliver as suspiciously convenient, and with every step towards the office, he was increasingly alarmed that he was hurtling towards a trap.

Despite its gloomy stairwells and exterior, the top floor of the building was airy and welcoming. The pale carpet on the landing felt soft beneath their shoes, and the walls were painted in calming magnolia. However, at the end of the corridor was a steel security door, hinting that casual visitors should go away.

"How do we get inside?" Kieran asked.

Oliver spotted a camera on the ceiling that was swivelling in their direction. It scrutinised them for a moment and then the steel door unlocked itself and opened slowly but purposefully.

"Please come in," barked a robotic voice. Oliver stepped forwards until the soothing carpet beneath his feet was replaced by a cold stone floor. He tried not to skid on the highly polished surface, which Kieran did anyway for fun. The youngster bumped into a shiny metal desk, which was the focal point of the ruthlessly modern and minimalist office. Even the sharply dressed woman perched behind the desk looked stern, especially as Kieran had upset her pencil tidy with the impact.

"Darran Kite I presume," she sniped.

"Yes ma'am," he replied, his politeness failing to mollify the ice maiden, who was mercilessly rounding up her non-stationary stationery. Her mood was already ill-tempered following a terse e-mail from her boss warning of the child's visit. It had no text, but the subject matter read: "If you want something done then do it yourself".

"Sit down," she commanded.

Oliver lunged for the nearest seat as if playing a Russian roulette version of musical chairs. Kieran was less hurried and adopted a bare metal stool that managed to be even less comfortable than it looked. He then produced a notebook with the calm menace of an assassin removing a rifle from its case; it seemed that reporting ran in his blood. Oliver knew that at least one of Kieran's parents was a journalist, and it was possible that both of them were.

"I believe you wanted to ask Dr Moore some questions," said Ms Potter.

"Yes ma'am, I'm doing a school project."

"I see, and why is your teacher so interested in defence firms?"

"She isn't; I was just told to find someone famous."

"I don't think Dr Moore would view himself a celebrity. He is a private man and usually avoids publicity," said his PA.

"My lad just wants to know a little more about him," Oliver clarified. Ms Potter replied that she could provide a basic biography, but would go no further.

"What else do you need?" she added.

"I want to know about Détente's latest weapons," said Kieran.

Ms Potter replied that new defence systems were not open for discussion.

"What about the HD Cotton Crater Plant?" he asked. Oliver's heart went into overdrive. Kieran had clearly inherited his mother's rashness, and while it had been her greatest asset, it was also her biggest failing, and had probably led to her death.

"That project is different," announced Ms Potter.

"What sets it apart?" Oliver asked.

"Let me show you," she said, as a flat screen television rose out of her desk and blinked into life. Kieran was poised with his notebook as the programme started. The words "HD Cotton Crater Plant" appeared, and were then replaced by Dr Moore standing beside a tangle of pipes and tanks that were roughly the size of a van. The contraption also had a large steel needle at its base.

"Ladies and gentlemen, I present Détente's latest creation in the pursuit of a peaceful planet."

Oliver tried not to snigger, and failed dismally.

"This is the HD Cotton Crater Plant," said Dr Moore. The camera then panned around the device as his speech continued. "Finally, mankind will have a quick, easy and safe method to put atomic weapons beyond use and reduce nuclear waste."

The multi-millionaire explained that it injected a 'high dose' – shortened to HD in the title – of localised radioactive energy. The pulse could incinerate 98 per cent of nuclear material, allowing warheads to be decommissioned in seconds, or reducing tons of atomic waste to a spoonful in a heartbeat.

"All that is left is a dusting of harmless white powder resembling cotton, and so we've called it the HD Cotton Crater Plant."

Oliver noticed an uneasy feeling in his stomach, which he'd encountered very rarely since his Fleet Street days. It took him a few moments to recognise it, but he did so before long – it was the sensation he felt whenever somebody was telling him a load of old bull. He glared back at the smiling scientist on the flat screen, clad in his trademark pinstripe jacket and white polo neck. Oliver then noticed a piece of paper protruding from Dr Moore's hip pocket. He recognised it at once, and it confirmed that he was being force-fed a banquet of lies. However, he wouldn't share his view with the youngster until they were safely out of the building.

The promotional film ended, and the screen retreated smoothly into the desk.

"As you can see, the device will make the world safer," said Ms Potter.

"Wow, what a cool invention," Kieran enthused. The uneasy feeling in Oliver's stomach returned, but only because the youngster seemed to be faking his awe. The boy then asked when it would enter production.

"It's only at the prototype stage," replied the PA. "We commissioned the video to attract potential buyers."

"Are you getting many orders?" Oliver inquired.

"We anticipate considerable demand," beamed Ms Potter.

"Enough to boost Détente's share price?" Kieran asked. The businesswoman was thrown by the question, which had been Oliver's intention when he wrote it down for the youngster before the meeting. However, instead of teasing out more details, it killed the inquiry.

"I thought your school project was about Dr Moore," she muttered.

"Clever hag," thought Oliver, who had to concede that eleven-year-olds would not be expected to investigate share fluctuations in their holiday homework.

"Is there anything else I can do for you?" she asked, which Oliver knew from countless previous interviews was corporate code for "sod off please".

"Yes, where is the HD Cotton Crater Plant built?" Kieran asked, consulting his notebook. The PA sighed at the question, replying that it was made in their research centre, and she couldn't reveal its location.

"Would this be the 'secret' facility in Honiton that's clearly signposted from the A30?" Oliver inquired. Ms Potter didn't reply, and simply smiled at her inquisitors.

"Please let me know if I can be of further help," she said. Oliver recognised this statement as corporate code for "sod off right now, or else". Kieran responded by flicking his notebook to a fresh page and chewing on his pen. Oliver assumed that he'd adopted the mannerism from Carmel, but then realised that he was also nibbling his biro. The tension in the office was reaching boiling point.

"One final question," said Kieran, using the time-honoured phrase that usually preceded a question that was capable of ending an interviewee's career. "Why did Dr Moore leave the Royal Navy?"

Ms Potter was totally wrong-footed. She couldn't deny that it was a vital part of his background. It would also be difficult to say that only Dr Moore could answer it, as the youngster might request another meeting. She had to respond herself.

"Some people are suited to military life, while others are not."

"Why didn't he like it?" Kieran asked.

The businesswoman had to think fast, and the feeling in Oliver's stomach that he was being force-fed balderdash was growing ever more intense.

"Dr Moore is a champion of peace, not a man of war," she said. "Now, might I assist you further, or are you ready to leave?"

Oliver knew that this was corporate code for "sod off before I call the police". Surmising that if he didn't head voluntarily towards the exit then he would soon be hurled through it, he opted to vacate his chair.

"Thank you for your time, ma'am," bid Kieran, as they both slithered across the polished stone floor towards the safety of the pale carpet. Oliver imagined the eyes of the stern businesswoman burning into his back in contempt as they left. Once they returned to the street outside, Oliver breathed a sigh of relief, but realised that their troubles were not behind them.

"Did you enjoy the film?" he asked.

"I think we're being lied to."

"You're a smart boy," said Oliver, "but what makes you sure?"

Kieran pondered the question, and replied that he didn't trust Détente.

"Neither do I, but we need evidence."

"Like what?"

Oliver asked Kieran what Dr Moore was wearing in the video. The youngster guessed that it was a suit, but Oliver was more precise.

"It was a pinstripe suit with a white polo neck. In fact, it was exactly the same outfit that he was wearing yesterday."

"Maybe he likes it," said Kieran. "I often wear the same stuff for two days."

"Mainly because you stuffed half your clothes in my bin," Oliver sighed. "Mind you, it wasn't his suit that convinced me that the video was a sham. Did you see what was in his right hip pocket?"

"A rubber chicken," muttered Kieran, kicking a pebble along the pavement.

"It was the programme from Buckfastleigh fete."

"That's no surprise, we saw him there yesterday."

"Precisely," said Oliver. "It was less than 24 hours ago, and what does that tell you about the video?"

"That he made it last night?"

"Exactly," beamed Oliver. "Now why would a chief executive spend a Sunday evening filming a cheesy corporate advert?"

"He's a workaholic?" Kieran suggested.

"That video wasn't produced for potential buyers. It was made for an audience of just two people."

Kieran and Oliver stared at each other, trying to come to terms with the fact that Détente had produced a film with the sole purpose of taunting them.

"Why did they make it?" the youngster asked.

"It's meant to throw us off the scent."

"But why go to so much trouble?"

Oliver was poised to reply, but was stumped. It made no sense that Dr Moore would expend so much effort in deceiving them. If he wasn't concerned then ignoring them seemed a more likely course of action. On the other hand, Carmel had paid the ultimate price for getting too close to uncovering the truth.

"He's playing with us," said Oliver. He then realised that they were caught in a dangerous situation. If they ignored Détente, it was possible that the truth behind the HD Cotton Crater Plant and Carmel's murder wouldn't be uncovered. If they came too close to unravelling what happened, then they could be the next targets.

***

"How much does he know?" the voice on the telephone asked. Ms Potter increased the volume on her headset – the words had been spoken softly, but with a hint of suspicion. One emotion that was lacking, though, was alarm. Indeed, the question was coaxed in a similar manner to a rotund aunt inquiring of a nephew's spelling test.

"They're either playing dumb, or genuinely stumped," the PA replied.

"Did they like my video?"

"Not as much as I enjoyed watching their faces. It's a shame you couldn't see them. It was like watching goldfish with learning difficulties in slow motion."

"I'm starting to realise why this Dart fellow quit Fleet Street. He might be just the man we're looking for," the gentle voice chuckled.

"Yes, but I'm worried about the boy. He asked lots of questions."

"You can't blame him, but as long as he doesn't find the answers, everything will be fine."

Sensing that the pressure was easing, the PA turned to the one frivolous item in her otherwise sanitised office. Unscrewing the lid of the liquorice jar, she asked what action should be taken, and then popped a sweet into her mouth.

"I want Tweedle Dum and his squire on a tight leash. Do not lose them again."

"I won't," she replied, muffled by the sweet.

"And don't get liquorice on the desk – it stains terribly," ordered the voice, which was verging on aggression for the first time. The line then went dead, which left Ms Potter free to enjoy what remained of her costly sweet.

***

As the Gordon Keeble rolled away from Dartmouth, Oliver noticed a small decrepit Fiat in the rear view mirror. He thought nothing of it until reaching the edge of Torquay forty minutes later, by which point it was still visible.

"We're being followed again," he warned. Kieran glanced in the door mirror and spotted the rusty runabout.

"Weedy," he scoffed, "let's outrun him."

Oliver waited until the next traffic lights. The moment the green light appeared he crushed the throttle pedal into the carpet and the V8 tore away from the junction. After the next bend, Oliver veered into a side street and came to a halt. The Fiat eventually clattered past on the main road, heading forlornly in the wrong direction.

"Détente's making it too easy," the youngster chuckled.

"Maybe another Audi was too expensive," Oliver suggested. He then placed a call on his archaic mobile phone. "Put me through to DS Ebwelle please."

Kieran asked why he was calling the police.

"I feel like we've been fighting this battle on our own. It's about time we had some help."

Following the call, the detective chose an unusual venue to meet Oliver and Kieran. Rather than their apartment at Edenhurst Court or the constabulary's HQ in Exeter, Kwame selected a neutral location. Furthermore, it was not a pub or café, but a children's funfair in Paignton, five miles south of Torquay.

"Why does your copper want to meet in a playpark?" Kieran inquired, as they cruised into the outskirts of the resort. Oliver replied that Kwame had promised to take his daughter to the venue and didn't want to abandon the trip. Kieran responded with a heavy sigh.

"I thought you'd enjoy the funfair," said Oliver.

"No, it's childish," muttered the youngster, with his head slumped against the passenger window in a sulk. It struck Oliver that his teenage persona was wrestling its way to the surface. He seemed to be evolving from the second stage of youth into the third. In Oliver's view, the first part was when children did nothing and smelt bad. Stage two was when they had too much energy and smelt bad. In their teenage years, boys usually became introverted and smelt bad. The final stage involved excessive consumption of cider and curry, which ensured they always smelt bad. It seemed that bringing up a boy was like living with flatulence for two decades. The theory underlined why he preferred to write books for children instead of having them around. Now a youngster had been sprung upon him, and his emotions lurched from believing he could cope to contemplating a surrender call to social services. Back at the apartment, the DNA letter from Exeter University would resolve the matter, but Oliver was uncertain what result he wanted.

After driving through the outskirts of Paignton, they reached the seafront. Its golden beach was larger than the tidal spit of sand in Torquay. The resort looked back across the gentle waves of Torbay towards Oliver's apartment block, which was just about visible in the clear afternoon sunshine. Along with the shore, Paignton's seafront was dominated by amusement arcades and a long terrace of pretty pastel-coloured houses. The beach was busy with children making sandcastles and the mood of the resort seemed cheerful. Meanwhile, Kieran was miserable.

"Why bother with the police? They don't know what's going on," he muttered.

"Perhaps they've made progress," Oliver replied, as he moored the Gordon Keeble in a parking bay near the funfair. The attraction was called The Paign Game, and was a short walk away, but Kieran was dragging his heels as if he had a sixth sense that they were wasting their time. Oliver begged to differ.

"Eighteen pounds please," grunted the wage slave in the ticket booth. Oliver was unimpressed that he had to pay for the privilege of speaking to a policeman. He led Kieran past several fairground rides until he found Kwame sitting outside a café. His daughter, who was around fifteen-years-old and dressed like a rap star's groupie, was also there, and looked even more dejected than Kieran.

"Hello Oliver," bid the detective. "This is my pride and joy, Saskia."

Oliver shook hands with the teenager, but she seemed neither proud nor joyful to meet him. Before that day he hadn't realised that Kwame was a father, but then press contacts rarely discussed their personal lives. In the detective's eyes, it probably seemed that Kieran had recently materialised from thin air. The difference was that Oliver knew this was precisely the case.

"You sounded jumpy on the phone, what's so urgent?" Kwame asked.

"What would you say," Oliver posed, as he took a seat and lowered his voice, "that I've been followed twice, chased once, and my life is in danger?"

"Don't support Spurs," chuckled the policeman.

"We're serious," insisted Kieran, who demanded to know what was happening with his mother's murder inquiry.

"Has your mum been bumped off?" Saskia asked, more out of nosiness than compassion.

"Yes, she was gunned down," Kieran replied frostily.

"Dad wouldn't mind a marksman killing my mum," the teenager announced. Kwame was clearly embarrassed by the revelation, not just because of its bluntness, but also that it exposed a subject that should have been off limits.

"Is everything okay at home?" Oliver inquired.

"Mum wants a divorce. She's taking me to America," Saskia boasted. Oliver was uncertain whether to pity her father, or the Americans.

"Sorry Kwame, I didn't know," he said, although he was only vaguely aware of the policeman's marriage, while his daughter was a bolt from the blue.

"Saskia's leaving next month, that's why I've brought her to the fair," the detective muttered, hinting that his gesture had fallen flat. Oliver felt equally duped in paying the entrance fee, but at least he wasn't facing a costly divorce. He'd also visited the fair for a good reason, namely to establish if Carmel's killer was any closer to justice.

"I've said before, it's a professional hit with no clues," the policeman sighed.

"So you've just given up?" Kieran asked.

"No, we put an appeal in the newspapers last week."

"That means you're stuck," Oliver observed, recognising that police only went to the media when they were desperate. The detective added that they'd traced most of the vehicles near the murder scene, and tried to establish the whereabouts of all recorded hit men when the shooting occurred.

"But if he's a pro, you won't know about him," said Oliver.

"Could be," muttered the detective, looking awkward. To alter the subject, he asked if they'd discovered anything more about Détente. Oliver told him about the experiments conducted by Graeme, and their efforts to interview Dr Moore.

"Good luck, he hates reporters," said the detective.

"He also has an axe to grind with the navy," Oliver added. "He was the bullied recruit in those disciplinary files, and that's why he left."

Kwame expressed no obvious surprise, and continued stirring his overpriced paper cup of weak tea.

"Everybody in the industry knows that Charles Moore has a naval grudge. It's the reason he exports most of his stuff," he said.

"He sells weapons to overseas powers?" Kieran asked, with alarm.

"I'm going overseas," interjected Saskia. Her announcement was not met with any protests.

"Could the HD Cotton Crater Plant be sold overseas?" Kieran asked.

"Almost certainly, that's how the business works," said Kwame. "Then again, a machine that disarms nuclear weapons could be a good thing."

"It doesn't destroy bombs, it *is* one," the youngster insisted.

"Of course," patronised the policeman, "or at least that's the view of your old professor in Bideford."

"And you've heard different?" Oliver asked.

"We have our sources," the detective replied.

"That's exactly why I'm here," Oliver said. "We need to share information to find Carmel's killer and establish if we're in danger."

The policeman took an extended sip of tea before he eventually answered. He started by repeating the impasse in the murder inquiry, and that Dr Moore's bad naval memories were an open secret. He added that Détente was legally entitled to build a machine to dispose of nuclear material, even if it had the potential to cause a major atomic disaster if used incorrectly.

"We don't stop cars being sold because people have accidents," he added.

"But this machine could kill millions," Kieran insisted.

"I can't jail a defence boss for building weapons, or a gunman we can't find," sighed the detective.

"So what next?" the youngster demanded, clearly unimpressed.

"If you're really spooked, I can arrange protective custody until the heat's off."

"And let Dr Moore get away?" Kieran asked.

"We can't prove he's done anything," said the detective. "Just do yourselves a favour and leave this to us."

Oliver suspected that if they left the matter to the police then nothing would be done. Kieran was absolutely convinced of the fact, but decided to bite his tongue. Kwame then rose to his feet after finishing his cup of tea.

"Saskia, do you want me to win you something on the rifle range?" he asked. In the absence of any protest he assumed that he'd obtained his daughter's blessing. He then walked across to the shooting gallery, which was opposite the café.

The detective paid for seven pellets and quickly set about demonstrating the effect of his weapons training. He vanquished the targets mercilessly, reloading the air rifle and firing without hesitation. The fruit of his labour was a small toy dog with an American flag. He gave it to Saskia, but without any reaction from the teenager. Kwame looked in desperation to Oliver, hoping for some parental empathy. While he was a beginner at fatherhood, he could understand Kwame's predicament.

"Fancy trying the rifle range, Oliver?" the policeman asked.

"Not really, I think I'll cut my losses," he said, before turning to Kieran to ask if he wanted a go.

"No thanks," he replied, staring at the detective, "I've seen enough already."

***

After leaving the funfair, Oliver was convinced that he'd shaken the decrepit Fiat from his tail, but on returning to Edenhurst Court he found the pathetic vehicle quietly rusting beside the entrance. A shadowy figure was behind the wheel, trying to look inconspicuous by reading a broadsheet newspaper, which was the wrong way up and millimetres from his face. Wary of confronting the driver, Oliver sped past and parked in the garages behind the apartment block.

"Why don't we capture him?" Kieran suggested. Oliver was baffled by the idea as he couldn't see any obvious use for a henchman with a penchant for reading the business pages upside down.

"We can torture him to discover Détente's secrets," said the youngster. Oliver was alarmed that Kieran could suggest anything so bloodthirsty.

"It's too risky, he might be armed," said Oliver, who added that they had nothing to torture the henchman with anyway.

"We could read him your books," Kieran suggested.

"I thought you liked them."

"Only when I was four; I'm much more grown up now."

Oliver was hurt by the remark. While he recognised that Spib's adventures would never scoop a Nobel Prize, he consoled himself with the idea that children liked his stories. Now he was being slated by a former fan, and worst of all, it was potentially his son. Feeling at odds with the world, Oliver placed a phone call to bring some misery into somebody else's life.

"Council parking department please," he said. Once the call was connected, he reported that a rusty Fiat had been abandoned outside his apartment block.

"Can you tow it away?" he inquired.

"Get them to crush it," Kieran suggested in the background.

"Your truck will be here later? That's marvellous," said Oliver, ending the call.

"Nice one," said the youngster.

"Don't mess with the kiddies' author," he replied. His attempt at being macho was premature as the Fiat driver wasn't the only person following him. Another pair of eyes had scrutinised his every move that afternoon, and Oliver had been none the wiser. This is exactly what his pursuer had intended, and the time was approaching when she would make her devastating presence known.

As Oliver led Kieran from the garages into the apartment block, the woman stepped from her vehicle. To maintain the element of surprise, she remained a few yards behind them, and sneaked into the building just before the door closed.

Oliver and Kieran narrowly missed the lift inside Edenhurst Court and took the stairs instead. Oliver thought it would be good exercise and save time. The latter was questionable, as the lift arrived on the sixth floor within seconds of him dragging his weary carcass up to the same level. A woman emerged from the compartment and followed Oliver and Kieran down the passageway.

As Oliver reached his door, he heard heavy footsteps echoing between the corridor's bare walls behind him. The noise was becoming louder, and he then felt a firm hand on his shoulder. He let out an involuntary yelp before spinning around.

"Hello Mr Dart," beamed Mrs Lightbody.

Oliver yelped again, which probably came across as rude, although the social worker carried on regardless as if it happened all the time. She then barged her way past Oliver and into his flat in the same manner that a runaway freight train enters an unsuspecting station.

"I've been watching you," she revealed. Oliver was about to apologise for the inevitable boredom associated with such a task, but then realised that his existence since meeting Kieran had been anything but tedious. To his considerable irritation, it had bordered on exciting at times.

"I must admit that I doubted your parenting qualities," she added.

"I'm only a beginner," he replied.

"Exactly," said Mrs Lightbody, who started pacing the apartment menacingly. "That's why I was shocked to see you at the funfair."

"Was that a bad thing?" he asked, sensing a feeling usually reserved for married men, namely being almost certainly in trouble without knowing why.

"It takes some believing that a bachelor could become a caring father within weeks," said Mrs Lightbody. "But you show great promise."

"Thanks," he replied, feeling slightly proud.

"However, before handing out any parenting Oscars, I need to see Kieran," she revealed, before lowering her voice so that only Oliver could hear her. "We need to ensure he's somewhere safe."

"I imagine so," Oliver replied, staring out of the window at the Fiat. He kept watching anxiously from his balcony as Mrs Lightbody led Kieran into a separate room. Her interrogation lasted some time, and was still taking place when the tow truck arrived. Oliver smirked as a colourful bit of street theatre unfolded below him. Using a lavish amount of emotive language, the driver told the council worker that his car hadn't been abandoned. The council man left grudgingly, leaving the figure in the Fiat to read the farming supplement of his paper sideways. Oliver was disappointed that the rusty runabout had remained defiantly in place. Even as a Fleet Street reporter, he'd never revelled in the prospect of being stalked. As a children's author, and possible father-of-one, he liked the idea even less.

Oliver trudged to the sofa and collapsed onto it in the way he used to when he did a proper job. When Kieran had arrived he'd been tempted to get rid of him. Now that a meeting was taking place behind closed doors that could decide whether he was taken away, he wanted to keep him. Oliver had never planned to have children, but wanted to believe that he could be a good father if the need arose. Then again, what sort of parent exposed their child to the risks they had already taken in pursuing Carmel's killer? Oliver didn't know if he could protect Kieran from Détente, and knew for sure that he couldn't safeguard him against Mrs Lightbody.

"Mr Dart!" she boomed, wrenching open Kieran's door, her interrogation having ended. "Kieran has told me everything."

"Oh dear," muttered Oliver, still collapsed on the sofa.

"I am quite amazed by what I've heard," she snorted. "In fact, I would say it was almost unbelievable."

"I'm a rookie at fatherhood."

"So you said, but I've heard differently," said the social worker, scrutinising the kitchen in case there was any grime she could complain about, and sighing when there wasn't any. "Kieran says you've kept him entertained during the holidays."

"You told me to keep him distracted."

"You've also bought him clothes, taken him on field trips to university and to watch science experiments, and learned to cook."

"Kieran told you all that?" Oliver gasped, insulted by the accusation of being a culinary calamity beforehand.

"Children never lie unless they want to, and if they're told to, it always shows," confided Mrs Lightbody. Oliver then asked the social worker if she believed Kieran.

"I think I can trust him," she smiled. "Perhaps you won't make such a bad father after all."

The social worker added that she would return before long, and then left with all the peaceful grace that had been so lacking on her arrival. As the front door gently closed, Kieran emerged from his room in the manner of someone leaving an air raid shelter after a blitz. His body language was timid as he assumed the chair next to the sofa.

"So, am I staying?" he asked. Oliver replied that he thought Mrs Lightbody had already given permission.

"She told me to ask you as well."

Oliver couldn't help marvelling at the social worker's psychology; he was hardly going to tell an eleven-year-old that he was evicted and effectively orphaned. As it happened, the decision was easy. Not only had Kieran been of invaluable help in the investigation, but the youngster had lied through his teeth to remain with him.

"You can stay as long as you like," said Oliver.

***

The morning after Oliver had told the youngster he could remain at Edenhurst Court, he woke to the smell of something horrible. His left hand reached for the alarm clock, which displayed a time suggesting the traffic outside would be heavy. More to the point, the odour in the immediate vicinity was growing worse by the second. He abandoned his bed, grabbed a dressing gown, and went to investigate.

"I'm cooking!" Kieran boasted, who was presiding over something resembling a nuclear meltdown at the kitchen stove. Either side of his smile, his cheeks were rosy from the heat, and a tea cosy was wedged on his head, which had clearly been the closest approximation to a chef's hat that he could find. Oliver surveyed the chaos.

"Magnifique," he grunted, although his semi-conscious state had not allowed for the wave of enthusiasm needed to humour the youngster sufficiently. It seemed as if Kieran shared his mother's cooking skills, which was saying like a bat had inherited its father's eyes. Undaunted by a complete lack of ability, the youngster had tried to create two full English breakfasts. Having deduced that the items needed to be cooked, he'd piled them high into a wok and drenched the relevant beans, bacon and bangers in a gallon of cooking oil. The multicoloured lump of 'food' was now crackling and hissing angrily, and would occasionally spit a small mushroom off the unsavoury heap onto the tiles below. It certainly looked distasteful – deep fried baked beans just weren't right.

"Do you plan to cook every morning?" Oliver inquired.

"Would you like me to?" Kieran enthused. Oliver wasn't sure how to respond without giving offence.

"No," he said, before adding that it would be unfair to expect Kieran to cook everything, and that household jobs should be shared.

"I don't fancy washing my own clothes," the youngster muttered.

"If you leave them in the trash, you won't have to."

Oliver then took over the cooking to sort the inedible from the unidentifiable. As Kieran patiently took his place at the table, Oliver suddenly felt more responsible for the youngster than ever before. Kieran had nailed his colours to the mast, and Oliver felt it was his duty to repay that loyalty. He wanted to look after the boy, and realised that investigating Détente was more likely to place Kieran in danger. It was his job to protect him, and as a result, the time had come to raise a difficult subject.

"I don't want you to feel unwelcome," he began, placing a truly horrendous breakfast in front of the boy, "but I'm worried that you're not safe here."

"Where are we going?"

Oliver said he was not going anywhere, and would continue the investigation into Détente. However, he suggested that it would be better if Kieran was taken into police protection.

"I'm not going with Kwame," hissed Kieran, folding his arms in disgust.

"What's wrong with him?"

"He's on their side."

Oliver was thrown by the response. At first he thought the youngster was referring to the police, but then realised that he meant Détente. The idea that Kwame was in the pay of Dr Moore seemed ludicrous, and he said as much.

"Then why hasn't he found my mum's killer?" the boy asked.

"He said it's a professional job."

"He isn't looking," Kieran claimed. "In fact, he might have done it himself."

"What makes you say that?"

"You saw him at the fairground, he's a crack shot."

"Yes, but he isn't a murderer," Oliver protested, who added that his friend was hardly likely to be an undercover assassin.

"He needs the money," reminded Kieran.

"Perhaps," Oliver conceded, "but not enough to become a killer, and certainly not badly enough to murder the mother of my son."

"But he didn't know she was my mum," said Kieran, who pushed his plate aside and rose from the table, "and I don't even know if you're my dad."

Oliver remained silent, as he couldn't deny or confirm that he was the boy's father. He glanced at the kitchen drawer where he'd hidden the DNA letter until such time as he had the courage to read it. The moment had now come to put the matter beyond doubt. He left the table, opened the drawer, and grabbed the envelope. He turned to show Kieran the letter, but stopped a fraction of a second before he opened the contents.

Kieran was gone.

Oliver then recalled hearing a door close as he reached for the letter, but had blotted it out, perhaps subconsciously assuming that it was the one to Kieran's room. However, he wasn't there, and on searching the rest of the apartment, the youngster was still missing. The only explanation was that Kieran had left altogether, and the noise Oliver had heard was the front door.

The DNA letter was thrust back into the drawer as Oliver put everything on hold to find the youngster. He grabbed his shoes from beside the front door, but ran down the corridor in his socks, skidding into the lift on the polished floor. As it took him down to the ground floor, Oliver forced his feet awkwardly into the shoes while sitting on the floor of the elevator compartment.

As the lift doors opened, Oliver sprinted from the building to fetch the car. He opened the garage door and then slammed it shut after reversing the vehicle onto the open tarmac. He climbed back behind the wheel, but his arm froze as he reached for the handbrake.

He had no idea where he was going.

Getting the car had been second nature, but Oliver didn't have a clue where to start looking. Kieran might be anywhere, and possibly where only pedestrians could go. Oliver realised that he had the wrong vehicle, and decided to swap four wheels for two. He put the car back in the garage, and leapt on his racing bike.

Oliver hurtled down the steep driveway from Edenhurst Court, fastening his helmet on the way. He then started to pedal furiously as he reached Parkhill Road. He could feel adrenaline bursting through his veins as he rode towards the marina. He picked up terrific speed heading towards the waterfront, slicing past a couple of slow cars. He then reduced his speed to look for Kieran but he wasn't there. Oliver continued cycling along the coast. The seaside was teeming with people, including a countless number of children. However, they were all accompanied by adults, and he couldn't see Kieran amongst them.

After a few minutes, Oliver had cycled along the northern side of Torbay and reached the point where the coastline turned south towards Paignton. He realised that Kieran couldn't have walked so far in such a short time. The youngster had taken a different path, but Oliver had no idea where to look. He was outside The Belgrave Hotel where the car chase with the Audi had begun. He then turned around and saw the rusty Fiat waiting patiently at the roadside for his next move. While Oliver had lost Kieran, he hadn't shaken his tail.

As Oliver resumed cycling, the Fiat dutifully continued its pursuit. He decided to ride towards the town centre and began wrenching his bike up Shedden Hill. The gradient was steep and the Fiat chugged along at walking pace. Having struggled to follow a sluggish bus in Weymouth, Oliver felt a tinge of sympathy for the driver. An idea crossed his mind, and he pulled up beside the kerb, which the Fiat immediately mimicked. Oliver strolled across to the driver's window and tapped on the glass. His pursuer, a stocky man dressed in black, sheepishly rolled down the window.

"Are you tailing the boy, or me?" Oliver asked.

"Ahem," muttered the man, looking embarrassed, "both of you."

"Well, he's disappeared," Oliver revealed, who then asked if he could help to find the youngster. The driver knew that letting one them vanish would mean trouble, and nodded to signify his co-operation.

"When he left my apartment, which way did he go?"

The driver insisted that he hadn't seen him, and followed Oliver as a result. It seemed hard to believe that Kieran could have given the motorist the slip, as he was parked right outside Edenhurst Court.

"Perhaps he's still at your apartment," the driver suggested. Oliver replied that he'd searched it from top to bottom. The driver agreed to resume his sentry duty at the building in case the youngster returned home. Oliver then rode towards the town centre to continue his search. He found himself retracing the route of the car chase as he cycled through central Torquay. However, he couldn't see Kieran, and decided to continue along the route of the chase.

Oliver looked for the youngster at the town hall and along the main shopping streets, but there was no trace of him. He became more worried as the minutes kept slipping past, knowing that Kieran could be further and further away from his home.

Leaving the town centre, Oliver continued the route of the car chase along St Marychurch Road. He had no idea where the boy was going. As he'd only been in Torquay a short time, it was hard to predict where he might seek solace and refuge. There was also the possibility that he was lost. Oliver didn't know if Kieran had taken any money with him. If he'd saved enough coins, he might have the means to skip town altogether. However, the quickest path to the railway station was along the coastal route, and Oliver had not found him there.

The racing bike turned into Windsor Road and then veered right into Victoria Road. Oliver's progress then slowed again as the terrain went uphill once more as he arrived in Pembroke Road. His legs started to burn as he turned into the sharper hill of Cavern

Road. He then realised that an even steeper climb was looming around the corner in Huxton Road. His muscles started to feel heavy as the adrenaline caused by Kieran's disappearance started to dwindle.

The wheels of the bike slowed to a crawl as Oliver hauled the machine up the unforgiving ascent of Huxton Road. While he was no stranger to climbing hills, the gradient would force all but the hardiest rider to give up, but he was determined not to quit. With every sapping turn of the pedals, the bike moved closer to the summit, inching its way to level ground. As he approached the top, the hill became less steep, and the wheels started turning more freely. At last he reached the summit, by which point his legs were burning from the battle. He then turned right into Warberry Road West and the machine started to freewheel gently down the slight incline. The speed built as the descent became steeper and he neared the one hundred foot sheer drop where the stricken Audi had plunged to its demise. Oliver applied the brakes and rode carefully onto the narrow patch of grass clinging to the hillside.

A boy was sitting on the edge of the precipice.

Oliver would not have seen the youngster from the road. He dismounted his machine and rested it on the ground before crouching down beside the youngster.

"Hello Kieran."

The boy didn't reply and kept tugging up blades of grass from the parched soil beside him. Oliver then asked how Kieran had managed to find the scene of the Audi crash, having only visited the location once.

"I'm good at remembering places," he muttered. Oliver was impressed by the lad's talent – it was presumably a similar gift that made him so good at anagrams.

"Why did you choose this spot?" Oliver asked.

"I like the view," said the boy. Oliver had to agree that it was impressive, with most of central Torquay visible, sweeping down to the waves of Torbay. After living in the resort for several years, he'd started taking the scenery for granted. Following Kieran's arrival, he now realised that he couldn't take anything for granted.

"I was worried when you left so quickly."

"Were you?" the boy muttered.

"Of course, I care about you."

"Why?" Kieran shrugged, genuinely baffled.

"I just do, okay?" Oliver replied, patting the lad's shoulder. "I didn't want to drive you away. I thought you'd be safer with the police."

"We can't trust them."

"What about Kwame?"

"He's one of the bad guys."

Oliver was about to protest his friend's innocence, but could tell by the boy's expression that he would never be convinced.

"Okay, we won't involve the police, but what next?" he asked.

Kieran had no answer. Oliver wasn't surprised by his silence as they were short of options. The police had made little progress and the youngster didn't trust them anyway. If they went into hiding, Carmel's killer would probably escape, and the HD Cotton Crater Plant could be let loose. Then again, even if they found the device Oliver didn't know what to do about it. The police couldn't impound it, and trying to destroy it could trigger a major atomic disaster. It seemed that while an assassin that had killed one person could be turned over to the law, a weapon that could murder millions could not. Oliver realised that they had to discover what Détente aimed to do with the device before it was too late.

"We need to track it," said Kieran. They weren't sure where the weapon was being stored, but the firm's research centre at Honiton in east Devon seemed the most likely place. The youngster suggested that they should go there, but Oliver was worried about being followed.

"By who?" Kieran asked.

"The Fiat driver who keeps tailing us," replied Oliver, gesturing to the road.

"I can't see anybody," said the youngster. Oliver stared at the totally clear road; he then remembered that he'd asked the Fiat driver to wait at the apartment block in case Kieran returned.

"What a numpty, we've given him the slip," chuckled Oliver.

"Then let's find the research centre before he catches up."

Oliver reckoned it would take an hour to reach Honiton by road, but first, they would need the car.

"But it's parked at the flat," said Kieran, who added that the Fiat driver would see them leaving the apartment block.

"We can't go by rail, I don't have any cash," Oliver conceded. The youngster said he was in a similar position, and asked where Oliver had left his money.

"Back at the flat," they chorused in grim resignation.

"You left so fast, I only just remembered my keys," said Oliver, adding that they'd have to return home unless Kieran wanted to walk to Honiton, or hitch a ride on his handlebars.

"Can't you borrow some money?" the youngster inquired. The question only reminded Oliver that he was desperately short of friends and the person he trusted the most was already sitting beside him. He wanted to return to the flat anyway to collect his wallet, phone, the Détente papers, and a change of clothes.

"How do we avoid the Fiat driver?" Kieran asked.

"You tell me, you've already done it," Oliver replied, adding that his departure from Edenhurst Court earlier that day hadn't been detected.

"I used the gap in the fence," Kieran revealed, who then said there was a hole in a timber panel behind the site.

"You climbed that huge bank behind the car park?"

"It was the quickest way here," said Kieran.

"Then it'll be the fastest route back."

***

Edenhurst Court, like many buildings in Torquay, was built into a steep hill. The fences behind it were level with the upper floors of the apartment block thanks to the gradient. Oliver peered over the wooden panels and saw the Fiat in the distance parked on the opposite side of the property. He was worried about being seen, and would have preferred to sneak into the block at night, but time was short.

"The hole in the fence is further along," said Kieran, walking towards the gap. Oliver followed the youngster, pushing his racing bike as he went. The aperture was large enough for a child, but a squeeze for an adult. Oliver peered through the gap and found that his view of the Fiat was obscured by the apartment block.

"He can't see us from here," declared Oliver, who then proceeded to clamber through the hole. Most people wouldn't have fitted, but given that he kept in shape, Oliver reckoned he would succeed if he tackled it headfirst. His plan worked until his hips became wedged in the fence, upon which he regretted spending more time eating ice cream than cycling since meeting Kieran.

"Can you stay here and watch my bike?" he asked.

"No problem," the youngster replied.

"And pass through the rucksack?"

"That'll be tricky if you're stuck."

"I could do with a shove," Oliver conceded.

Kieran sighed and grabbed the racing bike. He pushed it purposefully towards Oliver's wedged figure and the sudden impact of the front wheel striking him forced him through. He then fell forwards onto the top of the slope. Before he could recover his footing he began slithering uncontrollably down the steep bank. He plunged down it like a skeleton bobsleigh rider. His progress over the coarse and parched earth was as rapid as it was uncomfortable. The only consolation of the rough ground was that Oliver could grip some of it to slow his descent. He succeeded in reducing his pace from suicidal to swift by the foot of the hill, upon which he tumbled over the waist-high wall of the car park and crashed onto its unforgiving tarmac.

"That hurt," he groaned, lying on his back until his breath returned. He then heard something else careering down the bank behind him. At first he thought it was Kieran, but then remembered that he'd asked him to pass through his rucksack.

"Ouch," he complained, as it shot off the slope and bounced off his forehead. He then staggered to his feet before anything else toppled down the hill behind him.

Oliver arrived back in the apartment block through the rear doors and headed into the lift. As it doggedly elevated him to the sixth floor he dusted himself down and removed the fragments of stray flora squatting in his hair after falling down the bank. He then stepped from the lift and entered his apartment. It had an uncomfortable air to it, almost as if he shouldn't be there, or he'd broken into the place. Feeling oddly like a burglar, he decided to steal some fresh clothes from himself along with cash, credit cards, and a first aid kit. He also rounded up some garments for Kieran and a pair of binoculars to spy on Détente's research base. It then occurred that some food might be useful, and he began looting his kitchen. He then found himself beside the drawer containing the DNA letter. He took it out and stared at the envelope for a few seconds. He then realised that time was scarce, and stuffed the letter into the rucksack that had faithfully followed him down the slope.

The final things Oliver took from his apartment were a notepad, fountain pen, mobile phone and two carving knives. The blades were razor sharp, but he wasn't intending to threaten anyone. As he returned to the car park, he removed them from his bag and sank them into the foot of the parched bank above the waist-high wall. Using the knives, he hauled himself onto the slope. He then began mountaineering up the north face of the car park (as he dubbed it), using the blades to drag himself to the top. On reaching the summit, he returned the knives to the rucksack, and passed it through the gap in the fence.

"Nice climbing," complimented Kieran, taking hold of the bag.

"That's tougher than it looks," said Oliver, trying to squeeze back through the hole. "How did you manage it?"

"It was easy," replied the youngster, pulling his colleague through the gap. "I used the stairs."

Oliver poked his head back through the hole and spotted the flight of concrete steps at the far end of the bank.

"Damn," he muttered.

***

Oliver was already braced for how costly two rail tickets to Honiton might be, even if one was half price. All the same, he was still unimpressed at the figure when he reached the counter at Torquay Station.

"It's more for a return trip," the clerk advised. "Are you coming back?"

Oliver had to give the question some considerable thought.

"Yes," he finally announced, "we'll be coming home again."

Kieran nodded at the reply, although Oliver said it more for the youngster's sake than his own, as he couldn't be sure. He then wheeled his racing bike onto the platform and took a seat while waiting for the train. It was around lunchtime, but he was too anxious to feel hungry.

"I'm starving," complained the boy. Oliver didn't reply and simply produced a pack of sausage rolls from his rucksack. Kieran began to devour them, but Oliver was too nervous to join in. He felt helpless and vulnerable waiting for the train, and was desperate to leave town.

When the locomotive finally arrived, Oliver surged for the nearest doors and boarded the service. He secured his racing bike to the rack beside the guard's cabin and took a seat beside Kieran in the second carriage. He studied the faces of the passengers around him, seized by paranoia that they might be Détente agents. In fact, they seemed more interested in their puzzle books, newspapers, trashy novels, electronic gizmos, and everything else they'd brought to distract themselves from the beautiful scenery. Oliver relaxed into his chair as best he could, and breathed a sigh of relief as the locomotive pulled out of Torquay.

It wasn't long before they had to change trains and climb aboard the Honiton service. Oliver was starting to feel more comfortable, and now regretted surrendering all the sausage rolls to his young accomplice. He rummaged in the backpack and found a pork pie that appeared ripe for sacrifice. He started nibbling it as the Devon countryside, bathed in bright sunshine, drifted past the carriage windows. He spotted a school on the horizon, and reflected that he hadn't found anywhere yet for Kieran to study. Then again, while some families were anxious about an impending change of school, such worries were nothing compared to the danger they were facing.

It was mid afternoon when the train arrived at Honiton. It was a pleasantly bustling market town, and the last community of any real size on the Dorchester road before Dorset. While it was in the same county as Oliver's home, it had been a fiddly and tedious trip to Honiton. As a result, they'd gorged all the food from the flat on the way out of sheer boredom. In order to resupply, Oliver led them from the station and along New Street to the shopping area. The stores stood wearily to attention either side of the main road, which formed an east to west spine as straight as an arrow. As it was market day, every square inch of available pavement and parking was covered in benches and tarpaulins.

Oliver halted at the fruit stall, which Kieran skilfully by-passed to reach the pick and mix seller. Oliver glanced at the fruit but was reluctant to approach it as an army of wasps was guarding every last grape, cherry and kumquat. Any customers who ventured near the produce were promptly repelled by an angry and buzzing yellow and black squadron. Oliver hated wasps – they were the insect equivalent of bored teenagers. They did nothing of value and simply hung around making everyone's lives miserable. There was a similar assortment of buzzing things at the sweet stand, which deterred Kieran from buying anything that might cause the wasps to pursue him. Oliver eventually summoned the courage to buy some apples, along with bread, some seafood, and a suspiciously large amount of crisps for his colleague.

"Cheese and gherkin flavour," Kieran enthused, "that's one I haven't tried."

Détente's research base was on the edge of town beside the A30 London to Land's End road. The dual carriageway tore past the northern fringe of Honiton and cut the site off from the rest of the town. It was also surrounded by fences and trees, making it pointless to run the gauntlet of the 70mph traffic to peep at the premises. With no hope of a close view, Oliver and Kieran trooped around Honiton, seeking a high vantage point to observe the research centre. Eventually they found one, but it was a quarter of a mile away. Their viewing point was in a meadow above the town, and the base was barely visible with the naked eye. Oliver reached into his rucksack, which was overflowing with crisps, and extracted the binoculars he'd salvaged from Edenhurst Court.

"What's happening down there?"

166

"Not a lot," Oliver replied, who was lazily examining the site with the glasses. The property comprised several two-storey buildings with dull grey cladding. The concrete they stood upon was also drab, even in the sunshine, and the only sprinkling of colour on the site was Détente's logo beside the main gate. Even the car park looked dull, as if it were company policy only to drive vehicles that were grey, black, or a shade between the two. The monotony was broken when a royal blue BMW arrived at the gate and was promptly waved through the checkpoint.

"Fancy a look?" Oliver inquired, passing over the glasses, with the novelty of their stakeout wearing off. The boy, whose enthusiasm was yet to be tested, grabbed the binoculars and scrutinised the base. He followed the BMW as it prowled across the bare concrete and halted next to the reception building. The driver's door opened and a tall figure emerged. He was of African appearance, and was wearing a pastel coloured shirt and blue jeans. While being a long way from their observation point, Kieran was certain that he recognised him.

"Isn't that your police friend?" he asked, passing across the glasses. Oliver snatched them with urgency and fixed his gaze on the lone figure in the distance.

"I'll be damned," he muttered, as the binoculars settled on the detective. "What are you doing, Kwame?"

"I said we couldn't trust him."

Oliver told Kieran not to jump to conclusions, arguing that there was no proof that his friend was a traitor.

"Then why's he visiting the enemy?"

"He might be checking them out," Oliver replied, adding that they'd urged him to investigate Détente several times.

"Better late than never," said Kieran, who reclaimed the glasses and watched the policeman strolling towards the reception. The youngster asked if the detective was likely to be working undercover.

"I doubt it," Oliver shrugged, adding that Kwame's details had been in the media asking for witnesses to Carmel's death. As a result, if Détente had ordered her murder, they would already know the policeman's identity.

"Then if he's on duty, why is he wearing jeans?" the youngster posed.

Oliver took back the binoculars and studied his friend once more. Kieran was right about his dress code, and was impressed by the boy's attention to detail. The policeman then walked into the reception building and disappeared from view. Oliver put down the glasses and retrieved his mobile phone from the backpack.

"Calling your friend?" Kieran inquired.

"No, his office; we'll soon see if he's on duty." Oliver replied, who then asked to speak to Detective Sergeant Ebwelle.

"He's on a fortnight's leave," said the officer who took the call at the police HQ in Exeter. "Can I help you?"

"No," Oliver muttered. "I don't think anyone can."

He ended the call and returned his phone to the rucksack. By now, Kieran had liberated the binoculars and was combing the base for activity. He was frustrated by the lack of action.

"We need to get closer."

"There's no point, it's all covered by fences and trees," Oliver reminded.

"I meant inside the place."

Oliver was shocked by the idea of breaking into a military research facility. After giving Détente the slip in Torquay, he reckoned that risking capture while trying to enter one of their guarded bases didn't seem wise. However, he knew that Kwame would have to be challenged about his visit to the site. Then again, it would be hard to confront the detective while he was still inside the compound, unless they followed Kieran's suggestion of storming the fortress.

"I think I've spotted a way to break in," announced the boy. He added that the south west corner of the site was shielded by trees with a low fence. Without any sign of security cameras in that sector, and a clump of birches to hide their presence, they could sneak into the base.

"What then?" Oliver inquired, opening a packet of smoky bacon corn chips.

Kieran suggested that they waited until nightfall and then crept around the site to locate the HD Cotton Crater Plant.

"Always assuming it's there."

"You said this was the most likely place," the youngster reminded.

"What happens if we find it?"

"We could blow up it."

"And probably destroy half the town," Oliver warned. "I'm sure the good folk of Honiton wouldn't approve of that."

Kieran then asked if they could steal the device.

"I fear the checkpoint guards might have something to say about a young boy and a children's author waltzing off their base with a nuclear weapon."

"We could dress as Détente staff and say we're moving the bomb."

Oliver had to concede that it wasn't a ridiculous plan, but was still baffled over what to do with the device if they captured it.

"Sell it?" Kieran joked. Oliver smiled at the idea, but realised that the highest bidder was unlikely to be the cash-strapped British government. Even if they gave it to the Ministry of Defence, there was no guarantee they would order Détente to halt production. On the contrary, the armed forces might ask them to build a dozen more. What Oliver really wanted was for the device to cease to exist, but it was virtually impossible to make a weapon vanish once the technology existed to produce it.

"We can't win, can we?" Oliver sighed. "If we destroy that bomb, they'll only build another one."

"If they have the money," said Kieran.

Oliver replied that defence firms were seldom poor, and most of them 'made a bomb' in both senses of the word.

"But isn't Détente in trouble?" the youngster asked. The comment stopped Oliver in his tracks, and he put the remains of his corn chips to one side. Kieran was quite right – the company had apparently sunk most of its development budget into the device. Carmel's research had also identified that it had sold many bases, and even tried to offload its largest one in Portland, but nobody met the asking price.

"If we destroyed their prototype, the company might fold," said Oliver.

"Now you're talking," Kieran enthused.

Oliver finished his corn chips, wiped his hands, and asked for the binoculars. He then scanned the research centre again, and asked the youngster to recap his strategy for entering the site.

"It's simple really," he replied. Kieran then recounted his plan of waiting until nightfall to shin over the perimeter fence and comb the base for the HD Cotton Crater Plant. Oliver asked how they would find it, as the site was peppered with buildings.

"We'll borrow a Geiger counter from your friend at the university, and it'll lead us right to it," the youngster replied.

Oliver wondered if Lucas had fixed the device after the samples from Drake's Island had allegedly blown it up. He had to admit that using a Geiger counter was a smart move, but remained to be convinced that they could break into the building.

"They'll have locks, alarms, and guards," he warned.

Kieran was about to respond but stopped in his tracks. His idea of beating up some guards to steal their uniforms and stroll off with the bomb was a little optimistic. Not only would they be outnumbered, but the site personnel were probably armed.

"We only have cheese and gherkin crisps," Oliver reminded, "which are nasty, but not lethal."

"Okay, I've got another plan," said Kieran, who added that they would need a can of petrol and matches. Assuming that the eleven-year-old was conspiring to torch something, Oliver asked, with trepidation, what he had in mind.

"We set fire to the building," he replied.

Oliver was more than a tad concerned. In fact, he was petrified. Torching the military base would not only be a major crime, but could trigger a nuclear disaster.

"That's when the clever bit comes in," boasted Kieran.

Oliver was relieved to hear it, as the plan hadn't sounded very smart up to this point. Kieran revealed that they would call the fire brigade before the blaze took hold. He added that the firemen would find the bomb and then ask questions. Oliver wasn't so sure. His journalistic experience of fire crews was that they would ignore finding a weapon at a military research centre, but wouldn't ignore a blatant case of arson.

"If we're spotted then Détente will turn us in," he warned.

"So what do you suggest?" Kieran muttered, starting to sulk. Oliver resumed scanning the base with the binoculars.

"I think we should follow that truck," he announced, passing the glasses to his colleague. He took them grudgingly and searched for the vehicle, which was beside one of the endless grey buildings. Kieran watched a clutch of people in radiation suits emerging from the structure pushing a heavy trolley. Upon it was a tangle of pipes and tanks bolted to a fearsome steel needle at its base. He recognised it at once.

"They're moving the bomb!" Kieran exclaimed.

The party of six men – though it was hard to establish their gender from such a distance – handled the device as carefully as if it were resting on eggshells. Kieran looked on as they pushed it gingerly up the ramp and loaded it into the lorry. All six then walked away with a noticeable spring in their step.

"They look happy with themselves," Kieran observed.

"They're probably glad to be rid of it."

"We need to know where it's going."

"Let's get the car," said Oliver. The youngster looked baffled by his statement, and after a moment, he realised why. The Gordon Keeble was still in Torquay.

"Why don't we commandeer a vehicle, like in the movies?" Kieran suggested.

"It never works, nobody stops," Oliver sighed, before adding that an old friend once tried flagging down a pickup truck as a drunken birthday prank. "And it was two months before he could walk again."

"Well if you're too scared, I'll stop a car," declared Kieran, who instantly bolted towards the nearest road. Oliver rose to his feet at once to give chase but the boy's agility provided him with a significant head start. He called on Kieran to stop, but he slipped through the gate and left the meadow. Oliver reached it soon after and saw the youngster on the opposite side of the road with his arm outstretched. He then noticed a silver-coloured Mercedes speeding towards the youngster like a two-ton bullet. Oliver sprinted from the gate to rescue the boy. Far from being graceful, he grabbed him like an overweight prop forward and they plunged awkwardly into a roadside ditch. The car then roared past, blasting its horn in contempt.

"Never do that again!" Oliver scolded.

"I was just trying to help."

"Rash, impulsive and reckless, just like your mother," he complained, climbing slowly to his feet. Oliver then extended his arm to Kieran but he refused it, preferring to rise by himself. They trudged back across the road in silence.

On returning to the meadow, Oliver spotted a black Labrador that was off its leash. The dog was sniffing around his abandoned rucksack and soon became very excited. With its tail wagging eagerly, it buried its nose in the bag and then emerged with two packets of crisps in its mouth. The Labrador ripped them open immediately, scattering the contents. It then ingested the crisps like an industrial-strength vacuum cleaner. Oliver sighed at the spectacle.

"Greedy bitch," he muttered.

A speck in the distance, which was probably its owner judging by their frantic waving of arms, tried to appeal to the dog's better nature.

"Sasha, no!" the figure bleated forlornly.

"Yes, bad Sasha," Oliver added with resignation. On reaching the offending canine he tried to restrain it, but failed dismally as it buried its nose in the bag again to find a tastier flavour than prawn cocktail. The Labrador emerged with the last pack of Worcestershire sauce, and Oliver closed the rucksack while the dog consumed its swag. The forlorn figure, which turned out to be an elderly woman that would struggle to outpace a lame sloth, eventually arrived to retrieve her wayward pet.

"She doesn't usually do that," apologised the owner.

Oliver was tempted to ask if the dog usually ate tortilla chips instead, but didn't have the heart to be sarcastic.

"Don't worry," he soothed. "One of my friends had a Labrador, and it used to eat anything."

Kieran, who looked decidedly unimpressed that his stockpile of snacks was now contaminated with dog saliva, asked which friend Oliver was talking about.

"Kwame," he replied. His mind then returned to the detective, who was only a quarter of a mile away at the base. "Of course, that's the answer!"

"What is?" Kieran demanded, accompanied by the dog owner, who felt oddly compelled to join in.

"We're looking for a car, and Kwame has one," Oliver declared.

"I don't need a car," shrugged the dog owner. Oliver was tempted to suggest that she needed a slower pet, preferably one with a shell that was excited by lettuce.

"He won't give us a lift," said Kieran.

"Maybe not, but we have to try," Oliver resolved. He then led the boy from the meadow, leaving the dog owner to admonish her pet in private.

Oliver and Kieran ran down the hill towards the town, realising there wasn't a second to lose. Oliver soon switched to his racing bike to spare his knees any further damage from sprinting on the hard concrete. Once aboard, he had to use his brakes to avoid leaving the youngster behind. If left unchecked, the bike could have reached 30mph without any trouble. Eventually the terrain levelled out as they arrived back in the town centre, and they were soon at the dual carriageway.

"What next?" Kieran wheezed, trying to recover from the run. Oliver, who was not so jaded, watched as countless vehicles roared past at high speed. He knew they couldn't cross the road without risking their lives, but another option presented itself. There was only one way out of the base, which was a narrow spur road that fed into the dual carriageway. If they walked along the hard shoulder for two hundred yards, they could stand at the end of it without crossing the A30.

Oliver led the way after climbing off his bike. They soon arrived at the end of the spur road, which was far enough from the site so that the checkpoint was hidden by trees. More to the point, the guards couldn't see Oliver and Kieran setting up their own monitoring post beside the road. They'd arrived too late to intercept the lorry, but there was no sign that Kwame had left the base. Oliver took a piece of paper from the rucksack and wrote the policeman's name on it, along with the word "help".

"Do you think he'll see it?" Kieran asked.

"Even detectives can read."

"Will he stop the car?"

"He should do," Oliver replied, who added that he'd ask Kwame to follow the truck. Kieran then repeated his suspicion that the detective was a double agent.

"Then he should know where the lorry's going," said Oliver, who was growing tired of having to dispel rumours of Kwame being a traitor. He still couldn't believe his friend was a turncoat, even if Kieran seemed convinced of the fact.

It was late afternoon when they began staking out the spur road. The traffic was infrequent, and there was no sign of the detective. Oliver and Kieran decided to conceal themselves behind a gorse bush in case any guards came along the road to investigate. Oliver was starting to hope that they would, simply to relieve the tedium of monitoring a road that was hardly used at all.

By six o'clock they were both hungry and bored. Kieran was trying to amuse himself by casting pebbles towards a plastic cup in the nearby gutter. Oliver watched on with disinterest. He was ruing the fact that his car was unavailable, and with every minute, the HD Cotton Crater Plant was also getting away.

Shortly before seven o'clock, by which point the trickle of cars had turned into a drought, Oliver tried to summon the courage to suggest going home. He didn't want to give up, but waiting for Kwame seemed increasingly futile if they wanted to pursue the bomb. Then, in the distance, Oliver heard a performance engine. He looked over the gorse bush and saw a blue BMW heading towards them.

"It's him," he declared, picking up his crudely written sign. He plodded to the roadside with Kieran in pursuit. As the BMW approached, he held out the placard and waited for Kwame to stop. Oliver watched the car approach and then recognised the policeman behind the wheel. They made eye contact and Oliver then noticed an expression of panic on the detective's face. Instead of slowing down, the engine pitch increased and the vehicle speeded up. Oliver waved the sign at Kwame as he roared past, but the BMW failed to brake, and tore onto the dual carriageway.

"I don't believe it," Oliver gasped.

"Did he recognise you?"

"He must have done."

"Then it shows we can't rely on him," said Kieran.

Oliver had to concede that the youngster might be right.

***

With no idea of where the HD Cotton Crater Plant had been taken, Oliver and Kieran decided to find somewhere to stay. The light was fading when they arrived at the guesthouse near Honiton railway station.

Oliver decided to take a shower. He was still finding pieces of grass in his hair after tumbling down the bank at Edenhurst Court. Locked in the bathroom by himself, he began to contemplate his plight. He didn't trust the police anymore, and felt totally alone in his fight against Détente. His sole ally was Kieran, and he would have preferred to face the danger without him, as he didn't want to place the youngster in jeopardy. Then again, he had no choice. Ever since Kieran had appeared on his doorstep, and Carmel's notes had arrived, Oliver felt he'd been presented with one impossible decision after another. He couldn't ignore Détente but felt powerless to stop them. He also couldn't turn the youngster away, but was scared to face up to parenthood, especially as he wasn't sure that he was a father.

Oliver left the bathroom in a limp dressing gown that he found hanging beside the shower. It was faded pink, and designed for a female guest. Kieran was watching television and didn't notice his choice of garment.

"What's on the box?"

"Not a lot," muttered the youngster, his right fist pressed glumly into his chin.

"Most things on television are a joke."

175

Kieran then turned around and saw the pink dressing gown.

"Perhaps you should be on there," he diagnosed. The youngster then asked if Oliver had any idea where Détente had moved the weapon.

"It could be anywhere now," he sighed. He also feared that it was more likely that Détente's agents would catch up with them before they caught up with the bomb. He'd booked the most basic guesthouse that he could find to keep a low profile, but knew that time was running out. He also realised that staking out the research centre had increased the likelihood of being traced.

"Why did Détente move the weapon from their base?" he posed.

"So they can blow it up."

"I hope not," said Oliver, "but they'll need to test it somewhere."

Kieran asked if Détente could afford to sacrifice the prototype, given their lack of cash. Oliver replied that if the weapon was successful then the firm could expect to be bombarded by orders, which would solve its financial problems.

"Where can they test it?" Kieran asked.

"They can't use Drake's Island again," said Oliver, adding that if a miniature bomb contaminated the outpost then a full-size model would probably wipe Plymouth off the map. However, if the test failed, then the company could fold.

"We need to sabotage the bomb," resolved Kieran.

"We'll have to find it first."

They both stared glumly at the television, which was spouting rubbish. Oliver had no idea where to start looking for the weapon. Try as he might, he couldn't find a sudden burst of inspiration. As the evening dragged past, there seemed no option but to admit defeat and hope for a spark of genius the next day.

Oliver found that getting to sleep was difficult as his mattress was lumpier than a sack of deformed potatoes. The harder he tried to sleep, the trickier it became. He found himself staring at the ceiling in the darkness. There had to be some way to uncover Détente's plans, and he was sure that he missing something. He wondered if there was a vital clue in Carmel's notes that he'd overlooked. His brain was tired, but he focused on the problem as best he could. However, fatigue was now infecting his mind, and just when he didn't want to fall asleep, everything went black.

***

"Wake up!" Kieran urged.

In his semi-conscious state, Oliver became aware that the youngster was attempting to wake him, or perhaps trying to tear off his arm. He muttered something unintelligible, hoping that any sort of response would make him stop.

"You must get up!" Kieran exclaimed, making a renewed attempt to dislocate Oliver's shoulder. The incessant wrenching left him under no illusion that a lie in was now unlikely. He also detected that some kind of crisis, of which Kieran was already aware, had sneaked up on him during the night, and would be waiting for him when he dared to open an eye.

"What is it?" he burbled.

"We'll miss breakfast," warned the boy, clearly on the verge of panic.

Oliver wasn't impressed at being waken so forcefully at the mere prospect of economy baked beans and fried bread. However, he realised that the situation could have been worse. Then again, while Détente had not caught up with them overnight, he knew they still had to catch up with Détente.

Once Oliver had washed and changed, he headed to the breakfast room with his colleague. The dining area was a jumble of old furniture and kitsch, which looked like it had been assembled by a chain-smoking grandmother who owned a pit bull. Oliver hated it. They ordered two English breakfasts from the waitress, who judging by her Eastern European accent, had probably not been in the country long enough to know what an English breakfast was. Soon after she left, a succession of noises emanated from the nearby kitchen that sounded like a haggard mechanic changing the engine block of an Austin Montego.

When the breakfasts arrived they looked as if a hippopotamus had sat in them. Kieran ate his without protest, while Oliver pushed the button mushrooms around the lake of grease on his plate as if they were figure skaters on a winter pond.

After the meal, Oliver poured a large cup of coffee to neutralise the taste. His mind was still preoccupied with Détente, and the fear that he'd overlooked something very obvious about the HD Cotton Crater Plant

"It's a funny name for a nuclear bomb," said the youngster.

"It is unusual," Oliver replied, who then added that Dr Moore had explained in his video that it was named after the white powder that it left behind.

"Then why isn't it called the HD Powder Crater Plant?" Kieran asked.

"I don't know," Oliver shrugged, adding that the word 'plant' had always struck him as misplaced, given that 'device' or 'machine' would have been more accurate.

"Maybe the name is a clue," said the youngster. Oliver pondered the idea for a moment, then shoved his grease-ridden breakfast aside and rose from the table. In the corner of the room he uncovered a box of old toys, which were underneath a sign that read 'for our younger guests'.

"What are you doing?" Kieran asked. Oliver didn't reply and continued rifling through the box. Eventually he emerged with a wooden frame stacked with blocks, which had faded letters painted on their sides. Oliver dropped them on the table next to his colleague, who studied them with disdain.

"Those are for children," admonished the eleven-year-old.

Oliver started to extract the blocks and placed a few on the tablecloth. By finding the correct letters, he managed to spell "HD Cotton" with the faded cubes. Kieran now understood what was happening, and helped to find the remaining blocks needed to complete the weapon's name. Oliver then jumbled them up, spreading the letters across the table between the plates, preserves and sauces.

"What are you looking for?" Kieran asked.

"Some clue to where the weapon is going," Oliver replied, who added that the name of a town or military base might be hiding in the letters, for example Détente's test site at Drake's Island.

"There's no 'k'," reminded the youngster, surveying the faded blocks. He added that the absence of a 'y' also ruled out Plymouth.

"What about Honiton?" Oliver suggested, gathering some letters together until he found that, despite the small army of blocks, there wasn't a single 'i' available. He then recalled visiting Détente's base in Portland while looking for the security guards expelled from the navy. He picked out the letters and managed to spell its name.

"That works," mused Kieran, "but what about the other blocks?"

The youngster had a point – there were nineteen letters on the table and they had only used eight. Kieran started picking at the rabble of consonants and vowels and spelt 'the' before staring blankly at the remaining letters.

"These could spell anything," sighed the boy. Oliver looked glumly at the table before depressing himself further by gazing at the rest of the room's tasteless décor. It compelled him to reach for three of the unused blocks to spell 'tat', which prompted them both to snigger.

"There's also something this place lacks," Oliver stated, who added a 'c' to expand his creation into 'tact'. He then switched his attention to the four letters that were still seeking gainful employment.

"Ronc," he grumbled, studying the remaining blocks. Kieran busied himself rearranging the letters until he produced something intelligible. His best offering was 'corn'. All the blocks were now used, but the jumble of words made no sense. Oliver was beginning to wonder if they were wasting their time. Kieran continued staring at the letters, his hands pushed against his forehead in total concentration.

"I can make a longer word," he eventually announced, moving three blocks to extend 'tact' into 'contact'. Oliver then gazed at the orphaned 'r' that was squatting on the plastic floral tablecloth in sorry isolation. He picked up the faded block and placed it in the centre of the word that Kieran had just assembled. They both leaned back and studied the result.

"The Portland Contract," they said.

**

Oliver didn't need a good reason to leave the crummy Honiton guesthouse, but unravelling the anagram had given him added cause to check out. He led Kieran away from the hotel, unchained his bicycle from the lamppost behind it, and headed towards the railway station.

They took the Dorchester train. To reach Portland they would need to change services and head to Weymouth. It would be a fiddly trip, but presented Oliver with a chance to compose his thoughts. Even if the bomb was in Portland, he had no idea how to destroy it or render it harmless. It occurred that Graeme, the retired scientist, was the best person to ask. Oliver dialled his number but ended up conversing with an answer phone. He left what had to be the strangest message of his life.

"It's Oliver here; I hoped you might be able to call me back to instruct me how to dismantle an atomic weapon. It's quite urgent."

After hanging up, it struck Oliver that the scientist's wife would certainly have a fright if she picked up the message first. It probably wouldn't be music to Graeme's ears either, but his advice would almost certainly be required.

Oliver stared out of the window as the Devonshire countryside was exhausted and the train meandered into Dorset. The world outside looked perfectly tranquil. He envied the cyclists and ramblers that he saw from the carriage. They didn't appear to have a care in the world, while Oliver felt it resting heavily on his shoulders. Everyone he glimpsed seemed blissfully unaware of the murderous weapon that was lurking at the end of the train line.

Oliver glanced at Kieran, who was perched on the opposite seat. He was also watching the scenery but looked excited rather than nervous. Oliver guessed that the youngster had never glimpsed this corner of England. He was already familiar with it, and knew that the West Country's greatest asset was that very little happened there. Now that haven of calm was poised to be shattered.

Oliver wondered if Kieran really understood the danger that was likely to await them at the end of their journey. He would have left the youngster at home for his own safety if given the choice. However, he'd tried to leave him with the police before, with the result that Kieran had run away. He was worried that any attempt to detach the boy from the investigation – which it had to remembered was into his mother's murder – would lead to a repeat. Whether Kieran was safer roaming the streets or heading into Détente's lair was a tricky call. What was beyond doubt was that neither of them would be safe until Carmel's killer was behind bars and the HD Cotton Crater Plant was beyond use.

The train was nearing Dorchester. Kieran was still admiring the scenery. Oliver looked at the boy, studying him for any shared features. The youngster's hair was lighter than his, but exactly the same shade as Carmel's. He also saw traces of her in Kieran's nose and mouth, although the passing years had dulled his memory of precisely what she looked like.

Oliver had no photographs of Carmel as they'd scarcely been together long enough. He had none of Kieran either, as assembling a gushing album of inevitably out-of-focus snapshots hadn't been his immediate priority on becoming a dad. The letter that would resolve whether he was a father was in the rucksack beside him, but this wasn't the moment to open the envelope. To stand any chance of defeating Détente they would need to work together, and discovering they weren't related was certain to cripple their unity. Yet Oliver wanted some evidence of a link and was studying Kieran in the hope of finding one. Their eyes were the same colour, but that didn't prove much. He then noticed the boy's hands. They were a touch of the small side, quite rounded, and his index finger was noticeably shorter than usual. Oliver looked to his own hands, but already knew what he would find. They were almost identical. He then turned his gaze to Kieran again, but the youngster was no longer peering out of the window, but glaring at his companion with suspicion.

"Sorry," Oliver apologised, realising that he'd been caught staring. "I'd only just noticed that we have the same hands."

"That's hardly a surprise, you are my dad."

Oliver was stunned by the reply. The youngster seemed to have completely accepted that they were flesh and blood. Then again, many people had told him that, including his mother. If Kieran was convinced of the link then Oliver knew it was best to play along, at least until the current crisis had passed. There would hopefully be ample time later to read the DNA letter, if only Oliver could summon the courage.

They changed trains in Dorchester and took a connecting service to Weymouth. Now on the shorter journey, Oliver turned his mind briefly to what life might be like once the investigation was over. He only had two weeks to find a school for Kieran, yet somewhere was bound to have a place. If he needed to take the youngster on a 20-mile train ride then he'd take him each day, at least until the youngster said he was cramping his style. If the school was bad then Oliver would give the youngster extra tuition at home. Writing the *Spib* books and trips to the pub would have to wait, as the youngster had to come first. Oliver recognised that he was already prepared to risk his life on the boy's behalf. If that commitment led to Kieran's safety then he would make sure it was worth the effort. He was now determined to look after the lad. After all, if he didn't, who would?

***

On arriving in Weymouth, Oliver led Kieran away from the station to the bus stop. He then removed the front and back wheels from his racing bike to condense it into a complex tangle of metal tubes and spokes. From bitter experience, he knew that wheeling a muddy bike onto a bus usually triggered a look of contempt from the driver akin to if he'd just deflowered his only daughter. If taken to bits, he knew that he could usually avoid the glare.

The service they were waiting for was the X7 to Portland. Ironically it was the same one they'd followed from the island when tracking the security guards. When it arrived, Oliver placed his bike in the luggage hold. The vehicle chugged away from the town centre and began to retrace the route to Portland. Oliver recognised several landmarks, including the Town Bridge and a couple of the streets where he'd been forced to execute emergency three-point turns.

The bus plodded into the suburbs, heading south through Wyke Regis. Soon after, they reached sight of the English Channel and the windswept outpost of Portland. Even on a sunny day, the island still looked rugged and inhospitable, apart from the small cluster of buildings cowering on its leeward shore. Oliver felt his heart pounding as they approached Portland along the narrow causeway linking it to the mainland. His nerves had steadily built since leaving Honiton, but his pulse was now going into overdrive. In the past, he'd only be required to deceive, hide from, and occasionally infiltrate Détente. Now he would have to confront the firm directly and on its home territory. Then again, he couldn't be certain that the bomb was on the island, and even if it was, he still had no idea how to render it harmless.

Halfway across the causeway, Oliver's phone began to ring. He recognised the number on the display instantly, having dialled it earlier that day.

"I hear you need help defusing a warhead," said the retired scientist when Oliver took the call.

"Yes. I hope my message didn't scare anyone."

"Let's put it this way, my wife is currently building a shelter under the stairs."

"Sorry," said Oliver.

"Don't worry; it's given her something to do. Mind you, I doubt if hanging a tablecloth from the banister and filling the cupboard with crossword puzzles will offset a nuclear blast."

Oliver told Graeme about their journey to Portland, lowering his voice to avoid being heard by the other passengers. He advised the scientist that they might have located the weapon and needed advice.

"Tricky," the old man sighed, "I can hardly dismantle it over the phone."

Oliver replied that they might not have the chance, as even if the bomb was in Portland, it could be exported for testing at any moment. He added that he needed to know how to neutralise it without complex engineering.

"It must have an Achilles' heel," he added.

"There is one," the scientist mused, who said he stumbled on it when building his own version of the weapon. He said the bomb could be ruined, without a major atomic leak, if exposed to a large quantity of $H2O$ mixed with sodium chloride.

"What's that in English?" Oliver inquired.

"Salt water," clarified Graeme. He added that, having checked the chemicals listed in the Drake's Island prototype, the device wouldn't work if it became saturated.

"You'll need a large quantity of salt water. Do you have any nearby?" the scientist asked. Oliver glanced at the vast expanse of the English Channel lapping at the causeway.

"Might have," he shrugged.

The call ended as the X7 bus arrived on Portland. Oliver couldn't believe how calm Kieran was in the circumstances. Then again, the eleven-year-old shouldered the grief of his mother's murder like a grown man. He knew the youngster had emotions – he'd watched him doing badly at computer games – but he seemed able to rise above fear and despair. Oliver thought he had a duty to lead by example, yet it was him drawing strength from the youngster. He wondered if Kieran was bottling up his feelings. He was struggling to follow his lead, and feared that would crack at any moment. Infiltrating Drake's Island had stretched his nerves to breaking point, along with being stalked and the car chase. If tested again, he was worried that he would snap.

The bus dropped them in Fortuneswell, the village huddled beneath the steep rock face leading to Portland's summit. Oliver put the wheels back on his racing bike, although the operation didn't distract him from his increasing anxiety. He'd suffered the same condition in his journalism days when ordered against his will to pursue the families of murder victims and deceased soldiers for interviews. Now it was magnified several times and he felt awful. He'd changed jobs and moved to the West Country to

184

escape that stress, but it had caught up with him. His only choice was whether to be a hero or a coward; a quiet life was no longer available.

Working on the bike had covered Oliver's hands in oil, so they headed across the green in the middle of Victoria Square to find a washroom in a café. Afterwards he bought two sodas and they took a table beside the window. They could see all the vehicles entering Détente's base on the opposite side of the square. Traffic was light as they were between shift changes. Oliver needed a plan but couldn't think of one. Storming the base would be futile. Even if they were armed, Détente's guards would outnumber them in personnel and firepower. Sneaking onto the site would be virtually impossible. Oliver realised that there wasn't time to obtain a cleaning job at the base, or anything else that would allow legitimate access.

"How do we get in?" Oliver muttered, lowering his voice.

"Are you sure the bomb's over there?" Kieran asked, before blowing bubbles in his cola with the drinking straw.

"It's the most likely place," Oliver shrugged, "but I'd like proof."

"Can we spy on them, like in Honiton?"

Oliver tried to recall their previous visit to Portland, and whether there was a vantage point above the base. He then remembered the viewing area at the summit. Without a word he rose from the chair and paid for the drinks at the cash till. He then asked for several twenty pence pieces in the change.

"I hope you've bought your climbing boots," said Oliver, marching back to the table. Kieran rose reluctantly to his feet, realising they had a long walk ahead.

"What are those coins for?" he asked, pointing at the mountain of change that Oliver was feeding into his pockets.

"You'll see," he replied.

***

Shortly after emerging from the café, Oliver stopped at a convenience store to buy a copy of the *Dorset Echo*.

"Why do you need that?" Kieran asked as they left the shop.

"I like reading papers."

"But you don't even live here."

"If you're somewhere unfamiliar and you need to know what's going on, just buy the local rag," Oliver preached.

Kieran reluctantly led the way towards the looming climb of Portland. Even when Oliver had driven up it earlier that summer, he'd noted how steep it was. At the time he'd regretted not bringing his bike, thinking he would relish the challenge of tackling the ascent. Now that he had it, he felt no desire to assume the saddle. He preferred to wheel his bike up the climb. The youngster was already moaning about the gradient. His mood wasn't helped by the fact that several coaches were heading down the hill. They were packed with boys and girls, including some who waved at Kieran to taunt him about the climb.

"Why can't we take the bus?" he grumbled.

"There isn't one," Oliver replied, adding that the vehicles were hired privately, and judging by the passengers, it was a school trip.

"It's the summer holidays," Kieran reminded. Oliver conceded that it wasn't an obvious time of year for a school outing, but had no idea what else it could be.

"Why don't you check your great paper?" the youngster taunted sarcastically, adding that it supposedly had all the answers. He pushed the bike while Oliver leafed through the paper. He feared that Kieran would win the argument and the edition would prove useless. However, a small article on page sixteen spared his blushes.

"Read this," Oliver grinned, swapping the paper for his bike. Kieran studied the text, which revealed that Détente was holding a 'community day' for all children on Portland. The firm was paying for them to visit several theme parks. It had also funded several coaches to take senior citizens to the Kingston Lacy gardens near Dorchester. Kieran added that Dr Moore was quoted in the article.

"'Over the years Portland has given a great deal to me and I wanted to give something back'," he recited.

"If you believe that you'll believe anything," Oliver muttered, adding that Dr Moore's generosity was likely to be a cynical public relations' exercise.

"But if Détente's broke, how can he afford it?" Kieran asked.

Oliver didn't know and added that he saw little point in rewarding the islanders if the firm was already planning to sell its base. It seemed unlikely that the community day was an act of kindness, and its public relations' value was doubtful.

"Maybe Dr Moore wants them off the island," Kieran speculated.

"Perhaps, but why?"

"What if the bomb is here and he wants no-one to find it?"

Oliver replied that it was possible, but if it was being stored inside the military base then it would be locked away with armed guards.

"You wouldn't find it by accident," he added.

By now they were halfway up the climb and passing the unwelcoming gates of HM Prison, The Verne. It was perched on a tight bend in the road, which was one of several acute corners on the hill. While Oliver had initially been tempted to climb it on his bike, he didn't like the look of the way back down at all. It was riddled with treacherous turns. Then again, the comparative danger of a cycle ride was nothing compared with the challenge of neutralising a nuclear weapon.

As they reached the summit, two further coaches breezed past. Oliver had an uneasy feeling that all the traffic was heading the other way. It was as if everyone was fleeing some great danger, while they were dawdling blindly towards it.

Eventually they reached the summit of Portland. Coastal winds were tearing across the rugged grassland that clung desperately to the thin soil. The stiff breeze was battling with the heat of the late August midday sunshine, and Oliver realised that at least one of them was likely to burn his skin. He applied a little sunscreen and offered it to Kieran. He refused it, but Oliver smeared a handful onto his arms and face anyway, despite the youngster's vehement protests. A few weeks ago he would have left Kieran to make his own decision, but now he felt a greater duty of care.

"This climb better be worth it," the boy sniped, while picking excess factor 30 out of his left ear. Oliver wheeled his bike across to the picnic area and chained it to one of the vacant benches.

"I've been here before," said Kieran. Oliver was impressed that he recognised it, although his sense of direction was abnormally good, along with his talent for anagrams. Indeed, on his last visit, he'd mentally rearranged the picnic area sign to create 'panic, I care'. Oliver had focused on the scenery that day. Perched on the island's highest point, it commanded panoramic views of the English Channel. Once again Oliver saw the narrow causeway far beneath them which connected Portland to the mainland. He also saw Chesil Beach, the narrow shingle bank that stretched for miles into the distance along the Dorset coast. Weymouth was also clearly visible, where they had not only caught a bus, but tailed one as well. To enable visitors to admire the scenery in greater detail, the picnic area had a coin-operated telescope beside the picnic area. Oliver walked towards it and Kieran followed soon after.

"This is why we're up here," said Oliver, pointing at the telescope. He took one of the twenty pence pieces from the café and rolled it into the coin slot.

"That's why you needed so much change," Kieran muttered. "What are you looking for?"

Oliver replied that he was spying on Détente's base. Thanks to their elevated position, most of the buildings were visible, along with the entire quayside. He could observe them clearly with the telescope, along with tracking vehicles and personnel.

"If they move the bomb, we'll see it," he pledged.

However, it wasn't anywhere to be seen, and despite scrutinising the base for an hour, it refused to appear. By now, Oliver's stockpile of coins was starting to run out. The telescope had proved more frugal than Scrooge in a recession and hungrier than a student that had breached their overdraught several weeks ago.

"Git," muttered Oliver, half-heartedly slapping the eyepiece out of petulance as another coin expired. He hesitated before feeding the machine again, wondering if he should ration his observations to every fifteen minutes. Then again, if he spotted the bomb, he had no idea how to infiltrate the base and put the device beyond use. He hoped that the steady erosion of his wallet might provide some time to think, but no masterstroke had presented itself.

"Can I look?" Kieran asked, pointing to the lens. Oliver gave him another coin and relinquished the eyepiece. After standing aside he glanced at the handful of vehicles in the picnic area. They ranged from a couple of overloaded estate cars to an awkwardly parked juggernaut. Oliver guessed that its driver had tired of lunches at motorway service areas and craved somewhere scenic to savour his double round of cheese and pickle on white bread. Oliver then asked if Kieran had spotted anything with the telescope.

"No sign of the bomb," he shrugged.

Oliver suspected that the device was firmly under lock and key, having arrived in Portland the previous evening. He also feared that it wouldn't reappear until it was loaded onboard a ship, by which point it would be too late to intervene.

As Kieran monitored the base with the telescope, Oliver took the binoculars from his rucksack. As he suspected, the glasses weren't much use, as they were much further away compared with their viewpoint in Honiton. The telescope provided the only clear view, which left Oliver without much to do. He put away the binoculars and gazed at the car park. One of the overloaded estate cars had left while the other followed after its youngster passenger had finished relieving himself behind a nearby gorse bush. Before long, only the unmarked white juggernaut was left.

"This could take ages," Kieran sighed, losing patience with the search.

"Tell me about it," replied Oliver, staring blankly at the truck. He then noticed that its rear doors were slightly ajar. It looked as if they'd opened by accident as there were no signs of activity around the vehicle, including the driver's cab. Oliver decided to investigate to alleviate his boredom. The engine was silent and from a distance of fifteen yards it appeared that the cab was deserted. He was poised to check the rear doors when Kieran called him across to the telescope.

"Do you recognise that car?" the youngster asked. Oliver took the eyepiece and saw the royal blue BMW on the quayside. Magnified several times, he could see a tall man beside it, and while his face wasn't clear, Oliver knew it was Kwame.

"What's he doing here?" he muttered, puzzled that the policeman would risk two daytime visits to Détente within 24 hours.

"I said we couldn't trust him," Kieran gloated, before asking if the weapon had made a guest appearance yet. Oliver shook his head and relinquished the telescope to allow the youngster to continue the search. He then returned to the truck. The rear doors were still unlocked and there were no signs of life around the vehicle. Taking a deep breath, he approached the back of the lorry and then peered around the doors. It was fairly dim inside but he could see something in the shadows. It was a complex web of pipes interspersed with large tanks. As he opened the doors slightly wider, a beam of sunlight pierced the darkness. It settled on a large shiny needle in the centre of the device, which left Oliver momentarily dazzled. He slammed the doors in panic.

"Bloody hell," he wheezed to himself, shocked by what he'd found. Once his voice returned he called Kieran across to the lorry, which wasn't tricky as the frugal telescope had just withdrawn its services once again.

"What's so urgent?" the youngster inquired as he slouched towards the truck. Oliver had his back pressed firmly against the rear doors as if a ferocious bull was straining to burst out of the vehicle.

"It's in here," he announced, trying to remain calm.

"What is?"

"Have a look," he said, gingerly opening one of the doors. Kieran spied the contents and his eyes seemed to expand to three times their normal size. He pointed at the device in amazement and his mouth fell open but no words came out.

Oliver glanced around the lorry once more, and having confirmed that nobody was around, he summoned the courage to climb inside the trailer. Kieran followed his lead and they opened both doors to brighten the interior. They both stared at the bomb that was occupying most of the space. Oliver squeezed along the side of it to inspect the needle in greater detail. He had no idea how to dismantle the device, but recalled Graeme's suggestion that it could be neutralised if dumped in the sea.

"How do we get it there?" Kieran asked.

Despite being on an island, reaching the water would be difficult. They were on the summit of Portland and nowhere near the quayside or beaches. The weapon also weighed several tons.

"Can we shove it into the drink?" the youngster asked.

"Probably not," Oliver sighed, as he studied the trolley on which the device was mounted. He suspected that it would take several people to move it, and gave it a gentle push to satisfy his curiosity. It remained utterly motionless, which suggested he was right. While Oliver studied the wheels, Kieran continued to inspect the tanks and pipes.

"What would happen if we pulled a few tubes out?" the youngster asked.

Oliver said there were two scenarios, the first being that it would cause little or no damage, and Détente would just repair the device. Kieran asked what the second outcome might be.

"It'll destroy everything for miles, including us," Oliver replied, adding that their only option was condemning it to a watery grave. However, he still had no idea how to transfer it to the seafront.

"Why don't we steal the truck?" Kieran suggested.

Oliver had no experience of driving a juggernaut, much less pinching one. Then again, if they couldn't transport the weapon themselves, the lorry was the best option. He concluded that if he was going to steal a nuclear bomb then hotwiring a heavy goods vehicle was not, by comparison, a particularly heinous crime.

Kieran followed Oliver out of the trailer and they closed the doors. Two things started to worry Oliver as he walked alongside the lorry towards the cab. The first was his concern about stealing the truck. The second was that it made no sense that Détente would leave such a vital prototype unguarded. Its financial hopes rested on the device, and it was abandoned more than a mile from the base. The situation became harder to believe when the cab turned out to be unlocked.

Oliver climbed into the vehicle and started looking for the ignition keys. Kieran followed him into the cab and slid across to the passenger seat. Without any obvious means of starting the lorry, Oliver looked underneath the dashboard for any exposed wiring. All he found was a gearshift that looked alarmingly complicated. Then again, apart from struggling to start the juggernaut, everything else was going really well, or as Oliver feared, suspiciously well.

"Doesn't this seem too easy?" he asked.

"What?" Kieran muttered, nosing through the glove box.

"That Détente just leaves the bomb unguarded."

"Maybe it's good luck."

"I don't believe in it," Oliver replied, who added that the device might be a replica, or that several prototypes had been produced. He wanted to ignore the cynical part of his mind that kept screaming that something was badly amiss. As he resumed his search for the ignition keys, his worst fears were realised.

"And cut!"

Oliver wasn't sure who said it, but realised they were not alone. He reluctantly peered out of the cab towards a line of gorse bushes twenty yards away, which were moving around. Half a dozen security men then emerged, of which two were carrying video cameras. Following close behind was a stern-looking woman in a designer suit. Oliver immediately recognised her as Dr Moore's personal assistant, Ms Potter.

"What now?" Kieran asked

"We'll need to distract them," Oliver replied while trying to think fast. He then told the youngster that he would create a diversion and allow him to slip away. Oliver then charged out of the driver's door and stampeded towards the guards.

"Get down, it's going to blow!" he yelled.

What followed was a picture of total chaos. Four security men ran off while those with cameras plunged to the floor. Ms Potter dived behind a gorse bush. Oliver was stunned that nobody detained him, with his prospective captors more concerned about saving their own skins. He leapt behind a gorse bush that was a safe distance from Ms Potter and peered between the thorns for any sign of Kieran. He noticed that the lorry's passenger door was open. He then spotted the eleven-year-old sprinting in the opposite direction. Sadly he was running towards a sole figure in a pinstripe suit. He grabbed the youngster and held him still. It was Dr Moore.

"Oh no," Oliver groaned, realising that his moment of bravery had backfired with Kieran falling into enemy hands. He watched helplessly as Dr Moore produced a length of twine from his pocket and tied the boy's hands behind his back. He then wrapped more of it around his ankles to stop him kicking out. He then started shoving the boy – who could only shuffle slowly with his wrists and ankles tied together – back to the juggernaut.

As Dr Moore approached the truck, his minions started to resurface. The two cameramen in security uniforms came first, followed by Ms Potter who was brushing the dusty soil off her suit. The other guards did not reappear and Dr Moore glared at those who dared to come crawling back. He took Kieran firmly by the scruff of the neck. The youngster struggled to free himself, but his limbs were tied firmly together.

"Dart!" Dr Moore bellowed.

Oliver remained silent and totally motionless.

"I know you're here," he continued. "Reporters can't bear to miss the action."

Oliver was indeed watching, but not out of curiosity. He was trying to devise a plan to rescue Kieran but his options were limited. The situation became more urgent as Dr Moore issued a grim ultimatum.

"Come out, you want Kieran to see his next birthday, don't you?"

Oliver remained in his gorse bush, seething at the threat and frustrated by his inability to intervene. He felt totally powerless as turning himself in seemed to be the only way to save the youngster. Even so, it would not guarantee Kieran's safety, but Oliver knew that he couldn't sit back and do nothing. As a result, he took a deep breath and did what any responsible father would do.

"Okay," he shouted, "but let Kieran go first."

"How touching," beamed Dr Moore, although to Oliver's relief, he directed his comments in the wrong direction. The pinstripe-clad millionaire exchanged a few words with one of the guards who nodded and took both cameras out of sight. Oliver thought that he heard a van door being slammed before the guard reappeared. The security man was carrying a sword.

"This doesn't look good," Oliver muttered to himself. The weapon was passed to Dr Moore, and it seemed to be the kind issued to naval officers on receiving their commission. Oliver wondered if his aborted career in uniform still haunted him. He then watched helplessly as Dr Moore rested the blade behind Kieran's neck.

"You're in no position to negotiate, Dart," he warned.

Fury started welling up inside Oliver's veins. He couldn't bear to see Kieran threatened. He wanted to hurl himself out of hiding and take a running jump at Dr Moore. However, he realised that acting in anger was likely to make matters worse. In the heat of the moment, he knew that he needed a cool head. It then occurred to him that Dr Moore's behaviour was slightly strange. He'd recaptured the bomb and yet he wanted him to surrender. Why did he need him alive?

"Okay, come and get me," he shouted. Dr Moore and his henchmen looked in several directions to establish where the voice was coming from. Thanks to the stiff breeze, it appeared that they couldn't agree.

"Don't try my patience!" Dr Moore warned, still holding the sword in place.

"Don't come out!" Kieran yelled.

The millionaire tapped him on the neck with the blade, and whilst not breaking the skin, it reminded the youngster to watch his step. Oliver admired his courage, but realised it was his job to be brave and not Kieran's. He opened his rucksack and picked out the kitchen knives that he'd used to scale the Edenhurst Court bank. However, he was outnumbered and Dr Moore was holding a sword to Kieran's neck. Assuming that the guards would be armed, Oliver knew that brute force was likely to backfire, and the situation required stealth. He wrapped one of the knives in a handkerchief and tucked it into his right sock. After hiding the first blade, he decided to carry the second to show that he meant business. Then again, before emerging, he tried to bargain for the youngster's release one final time.

"Let the boy go and I'll give myself up."

"Don't do it, he'll double cross you," Kieran warned. Dr Moore tapped him with the sword again, but harder this time. He then spoke to the nearest guard who began walking out of view. Oliver then heard an engine starting, presumably of the van that he suspected was just out of sight. Ms Potter then led Kieran towards the vehicle.

"Where are you taking him?" Oliver demanded.

Dr Moore replied that he was being led to a minibus which would return him to Torquay unharmed if Oliver gave himself up. He could hear the vehicle's doors slam to indicate that Kieran was probably aboard with Ms Potter and the guard.

"The bus is blocking the road, so don't try playing for time. Nobody's coming to help," added Dr Moore.

Oliver knew that Kieran was still in danger, but the situation was a little better than before. The weapon was only guarded by one security man and Dr Moore. Oliver knew that the odds were unlikely to improve. He took a deep breath, put the second knife in his right hand, and stepped into the open. He was soon noticed but continued walking towards the enemy.

"Drop the knife," ordered Dr Moore.

"You first," he replied, now a mere twenty feet away.

"Very well," said the millionaire, who stabbed his sword into the parched soil. He then extended his right hand towards the guard who obediently placed a silver-coloured pistol into his palm.

"Now it's your turn," he said, aiming the gun at Oliver's head. He recognised there was no choice but to discard the knife, but he'd expected to lose it anyway. The one in his right sock was his trump card and he kept striding towards Dr Moore until they were just six feet apart.

"Close enough; now get on your knees," ordered the millionaire. He told the guard to search him, and he frisked him with the delicacy of an enraged bull. Oliver hoped desperately that the second knife wouldn't be detected, but the security man found it within moments. The guard then confiscated his rucksack, and dropped it a few yards away beside the truck.

"Naughty boy," patronised Dr Moore, studying the concealed knife. He then tucked the pistol into his waistband and picked up the sword. He rested it on the peak of Oliver's skull. Oliver closed his eyes and tried to ignore the blade's presence but it proved impossible. In the circumstances he would have expected to be petrified but surprised himself, as he felt stupid and angry. It would have been easy to ignore the package from Carmel and scrap the investigation. His common sense kept telling him to walk away, but through a mixture of guilt and uncharacteristic bravery he was now facing death. His courage stemmed from Kieran, and his priority was to protect the youngster, but his bravery had backfired. He felt stupid for being caught and angry that he'd failed to save the boy.

"What are you doing with Kieran?" he asked.

"We'll need to uncover how much he knows," said Dr Moore.

Oliver replied that he led the investigation and the youngster knew very little.

"That's not what I heard," Dr Moore replied, who threw a telling glance to Ms Potter. "He made all the running by the sounds of it, which is hardly a surprise, given your incompetence."

"My what?"

"You couldn't find a reflection in a hall of mirrors," scoffed the millionaire, still dangling the sword above his victim. "That's why you were virtually ideal."

"For what?"

Dr Moore said details of his project had leaked several months ago, and when it was on the verge of being exposed, he had the journalist killed.

"You mean Carmel?"

"No, she was the second one," said Dr Moore, who added that she inherited the story from a deceased friend in Fleet Street. "Once the details leaked out, I knew that at least one member of the scum would be sticking their snout into my affairs. All I had to do was to wait for the documents to wash up with a hack that was too dim or lazy to solve the case."

"You mean me?"

"How does it feel knowing you only came this far because you're hopeless?"

Oliver wanted to protest that he was cautious rather than incompetent, but the millionaire wanted to continue gloating.

"I said you were virtually ideal," he announced. "You would've been perfect if it wasn't for that meddling little sidekick of yours."

"He just wants to know who killed his mother," said Oliver.

"How sweet," patronised Dr Moore. "Well, the little mite will be able to see him soon. I've been told that the gunman's coming here to demand his cash."

"You mean DS Ebwelle?"

"Maybe you're not so clueless, or perhaps Kieran worked that one out."

Oliver was stunned. He'd never wanted to believe that his friend in the police was a traitor. However, he was a crack shot, and facing a crippling divorce. Oliver wondered how many other people the detective had eliminated for cash.

"The detective is one of the best in the trade," Dr Moore revealed. "He knows how the forensics people do their job, and how to deceive them. Unfortunately he also knows too much about me. That's why I've invited him here."

Oliver then asked if the device was going to be detonated while both he and the detective were nearby.

"It won't just be the two of you," the millionaire warned.

"You're going to murder the whole island?" Oliver gasped.

"Given time," replied Dr Moore. "Those nearby will die in seconds, so consider yourself lucky. Anyone on the coast will languish for hours, if not days."

"What about your staff?"

"That's the beautiful part. When closing the Portland base, it would cost about the same in redundancies as if they all died in a work-related accident."

"But they're your own people."

"They're hand-picked," said Dr Moore. "All of my most useless, incompetent and worthless employees are stationed here."

It occurred to Oliver that Carmel's paperwork had included some personnel documents from Détente, which perhaps included details of the transfers to Portland.

"Is that why the four sailors who bullied you in the navy work here?"

"They were among the first names on the list, along with the members of my research team who leaked my plans to the press," said Dr Moore, who added that the fallout from the device would make the base uninhabitable for decades.

"Then who's going to buy your land?" Oliver asked, who added that nobody met the asking price earlier that year.

"I'll claim on the insurance, which is much easier," said Dr Moore.

"What about the civilians?"

"I'm not a monster," shrugged the millionaire. "This is just business. You must have seen the coaches taking the children and pensioners away for the day. Virtually everyone else is working on the mainland apart from the lame and feckless, and I'm doing taxpayers a favour when it comes to them."

"You'll murder millions."

"Don't be so dramatic, it's only around two thousand," dismissed Dr Moore. "Besides, testing the weapon on live subjects will underline its power. Orders should come flooding in afterwards."

"You're doing this just to save your firm?"

"It's more than that," said Dr Moore. "Being an old hack, I'm sure you bought a copy of the local rag this morning."

The millionaire clicked his fingers and the guard rifled swiftly through Oliver's rucksack. He emerged with a copy of the *Dorset Echo*, which he passed to Dr Moore.

"How predictable," he gloated, "if it wasn't for journalists buying these things, nobody would at all."

The millionaire then discarded the edition into Oliver's lap and ordered him to read the article about Détente taking children and pensioners off the island.

"I've already seen it."

"Then read my quote aloud, one more time," ordered Dr Moore.

" 'Over the years Portland has given a great deal to me and I wanted to give something back'," he recited.

"This island left its mark on me," said the millionaire, who loosened his jacket and unbuttoned the top of his shirt. Oliver could see the scars on his chest left by the scissors attack during his time at the naval base. "When I said I wanted to give something back, I really meant it."

Oliver glanced at the juggernaut containing the bomb. His mind then returned to the issue of Dr Moore being so determined to capture him alive, which had baffled him earlier. While reluctant to know the answer, he had to ask the question.

"My dear Dart, you're vital to my plan," beamed Dr Moore. "After all, how else can I explain a nuclear disaster to the authorities?"

"You can't blame me."

"Oh, but I can. You were trying to be a hero by sabotaging the device, but you only managed to activate it instead."

Oliver replied that nobody would believe him.

"But I have proof," said Dr Moore, who added that he had camera footage of him confronting the guards, trying to steal the truck, and tinkering with the bomb.

"I only examined it," Oliver protested. "Any scientist worth their salt could see that I had no idea how to dismantle the bloody thing."

"Exactly," the millionaire smarmed, as he crouched to look his prisoner in the eye. "Can you see the headlines? 'Scoop-hungry hack kills thousands' would fit well, don't you agree?"

Oliver fell silent and stared at the newspaper in his lap. He noticed that the fountain pen he'd brought from Edenhurst Court was clipped to the edition. He'd used it to tackle the crossword while hiking up the hill, but quit after being stumped by one across. While Dr Moore continued his rant, Oliver spirited the pen into his right sock.

"The only thing I hate more than reporters is this place," he complained. "Still, today should settle my score with both."

Oliver then noticed three more guards coming over the hill. They were leading a large man in handcuffs towards Dr Moore.

"Ah, it's always amusing to see a policeman under arrest," he cackled.

"What's the meaning of these?" Kwame protested, raising his arms so that the handcuffs caught the light of the midday sun.

"Never mind that, you've got some explaining to do," Oliver muttered, as the detective was cast down to his knees beside him.

"I needed the money."

"Don't you realise who you shot?" Oliver asked.

"Some woman, I never met her," Kwame protested.

"It was Kieran's mum."

"I know that now, don't I?" Barked the detective, trying to wrestle free of his handcuffs. Dr Moore simply looked on with amusement as the former allies bickered amongst themselves.

"You're a policeman, or did you forget?" Oliver sniped.

"I only kill criminals. Carmel was an industrial spy who tried to sell the device to foreign powers."

"Who told you that?" Oliver asked.

"He did," said Kwame, pointing his shoulder towards Dr Moore.

"If you're a rich man, you can always rely on the gullibility of the British plod," grinned Dr Moore, "and his fair-weather friend, the miserable hack."

"I write children's books."

"I know," sighed Dr Moore. "I forced my PA to read one. It was dreadful."

"At least I don't kill anyone for a living."

"Unlike your old pal," said the millionaire, turning his gaze to Kwame. "You'd have such a rough time in jail that I'm almost tempted to release you."

"But I know too much, don't I?" the detective murmured, staring desolately at the parched ground.

"Cheer up, after this bomb detonates you'll be a hero," said Dr Moore.

"How do you figure that?" Oliver asked.

He replied that DS Ebwelle would be the man who valiantly tried to prevent Oliver triggering the device, but tragically arrived a few seconds late.

"I've nothing against the police," he added, returning to the detective, "and I'm sure you'd rather be a dead hero than a live criminal."

"I'd like to choose myself," said Kwame, resuming his futile efforts to wrestle free of the handcuffs. Oliver's wrists and ankles, by contrast, were unbound, and he assumed that Dr Moore no longer saw him as a threat. He was determined to prove him wrong.

"I could stay here all day rubbing your noses in your stupidity, but this isn't the safest place to hang about," mocked the millionaire, who added the countdown to the weapon's detonation had already begun.

"Let me guess, there's enough time for you to escape while we sit here until it explodes," Oliver speculated.

"Something like that," shrugged Dr Moore, who added that there would be a roadblock on the causeway to prevent anyone leaving the island, especially them. He also warned Oliver that the device was monitored by security cameras, and if he tried to defuse it, the bomb would be triggered prematurely.

"So forget the heroics," he added. "Just enjoy the view and jot down your last will and testament."

Dr Moore then handed his sword to one of the four guards, who rested it on Oliver's head once more.

"If he moves, slice a few pieces off until he stops," added the millionaire, who started walking away. Kwame let out a hopeless sigh and seemed to be on the verge of tears. Despite being outnumbered, Oliver held himself together. He did not want to buckle, and had one final card to play.

"I wouldn't detonate that bomb," he warned, "not after what I did to it."

Dr Moore stopped walking and turned around.

"You know nothing about science. Just moments ago, you said you'd have no idea how to dismantle it."

"Exactly," Oliver replied. "But that didn't stop me trying. Who knows how much damage I did?"

Dr Moore was about to respond but fell silent. He shook his head in frustration and marched towards the juggernaut, before pausing briefly as he passed Oliver.

"If you think I'm aborting the countdown, you've got another thing coming," he warned. "I designed the device myself, so if there's a single wire damaged, I'll know. I won't need to ring an electrician."

He then climbed into the trailer and opened a tool box beside the bomb. He picked out a torch and an electric screwdriver. He then took the twine from his pocket that he used to capture Kieran and threw it towards one of the guards.

"Tie that chatterbox up, and gag him while you're at it," he ordered, before climbing out of sight to investigate the device.

"If you have any bright ideas, now is a good time," Kwame muttered.

"Sadly, it's difficult to think with a sword resting on your head," Oliver replied, staring at the security man that was holding the blade. He then looked at the guard to address him. "You know, they say the pen is mightier than the sword."

"Prove it," teased the security man.

"Very well," said Oliver, who rolled onto his side in a flash. The security man thrust his blade into the ground where Oliver had been crouching, having reacted too slowly. Oliver then produced the fountain pen from his right sock and stabbed it into the guard's ankle with a ferocity that only came from pure adrenaline. He collapsed to the ground in anguish, releasing his grasp of the sword. Oliver wrenched it out of the parched earth and waved it towards the three remaining guards. To his horror, one of them was armed, and reaching for his gun. Oliver rushed towards him and held the blade to his throat before he could raise the pistol.

"Throw it to the guy in handcuffs," he ordered.

The guard reluctantly cast the gun aside, which landed next to Kwame. While his wrists were bound, he was able to pick it up, and pointed the weapon towards the security man.

"Don't bother me, it ain't loaded," shrugged the guard.

Kwame then belted the security man around the face with the firearm and laid him out cold.

"It doesn't have to be," said the policeman, who examined the gun but found no bullets. The other two security men then produced hunting knives and converged towards Oliver and Kwame. With only an unloaded gun and antique sword between them, they decided to take cover behind the juggernaut.

"Why are there no bullets?" Kwame complained, studying the gun.

Oliver replied that gunfire might alert the authorities, and Dr Moore would not want policeman swarming over his nuclear test site.

"How do we destroy the bomb?" the detective asked.

"By dumping it in the sea," Oliver replied. He then saw the two security men running around the corner of the truck. He leapt to his feet in a rush of adrenaline, drew his sword, and stopped the guards in their tracks. They were now just three feet apart from each other. Oliver started to feel his bravery draining away and needed to think fast.

"What are you paid per hour?" he asked.

The security men looked baffled by the question. One of them eventually replied with a pretty derogatory rate.

"Cleaners earn more than that," said Oliver, who kept his sword pointed at the men. "Is it worth dying for?"

The security men looked at each other and then backed off. Oliver then heard a rumbling inside the lorry, which he assumed was Dr Moore checking the device.

"What's going on out there?" he shouted from inside the truck. Oliver realised that Dr Moore might call for back up at any moment and there was no time to lose.

"Ever stolen a truck?" he asked the policeman.

Kwame and Oliver climbed inside the lorry cab. The detective took the driving seat while Oliver put his sword on the floor and began looking for the keys. He couldn't find them anywhere but noticed that the policeman had produced a large set of keys from his pocket and was studying them in great detail.

"This should fit," he declared, and rammed the selected key into the ignition.

"Are those police issue?"

"Not entirely," the detective replied, who then turned the key and the engine immediately fired up. With his wrists bound, Kwame struggled to find a gear and the juggernaut jolted forwards. Little did he know, but the sudden movement caused Dr Moore to lose his footing while perched on the device in the back of the trailer.

"My foot's stuck. Help me," was the forlorn cry on the walkie-talkie that was left on the juggernaut's dashboard. Oliver and Kwame looked at each other and laughed. The detective then restarted the engine but made no attempt to engage first gear. Instead he picked up the sword and pointed it towards Oliver.

"Get out of the truck," ordered the policeman.

"Is this a joke?"

"I mean it, get out."

Oliver nervously shuffled towards the door and then climbed off the vehicle. He looked back towards Kwame, who was impassively sitting behind the wheel.

"What are you doing?"

"If I'm a hero, it'll be my choice," said Kwame. He then engaged reverse gear and rammed his foot onto the accelerator. The passenger door swung shut with the sudden momentum and the juggernaut began to tear backwards. Oliver looked on in disbelief as the lorry careered through the car park, over the main road, and onto the grass verge. He started to run after it, and was soon sprinting to keep up. He was worried that Kwame was about to do something completely reckless. He tried waving his arms to urge the juggernaut to halt but its speed continued to build. It then began to accelerate even more sharply as it careered across the verge and onto the steep bank behind it. Oliver continued running, but was now falling behind.

In the trailer, Dr Moore was still trying to release his foot, which remained trapped in the device's complex web of pipes. He was hammering on the side of the vehicle and yelling for the driver to stop. The policeman did not hear him.

Oliver was now on the grass slope, and realised that any hope of catching the juggernaut had vanished. It was hurtling down the deserted hill and plunging towards the cliff edge, which was less than a hundred yards away. He stared at the cab and saw Kwame remaining resolutely behind the wheel. He was calm and expressionless as the lorry careered towards the English Channel far below. Oliver now realised what his former pal was doing.

"Goodbye old friend," he murmured. Unable to prevent what was destined to happen, he looked on helplessly as the truck retreated over the cliff edge. Once the trailer's rear wheels had lurched over the side, the lorry started to tip backwards. With a deafening shriek of tortured metal, the HD Cotton Crater Plant fell out of trailer.

Oliver watched the device plummet towards the crashing waves. Dr Moore was still caught in the pipes, his arms flailing in desperation as the weapon plunged towards its demise. Oliver continued watching until it smashed into the sea. He took no pleasure from his enemy's fate, but wanted to ensure that the barbaric invention that turned his life upside down was destroyed. His eyes then turned to the truck. The wheels beneath the cab had reached the cliff edge. Its speed increased as the weight of the trailer began dragging the front of the lorry towards a watery grave. Oliver was powerless to act as the vehicle driven by his former friend lunged over the precipice.

Oliver had no wish to see Kwame die. Instead, he focused on the HD Cotton Crater Plant, which was rapidly sinking into the depths. It disappeared just before the trailer crashed into the sea behind it, which sent water flying in every direction. The impact was so fierce that it generated a wall of spray that charged up the cliff before sinking back to sea level. The impact also forced the juggernaut to tip backwards and it started falling towards the water. The oxygen in the trailer was soon exhausted and the vehicle began sinking into the sea. The water then reached the cab, and within a few moments, there was nothing to see but a gradual flow of bubbles drifting towards the surface.

Oliver was motionless as he watched the waves that lapped gently over the final resting place of Dr Moore and his wretched device. He couldn't celebrate because a friend had perished with them. He then realised that someone else, a person much more important to him, was also in danger.

"Kieran," he gasped, and then turned around and started charging up the hill. Within seconds he was back in the car park, and saw the Détente minibus in the distance. Kieran was onboard and the vehicle was driving away. He could see the youngster hammering on the side windows with his hands bound. Oliver felt enraged. His anger increased when he realised that his car was absent. With the road blocked further down the hill, there were no other vehicles available to give chase. The only option left was his bike.

Oliver picked up his rucksack and the knife that he'd plunged into the parched ground. He threw the bag over his shoulders and tightened the straps before leaping onto his racing bike. He felt adrenaline bursting through every vein, and more so than when Kieran went missing in Torquay, as this time Oliver knew he was in danger. He cycled through the gravel car park with such fury that a haze of dust and grit was left in his wake. He then arrived on the road, and the speed continued to rise as the tyres gripped the asphalt and provided much better traction.

After his initial burst of energy, Oliver settled into a brisk rhythm on the pedals instead of a desperate sprint. He realised that the chase would be long, and the road was poised to plunge downhill. His struggle would not be maintaining the speed, but staying on the road.

The first bend was a right-hand curve. It was wide enough to avoid braking but Oliver knew that tougher turns lay ahead. While hiking up the climb he'd noticed how sharp the corners were, and now regretted not memorising the sequence. Within moments he was ambushed by a savage right-hander. If he kept going, his machine would crash through the barriers towards the cliff edge. Oliver squeezed the brakes and hoped that his tyres would grip the road. The narrow wheels turned in a heartbeat. The rear tyre snaked under braking, but didn't break away. Oliver rode around the outside of the corner. He was inches from disaster but had lived to tell the tale. However, he'd sacrificed his momentum, and had to sprint to build up his speed.

The bike continued to charge down the hill. It wasn't long before another sharp turn was looming. This was a left-hander, and tight enough to be a hairpin. It was outside HMP The Verne and Oliver remembered it from hiking up the climb. The speedometer on his handlebars was rushing towards 40mph. He knew that he was in trouble. Making a split-second decision that he wouldn't make the corner if he stayed on the inside, he swerved across the road. To stand any chance of making the turn, he realised that he'd need to apex the sharp corner. However, this would involve lurching into the oncoming traffic on a blind bend. His only hope was that Détente had managed to keep the road blocked. However, he could already hear engine noise and horns blaring further down the hill. The traffic was not far away.

Oliver was now past the point of no return and he touched his brakes as he arrived at the hairpin. Any attempt to slow down further would have locked the tyres and caused a horrendous accident. He set up for the corner by going to the extreme right-hand side of the road. He then dived left towards the inside of the bend. Oliver knew he was right on the limit and even the smallest speck of grit or moisture beneath the tyres could seal his fate. The bike remained upright as it flashed past the apex, but then sped towards the intimidating prison wall across the road. Oliver turned the handlebars further left, and well past the safety margin, just hoping that the tyres would stick. The camber of the road then changed and he found extra grip. He steered away from the wall, and avoided it with just inches to spare.

Having negotiated the hairpin, Oliver looked forwards to see if any traffic was hurtling towards him. It seemed that his gamble had worked, as there was nothing for two hundred yards. Beyond that point, there was a melee of cars and trucks caught behind a Détente low-loader truck blocking the road. It was reversing slowly, but only to allow the minibus carrying Kieran to pass through the roadblock. Oliver's bravery at the hairpin had reduced the gap, but he needed to maintain his speed.

The racing bike was now tearing towards the roadblock at 40mph. If the truck had stayed put, there would have been acres of space to pass it, but the driver had other ideas. He was now moving forwards, seemingly intent on following the minibus and releasing the angry queue of vehicles. As the truck slowly accelerated, Oliver closed on it with alarming speed. He couldn't overtake it, as the opposite side of the road was jammed with traffic. He was facing a wall of vehicles and had nowhere to turn. The only escape was the pavement beside him. He couldn't risk jumping the kerb as he was riding too fast, but there was a dropped section further down the hill. Oliver had to hope that he could reach it before smashing into the back of the low-loader. Heavy braking was out of the question, as the minibus carrying Kieran would get away. Oliver focused on the kerb as he plunged towards the truck. It seemed to lose even more speed with a sluggish gear change, but then lurched forwards at the critical moment. Oliver was able to swerve around the truck and onto the pavement. Now he just had to hope that it was clear of pedestrians.

The racing bike zoomed along the side of the low-loader. Its driver was totally unaware of Oliver's presence until he overtook the vehicle. With the truck negotiated, Oliver was now looking for another dropped kerb to rejoin the road. He was not concentrating on the pavement, and when he glanced along it, he found himself hurtling towards a pensioner struggling up the climb.

"Gangway!" Oliver yelled.

The senior citizen defied his years by leaping into the porch of a convenient house. He even had enough energy to shake his stick in outrage and serenade the speeding bike with a shower of abuse. Oliver knew that he was breaking every rule in the Highway Code but he didn't care – Kieran was in danger.

The bicycle dived back into the road when the next dropped kerb appeared. Oliver's bravery in overtaking the low-loader had reduced the gap to the minibus, which was only thirty yards ahead. He also had more speed, but the route was treacherous and twisty. They were now in the outskirts of Fortuneswell and both sides of the road were hemmed in by weather-worn stone buildings. He knew that any mistake would leave him skidding towards a wall at

40mph. The traffic was also heavier, and Oliver knew he was going too fast. However, if he slowed down, the minibus would escape.

Darting between sharp bends and slower cars, Oliver kept charging down the hill. He knew they would soon arrive in Victoria Square and the terrain would level off. While this would be safer, the bicycle would lose its speed and the minibus would pull away. Unless he caught it within the next few turns, Kieran would be out of reach.

Against his better judgement, Oliver began to sprint, realising that he only had a few corners left. Every bend he took was at greater speed than the last, and crucially, he was gaining on the vehicle. There was one final corner before the square, which was one of the tightest on the climb. The minibus slowed and was agonisingly close; Oliver felt that he could almost reach the rear doors. Then he spotted the corner, and was forced to brake, but was determined to carry more speed around the turn. As the minibus headed towards Victoria Square, the bicycle was still closing the gap.

Oliver stared at the rear doors of the vehicle. His legs were pumping like pistons in a sports car and he was totally focused on his prey. From behind his sunglasses, he then saw one of the Détente guards who was sitting by the rear doors and gazing out of the window. He seemed to be urging the driver to accelerate. The terrain was now virtually level as they sped through the pretty village square. Just the length of a bicycle separated Oliver's machine from the minibus. He knew that one final effort was needed to catch the vehicle and he pedalled even harder. He then leaned forward and his right hand grabbed the handle of the rear doors.

"Please be unlocked," he said to himself, while detaching his feet from the pedals. The issue was academic as the guard took matters into his own hands and opened the door. As the security man intended, Oliver was immediately thrown off balance. The rear door, to which he was clinging desperately, swung him off the bike and violently to the right. The speed nearly shattered the hinges, and stretched every muscle in Oliver's shoulders to breaking point. He was now dangling helplessly to the right-hand side of the vehicle, staring at a long line of vehicles heading towards him. He then glanced over his shoulder and saw his bicycle freewheeling across the road towards the village green. It was on a harmless collision course with the ornamental pond, but Oliver knew he was in much greater jeopardy. Unless he could swing back the other way, he would collide with the vehicles coming towards him. Just for good measure, the X7 bus from Dorchester was leading the pack.

As Oliver struggled for survival, he heard laughter. The guard was leaning out of the bus and gloating over his handiwork. Oliver stared at the X7 service coming his way. Its headlights were flashing as the driver tried to alert the minibus to the danger. Oliver stared at the vehicle, and realised that instead of sealing his fate, it might just save his life. He dragged his heels on the tarmac, which awkwardly bounced around as the vehicle picked up speed. He was now close enough to the minibus to avoid the X7 and waited until it was alongside. As it passed, Oliver swung his legs towards the bus. Once his feet made contact with the side of the X7, he pushed against it with every ounce of energy left in his sapped calves. The effect was to swing the door violently back towards the security man. He was too busy laughing to notice what was happening, and the door smashed into his head with enough force to crack the glass. The guard slumped to the floor unconscious. Oliver then reached for the other door handle and wrenched himself onto the back of the vehicle. He then opened the door with the shattered pane and crawled inside the minibus.

He was aboard.

Oliver didn't have long to catch his breath. Three guards were on the minibus, and while one was driving and the second was out cold, the third was charging his way. He was a large and athletic man and was brandishing a night stick.

"Look out!" Kieran urged, who was tied to his seat near the driver.

Before Oliver could peel himself off the floor he felt an almighty blow to the head. Thankfully his cycle helmet absorbed the impact of the night stick, which bought him enough time to struggle to his feet. He then realised that his headgear could be turned from a means of defence into attack. He lunged towards the guard, ducking a second swipe from the stick, and barrelled headfirst into his stomach. Oliver barely felt the collision but the guard was winded and sank to the ground.

"Tie him up," said Kieran, who was told to shut up by the driver.

While the security man was rolling around in pain, Oliver removed the belt from his jeans, looped it around a nearby chair, and then bound the guard's hands to stop him escaping. He then marched up the aisle of the minibus.

With two guards neutralised, Oliver's remaining opponents were the driver and Ms Potter, who was sitting opposite Kieran. She rose to her feet and tried to block his path.

"That's far enough," she said calmly, as Oliver stomped up the aisle.

"Release the boy and stop the bus," he ordered.

"Not until we reach the airport," she replied, as the bus left Fortuneswell and started driving along the causeway back to the mainland.

"Your boss is dead, you might as well give up," said Oliver.

"I can't do that," said Ms Potter.

"Just slap her one," suggested Kieran.

Ms Potter scowled at the boy, making her look even sterner than usual. She then turned back to Oliver.

"I don't know why you're so desperate to save him," she sighed.

"What makes you say that?"

"Well, he isn't even your son," the PA chuckled. Oliver didn't join the hilarity, and could feel his blood starting to boil at the jibe. Ms Potter's laughter ebbed away when she sensed the anger levels rising.

"Come now, you wouldn't hit a woman wearing glasses?" she soothed, batting her eyelids behind her designer rims.

"No, I wouldn't," he conceded, before taking off his shades and letting fly with a thunderous left hook that catapulted Ms Potter clean off her heels.

"I'd remove my glasses first," he added.

Kieran cheered as she tumbled awkwardly to the front of the vehicle. Oliver surprised himself with the strength of his punch – for a man who disliked violence it was a commendable effort. He could only explain it as a heat of the moment phenomenon fuelled by his determination to rescue Kieran. He was about to start untying him when he felt the minibus starting to swerve.

"Look out," said Kieran, pointing at the driver. Oliver span round and saw that Ms Potter, now unconscious, had fallen onto the remaining guard. He was fighting a losing battle to keep the vehicle pointing ahead and the minibus was swerving across onto the wrong side of the road. A large blue van speeding the other way flashed its lights and blasted its horn. The minibus driver continued wrestling with the wheel and missed the oncoming van by inches. He then zigzagged along the causeway road in a forlorn effort to regain control. He tried to push Ms Potter into the gangway, but was unable to move her while keeping one hand on the wheel.

While the minibus darted from left to right, Oliver rifled through his rucksack. After finding one of the knives he turned to Kieran to cut the twine around his arms and legs. The youngster was watching the oncoming traffic with alarm. The minibus veered violently left and charged towards the kerb. As its front wheels mounted the pavement, Oliver was thrown off balance and dropped the knife, which rattled down the aisle to the rear doors. Kieran watched the vehicle skidding across the pavement and hurtling towards the narrow beach beside the causeway road.

The bus was going to crash.

"Get a seatbelt!" Kieran shouted. Oliver stopped looking for the second knife and threw himself onto the nearest chair. He wrenched the seatbelt towards him, but it jammed with the excess force. He then saw the beach looming through the front windows of the vehicle. The driver was still fighting to regain control of the bus, which was leaving a helpless cloud of tyre smoke in its wake. Everyone onboard that was still conscious was yelling in terror except Oliver, who was focused on the seatbelt. He pulled the strap across his chest and tried to force it into the socket.

As the front wheels of the bus reached the stony beach, Oliver still wasn't strapped in. He tried to secure the belt one last time. He felt the minibus leaning to the left as it careered down the beach towards the sea. The left-hand wheels were sinking into the pebbles, while the right-hand ones were off the ground. Oliver felt the minibus starting to roll. It seemed inevitable that it would tip over. He tried frantically to plug the seatbelt into the socket, and finally, it clicked into place.

A heartbeat later, the vehicle passed the point of no return. It was tipped more than 45 degrees and the speed of the roll began to build. Debris on the floor started heading towards Oliver's side of the bus and away from Kieran's. The engine revved wildly as the stricken vehicle crashed onto its side. Oliver braced himself for the hail of objects, hoping that his knife was still at the back of the bus. The window beside him then smashed as the vehicle rolled onto its side. Some of the shards grazed him, but he didn't notice. The impact of the crash was so violent and deafening that he could no longer think straight. He then sensed the vehicle was leaning further left, and his legs were almost weightless. The vehicle was tipping onto its roof.

As the minibus continued to roll, Oliver clung to the chair in front to stay in his seat. Kieran was tied in place, but Ms Potter and the guards were rolling around like marbles in a jar. The noise of the crash was deafening as the windows continued to crack and the engine revved wildly. It seemed like the accident was never going to end. The bus was now on its roof and starting to slither down the beach upside down. The screeching was unbearable as the coarse shingle and flints tore the paint off the roof. Oliver kept hanging on for dear life. The vehicle was still moving and now sliding helplessly towards the sea.

Eventually the minibus reached the water. Oliver wasn't sure if it would slip beneath the waves. As it transpired, the sea provided a cushion to slow it down. The engine noise abated, but water was now flowing in through the front windows.

Oliver jammed his knees against the next seat and released his seatbelt. For a moment he hung upside down awkwardly like a drunken bat. He then grabbed the chair and swung himself around before dropping noisily to his feet. He immediately went to Kieran who was still bound to his seat and nervously watching the water flowing into the vehicle.

"Keep calm, you'll be okay," said Oliver, picking his knife off the ground. He then severed the twine around Kieran's arms and legs before unclipping the seatbelt and catching the youngster as he fell, clutching him to his left shoulder.

"Don't worry, I've got you," assured Oliver, who was now carrying the boy in a fireman's lift. He then glanced back and noticed that the water had stopped pouring into the bus and only part of it was submerged. Satisfied that nobody would drown, he kicked the rear doors open and staggered into the sunshine. He struggled on for a few steps before laying the boy onto the ground and keeling over in exhaustion.

***

Within minutes the causeway was swarming with police. Oliver was sitting on the beach wall beside Kieran. The police had already retrieved the racing bike from the pond. Having inspected it, Oliver found that, like himself, it had survived with only a couple of scratches.

Two ambulances arrived to collect Ms Potter and the guards. Their conditions ranged from unconscious to walking wounded, but they would all be healthy enough to face detectives before long.

The police also wanted to interview Oliver and Kieran, but allowed them a few moments to catch their breath. The officers had arrived after several holidaymakers had watched with horror as the Détente lorry plunged into the sea. While responding to the call, some had stopped on the causeway to investigate the stricken minibus.

Oliver wondered what the police might ask, but wasn't overly bothered. The question that had plagued him was his safety, which was resolved. Kieran had also found out who murdered his mother and who ordered it, and neither man had lived to tell the tale.

"So what's it like being a hero?" Kieran asked.

"You tell me, I just write children's books."

Oliver certainly didn't feel like a hero, after all, they sailed into the sunset with the leading lady sipping champagne. All he could muster was a bicycle strewn with pond weed. The police hadn't even brought him a cup of tea.

"If this is the hero lifestyle, count me out," he muttered.

"What's so bad about it?"

"An old friend double crossed me, I've feared for my life, several people have tried to kill me, and I was nearly incinerated by a nuclear bomb."

"Exactly," the youngster grinned. "Great, wasn't it?"

"I'd prefer a pint."

Oliver rose gingerly to his feet and leaned on his trusty bicycle. He opened his rucksack to search for something to clean the frame. The only option was his clothes, which he wasn't prepared to sacrifice. In his opinion, he'd already sacrificed enough since the Détente inquiry had ruined his once peaceful existence. However, he'd also gained something very important from the experience, and it was so valuable that he wouldn't even dare to put a price on it.

"Tell me, is parenthood always this dramatic?"

"Why are you asking me?"

"In a way, you're more experienced," Oliver remarked.

"Not when it comes to having a dad."

Oliver's attention immediately turned to his rucksack, and the DNA letter that was nestled amongst the battered contents. He removed the envelope and studied it one last time. He then threw it away.

"Let's go home, son."

THE END